Eric Wilder

A Gathering Of Diamonds

Gondwana Press

Edmond, Oklahoma

Other books by Eric Wilder

Ghost of a Chance
Murder Etouffee
Name of the Game
Over the Rainbow
Big Easy
Just East of Eden
Lily's Little Cajun Cookbook
Of Love and Magic
Bones of Skeleton Creek
City of Spirits
Primal Creatures
Black Magic Woman
River Road
Blink of an Eye
Sisters of the Mist

This book is a work of fiction. Names, characters, places, and incidents either are products of the author's imagination or are used fictitiously. Any resemblance to actual events or locales or persons, living or dead, is entirely coincidental.

© 2006 by Gary Pittenger

All rights reserved, including the right of reproduction, in whole or in part in any form.

Gondwana Press
1802 Canyon Park Cir. Ste C
Edmond, OK 73013

ISBN: 978-1-946576-05-7

For Marilyn

Foreword

I grew up an avid reader of adventure fiction, glued to the words of writer's Jules Verne, Edgar Rice Burroughs, and H. Rider Haggard as they took me on flights of fantasy to the bottom of the ocean, the plains of Pellucidar, and the lost mines of King Solomon. Later, I spent time as a foot soldier in a needless war that left me wondering about humanity. A *Gathering of Diamonds* is my tribute to all the writers of great adventure fiction, and to the foot soldiers that experienced their own brand of adventure.

Don Yaw, a dear friend and early reader of this novel informed me he loved most of the book though the flashbacks of Vietnam made him so uncomfortable that he skipped over them. When I reread those passages, they also make me uncomfortable. I left them in the book because they detail how post-traumatic stress can debilitate the bravest of people, and how some manage to cope with the ongoing pain.

I hope you love the mystery, adventure, and romance of *A Gathering of Diamonds*. If the passages of war disturb you, then please feel free to skip over them just as did my dear friend. Don't ever be afraid to travel places you've never been, and whatever you do, never stop seeking that next great adventure, even if it's only in your mind.

~Eric Wilder~

A Gathering of Diamonds

A novel by
Eric Wilder

Chapter 1

A white-tailed doe racing across the road roused me from a flashback and sent adrenaline buzzing through my brain. Slowing the red Mustang, I clutched the wheel as pain behind my eye nudged me back to reality. Beyond the hood stretched the foothills of northern Arkansas. It was early autumn, the colors around me as bright as a fresh coat of paint.

I'd left the Big Easy at dawn, stopping only once in Little Rock for gas and a cold drink. Though the last few miles were missing from my memory, the narrow highway forced me to concentrate on driving and forget the reason I'd come here in the first place.

Heat devils rose off the blistered blacktop. Early October sun warmed the skin on the back of my neck. After cresting the next hill, I saw a tall building topped off with a clock tower crowning the horizon. Its windows glimmered in the afternoon sun, and I didn't have to check the map to know I'd reached Brannerville.

The college town lay nestled in a bowl-like valley in an ancient range of rolling hills. It had weighed on my thoughts for the past thirty days as I pulled into a filling station to stretch my legs and top the gas tank.

A massive sandstone courthouse occupied one corner of the town square. Shops and stores rimmed its periphery, people in shorts and casual clothes browsing store windows and soaking up the late afternoon sun. A man clad in overalls and clutching an oily red rag interrupted my thoughts.

"Help you?" he asked, his hillbilly twang making his question sound foreign.

"Fill it up," I said, leaning away from his black-toothed grin.

He used the oily rag to dab his sweaty neck, a rumpled welder's cap crowning his bald head. I could smell his breath, stale from last night's whiskey when he rested his hairy forearms on the door of my car. The dagger tattoo on his hand looked as if he'd put it there himself.

"Where you from?" he asked, likely as curious about my accent as I was of his.

"New Orleans."

"Kid in school here?"

"Something like that. Which way is the college?"

"Down the road a piece," he said, pointing his nicotine-stained finger.

"Is that the courthouse next door?"

"That and the police station."

"I wouldn't think you'd have much crime around here."

"About the same as the hair on a mangy yellow dog," he said.

I waited for him to smile. He didn't. Instead, he stole a cockeyed glance at me to see if I had. When I obliged, he rubbed his chin and spat a glob of tobacco juice on the concrete.

"What's the population?" I asked.

"Bout thirty thousand when school's out. Twice as many counting college kids," he said, wiping his mouth with an oily hand.

"Is there someplace nearby to get a sandwich and cold drink?"

"College strip around the corner," he said. "Can't miss it."

"Thanks," I said, saluting him as I drove out of the parking lot.

I cruised down the brick pavement. It didn't take long to find the bustling square that reminded me of a similar area near the LSU campus in Baton Rouge. Fall semester had begun, scores of students in cars, on bicycles and more on foot, crowding the four-block quadrangle. After parking in a vacant alley between a tee shirt shop and barbecue joint, I went inside for a sandwich.

Boisterous students were still pouring into the café when I exited a half hour later. Though late afternoon heat remained, the sky had begun turning the color of turquoise, the humidity so high it almost felt like a kick in the groin when I took a deep breath. I had only a moment to think about it as I noticed a uniformed woman gazing into my car, frowning as she scribbled something on a notepad.

"Problem, officer?"

"Your vehicle's in a no parking zone."

She had a pleasant voice and spoke in neutral Midwestern tones instead of the pervasive twang of the man at the filling station.

"I didn't see a no-parking sign," I said.

"Because there isn't one. You're blocking an alley," she said. "I could have had you towed."

"Sorry. I'm from out of town."

The young cop stared at me and shook her head. "You know what they say about ignorance of the law?"

Glancing away from her cool stare, I read the tag on her uniform that said her name was Armstrong. Officer Armstrong was no taller than five-three, her short hair sun bleached almost white. She had expressive eyes the same hue as the darkening sky. I marveled at how every straight seam of the young woman's uniform defied the heat and humidity.

"Uncle," I said.

Officer Armstrong didn't smile. "Can I see your driver's license?" I fished it out of my wallet and handed it to her, waiting as she made a notation on her pad. "Is this your car, Mr. Logan?"

"I'm renting it."

She returned the license to me, along with a traffic ticket.

"The courthouse is closed for the day. You can pay this tomorrow when it reopens."

"Thanks, Officer Armstrong," I said.

She didn't react when I used her name. Ignoring my eye contact, she said, "Next time watch where you're parking."

I watched as she strolled to a tan and white police cruiser, her tires spinning in loose gravel as she hurried away and disappeared over the hill. Raising my car's canvas top, I switched on the air conditioning full blast.

It was late when I reached the hillside college, shades of crimson and pink already draping the surrounding hills. Though the person I was looking for had likely left for the day, I decided to give the place a look. As I parked and walked toward the largest of several stone buildings, hazy clouds began masking the sky and a sudden chill permeated the air.

Overhead, a hawk floated in a thermal updraft as cyclists, laboring up the steep grade, passed on the street. A jogger brushed past on the sidewalk, almost knocking me down. It wouldn't have taken much. After thirty days flat on my back in a hospital bed, my muscles labored from the strain of the hilly campus. Finding the front entrance locked, I found an open door in the back.

Down a darkened hallway, someone hummed as he pushed a broom across the floor. The tune echoed inside the empty building, reminding me of the interior of a cave. For a moment, it threatened to overload my fragile mental state.

The cleaning person could have been on the third floor or ten feet away. It didn't matter. The drifting sound caused a predictable reaction. I began to feel the madness starting to return. Against my will, my thoughts started racing back to distant murky memories. This time, it didn't happen.

The red glow of a nearby fire alarm returned me to reality, though it left me with a throbbing head. I was looking for a water fountain when a light radiating from an open door revealed a name on the glass that read Dr. Theodore Fridel. I rapped on the window to get the attention of the man sitting behind a desk.

"Help you?" he said, opening the door.

Dr. Fridel looked nothing like I had imagined. Instead of old and gray, he was probably on the front side of thirty. Didn't matter because he seemed older as he gazed at me with myopic eyes trapped behind thick-framed glasses. His hair and mustache were coal black, the same color as his eyes. They clashed with his peach-colored sports jacket and zigzag tie he'd probably bought at a garage sale.

"I'm Tom Logan," I said. "You were my brother's thesis adviser."

Understanding replaced Fridel's initial disbelief as he pointed to a chair in front of his desk.

"Your brother?"

"Half brother. Much younger."

"I see," he said. From the way he blinked his eyes and frowned, I could tell he didn't. "How can I help you?"

"I'm trying to find out what happened to Bill."

"I'm sure you read the police report. . ."

I held up a hand to stop him. "I was hoping you could add something. Explain why my brother seems to have vanished without a trace."

"Regrettably, it's as much a mystery to me as it is to you. Though I was Bill's thesis adviser, we were never close. Your brother was quite secretive."

Our father and both our mothers were young when they'd died. Old enough to be Bill's father, I was present during most of his formative years. Secrecy was only one of his unusual traits of which I was well aware.

"Maybe you can tell me something about this," I said.

Reaching into my shirt pocket, I pulled out a small leather pouch. Professor Fridel's mouth opened when its sparkling contents rolled across the desk.

When he regained his senses, he said, "Is that a diamond?"

Chapter 2

The sight of the large black diamond mesmerized Professor Fridel. For a long moment, he sat unmoving in his chair.

"Is it real?" he finally asked.

"Very real. Bill sent it to me."

"Where did he get it?"

"Don't know. I thought that you might."

Glancing up at me with an appraising stare, he shook his head as he turned the large crystal in the palm of his hand. Blue light reflecting from the stone formed dancing patterns on the wall behind him.

"This looks uncut," he said. "A single crystal the color of which I've never seen. Where in the world did Bill get it?"

I interrupted him, realizing he knew no more of the origin or significance of the uncut gem than I did.

"Perhaps you can tell me something about Bill's thesis. Maybe it'll shed light on his disappearance."

"I've gone over this with the police a thousand times. Surely there's no more I can add," he said, irritated by my insistence.

Fridel's buckshot eyes seemed to question just what I might possibly accomplish by hearing more than the reams of information he had already given the police. I'd read the report. I wanted to hear it from him. Deciding bluster wouldn't work, I tried reason instead.

"I was the closest thing to a father Bill had. I was in the hospital when he disappeared. For my own piece of mind, I need to find out what happened to him."

Fridel didn't mention the guilt I'm sure he could see in my eyes and hear in my voice.

"Sorry, Mr. Logan," he said as his eyes returned to the diamond still clutched in his hand. "Your brother was involved in an anthropological study of Arkansas hill people. These people are direct descendants of first-generation Europeans, and because of the region's secluded nature, little interaction with the outside world has occurred. Even after three hundred years. Bill felt their craft, culture, and art might mirror the past, and that's what his thesis sought to determine."

Such an obscure quest was exactly what would have excited Bill's passion and sense of adventure. Once, we'd spent three days searching for and cataloging arrowheads found in a meandering streambed; three laborious days beneath hot Texas sun. A study of Arkansas hill people was exactly what would have excited Bill's curiosity.

"The police report said his truck turned up in central Arkansas."

"Abandoned," Fridel said. In the wilds of the Ouachita Mountains."

I found myself wringing my hands in anticipation of his explanation. Instead, he grew silent, his eyes still locked on the diamond.

"Bill's effects were sent to me in Louisiana. Mostly his clothes and a few items like a broken tennis racquet, textbooks and chipped china. I received none of his thesis material. Do you have it?"

Fridel removed his milk bottle glasses and rubbed his eyes. "No, I assumed. . ."

"I know how thorough Bill can be, Dr. Fridel," I said, raising my palm. "You said his thesis was almost complete. Surely he kept detailed notes."

"I'm so sorry. Bill maintained a detailed account of his work and volumes of notes and recorded interviews with the hill people. I assumed they were in police custody."

"No problem," I said, seeing Fridel was at a loss. Did Bill have a base of operations, someplace he always stayed while working on his thesis?"

Though the diamond continued to lock Fridel in its spell, my question awakened him from his distraction. Shaking his head as if he had a bee on his nose, he pushed the crystal across the desk to me.

"Like most college students Bill was usually short on cash. When he worked on his thesis, he always camped out to save money." Fridel opened his desk drawer and fumbled around until he'd found a loose piece of paper. "He left this note for me in case I needed to contact him. He always stayed at the Chaparral Camp Grounds in Turkey Gap."

⬥

Turkey Gap. The name sounded exotic and foreign. Landlocked, deep within jagged Ouachita Mountains peaks, it seemed as far away from my former life in New Orleans as Beijing. Still, I rolled the name over in my mind as I parked the red convertible outside the county courthouse.

Rain had fallen during the night and water lay in puddles in worn indentions in the limestone pathway leading to the front door. Joggers were everywhere, despite early morning sun already hot enough to raise a fine mist off the grass and muddy puddles. The courthouse still lacked much human activity at this early hour. A sign directed me to the basement for payment of my parking ticket. Taking a deep breath, I pressed the down button and waited for a slow-moving elevator to arrive.

The musty basement was tomb-like, devoid of windows. Dim lighting from corroded fluorescent fixtures imparted a seedy appearance to its flaking plaster walls. Mustering my courage, I hurried to a closed door at the end of the hall. Sitting behind a gray metal desk, I found a suspender-clad man.

The old man either didn't hear me when I entered through the creaking door or else didn't care. As I waited in front of his desk, he continued writing in a leather-bound book. Finally, ever so slowly, he glanced up from his work.

"Help you?"

His voice sounded like a cracked record, vintage 78 RPM.

"I need to pay a parking ticket," I said.

The old man nodded and walked with a pronounced limp to a row of gray filing cabinets crowded against the wall. He returned with an armload of filings bound together with cardboard.

A tie of purple paisley clashed with his white shirt, yellowed with age. Despite the room's stuffiness, he appeared perfectly comfortable. A living mummy, I thought, already entombed.

"Three dollars," he finally said.

Handing him a five, I regretted not having correct change. Five minutes later, he returned from the file cabinets with six quarters, one Kennedy half-dollar, and a hand-scrawled receipt. Thanking him, I hurriedly caught the express back upstairs.

The basement had seemed like a dungeon. Upstairs, wonderful sunlight reflected through windows and doors. Taking a deep breath I glanced outside, studying lines of the massive old sandstone building as I attempted to relax from my trip into darkness. Concentrating as the doctors at L.S.M.H. had taught me, I blocked out the cause of my suddenly palsied hands. This time the exercise proved useless, failing to prevent my blackout. Instead of the darkness of Vietnam, my mind returned to the streets of New Orleans.

I was standing on a second story balcony above a Chartres Street antique shop looking out over similar, seamless buildings across the street. Near the flat roof of one of the buildings grew a stunted palm, a tropical plant protruding from the vertical wall, surviving like a weed between decaying bricks, and sustained and nourished with water from a cast-iron rain gutter.

The palm was an anomaly. Unlike the agglomeration of hanging and potted plants, azaleas and groomed magnolias, and even tourists and residents populating the Quarter's ancient brick valleys, the palm was free and wild. Nothing owned it, and it owned nothing except for its place in the brick and mortar.

Unlike most of my seizures, this one was brief. As I opened my eyes, I remembered the fading dream and wondered what it meant. Gazing out the window, I realized that somewhere between Louisiana and northern Arkansas the natural sequences of the two locales had reversed. In Brannerville, unlike New Orleans, plants and creatures surrounded man-hewn stone. In stark contrast to the French Quarter's tame streets, nature surrounded man instead of the reverse. The thought frightened me.

A door slammed, and I wheeled around to find courthouse halls suddenly brimming with activity. Taking a deep breath, I leaned against the wall until my heart quit pounding. When it did, I recognized Officer Armstrong standing just inside the doorway. Having for a moment forgotten my trip into the musty basement, I walked up behind her and tapped her shoulder.

"Arrest any dangerous felons lately, Officer Armstrong?"

At first, she didn't recognize me. Then she smiled and said, "Every now and then, the Sheriff lets me run in a drunken college student."

It was my turn to smile. "Buy you a cup of coffee? I'd like to hear all about the Brannerville crime wave."

"There's a machine down the hall," she said, motioning me to follow her.

We reached a tiny snack bar that wasn't what I'd in mind. Coffee from the quarter machine was as dark and strong as last month's oil change. As we sat at a Formica-topped table jammed in a rear corner, I found it tasted much like it looked.

Officer Armstrong was direct. "What are you doing in Brannerville, Mr. Logan?"

"Tom," I said. "Someone I needed to talk to at the college."

"Are you enrolling?"

"I'm a little old for that."

"You don't look that old," she said.

"I'm probably old enough to be your father."

"I don't think so," she said. "I'm over thirty."

I felt guilty for prying into the life of someone I'd known only briefly even though I was attracted to the young woman. It was a feeling I hadn't experienced in what seemed like many years and its sudden and inexplicable appearance greeted me like a long-departed friend.

"You're Bill Logan's brother. I saw your picture in the paper. I'm sorry."

Her recognition caught me off guard. "I was in the hospital when he disappeared." The Louisiana State Mental Hospital. I found myself hoping she hadn't read that part. "Did you know Bill?"

"No, though I'm familiar with the facts of the case," she said.

"Such as they are. Bill's body was never found."

"You think your brother is still alive?"

"I wish I could believe it. He's never purposely stayed away from home this long."

She must have sensed my pain because she leaned across the table and took my hand.

"Tom, I'm so sorry."

"Let me show you something," I said, reluctantly extracting my hand from her gentle grasp. "Bill sent this to me in the hospital just before he disappeared."

I dumped the diamond onto the table between us.

"It's beautiful! Is it a diamond?"

"Yes. Any ideas?"

Officer Armstrong continued staring at the diamond as sunlight reflecting off whitewashed walls penetrated its angular surface, sending shimmering beacons dancing on the vertical face of the coffee and beverage machine.

"You think this is somehow important to your brother's disappearance?"

"I have no idea what it means. I was hoping someone here could tell me."

She shook her head while continuing to stare at the diamond. "Maybe Professor Quinn could help."

"Professor Quinn?"

"He teaches geology at the college. He won't know about your brother, though I bet he knows all about diamonds."

"Will he see me?"

"If I ask him for you," she said.

She fumbled for her cell phone, excused herself for a moment, and walked a short distance up the hall. When she returned to the table, she winked and smiled.

"You can go over now. Professor Quinn's office is in the geology building on campus. You can't miss it."

"I don't know how to thank you, Officer Armstrong."

Her neck flushed and she looked at the floor. "Don't worry about it. And Tom," she said. "My name is Amber."

"You're a thoughtful person, Amber. I would like to repay your kindness. Dinner later? Bowl of gumbo, maybe?"

She made a face and said, "I'm working tonight and I don't eat gumbo. If you'll settle for something else, I'll do the cooking. My place? Tomorrow night?"

Her unexpected invitation caught me by surprise. For a moment, all I could do was gaze into her big blue eyes. My voice had deserted me.

She quickly broke the spell, glanced at the clock on the wall, and said, "Where are you staying?"

"Holiday Inn, on the main highway."

"Pick you up at seven," she said. With the swaggering gait of a cop on the beat, she walked away down the long hallway. Halfway back to the open office door she turned around and said, "Good luck with Professor Quinn. He may be an old bear, but if anyone can tell you about the diamond, it's Uncle Enos."

Chapter 3

The tiny building housing the geology department did little to inspire visions of intelligence or imagination. It did make it easy for me to locate Quinn's office at the end of a long hallway. The door was open, the office empty. After a passing student informed me I could find the Professor in the basement, I drew a deep breath, closed my eyes and started down the steep stairs.

Though the coffee room was homey and well lighted, the concrete walls made me feel like I was entering a bomb shelter. I blocked it from my thoughts when I found Professor Quinn locked in a heated conversation with three graduate students. The students departed near the top of the hour, their discussion unresolved. Saved for their next coffee break, I guessed.

An old brown western shirt, probably the same vintage as the geology building, draped Professor Quinn's rounded shoulders. The shirt and his buckskin sports coat of the same vintage. The turquoise-ornamented bolo tie complemented his scuffed cowboy boots. When he stood to shake my hand, I saw just how short he was. He was stout and had jowls like a bulldog that imparted a look of perpetual irritation. I soon learned his appearance was a close reflection of his personality.

"I'm Tom Logan. Amber Armstrong called on my behalf."

"Yes, she did. How can I help you?"

Glancing around the windowless coffee room, I pondered retiring first to the privacy of his office. Since we were the only two people in the basement, I decided it probably wasn't necessary.

"Amber said you might shed some light on this."

Dropping the black diamond into Quinn's hand, I waited as he removed an antique pair of wire-rimmed reading glasses from his shirt pocket and perched them on his stubby nose. A minute passed before he raked his hand through thin brown hair.

"Where did you get this?"

I explained having received the diamond from Brother Bill. Professor Quinn had heard all about Bill's disappearance. In broken sentences, he began commenting on the stone.

"This is at least ten carats. Uncut. Rare color. Probably very valuable. Let's go upstairs to my office."

My heart was racing when we reached the top of the stairs, and not from exertion. Thoughts triggered by my sojourn into the basement suddenly replaced my preoccupation with Bill's diamond. Dark thoughts from another place and time. I struggled to divert the mind-numbing flashback already filling my head with visions of a tunnel in the jungle. This time, a blackout didn't happen.

"Are you all right?" the professor asked.

Quinn had grabbed my shoulders and was shaking me, causing my eyes to focus. Light from the window behind his desk flooded through, temporarily freeing me from the dark bonds of a not-so-distant past.

"Sorry, I sometimes have these spells."

"Sit down, Mr. Logan. Maybe you should see a doctor."

Quinn quickly forgot my problem and began thumbing through reference books that occupied shelves on most of two walls. He returned with one yellow-paged volume. I waited through ten wordless minutes until he pushed the reading glasses up on his forehead, folded his construction-worker hands and gazed across the desk at me.

"Mr. Logan, are you sure you're feeling okay?"

"I'm fine," I said. "Please tell me about the stone."

You obviously know this is a diamond. What else do you want to know?"

"Bill was working in the Ouachita Mountains, near Turkey Gap. I think he may have found the diamond there. Maybe, it somehow caused his disappearance. You think it's possible?"

"Diamonds in Arkansas? Yes. Related to your brother's disappearance? That I don't know."

I ruminated briefly over his words. "Then there are diamonds in Arkansas? Not just quartz crystals cut to resemble diamonds?"

"Real diamonds, Mr. Logan and not quartz imitations. Except for a very recent find in the western United States, diamonds occur in situ at only one location in the United States and that place is in Arkansas."

"In situ?"

"In place or at the source," Quinn said.

"Where in Arkansas?"

"Murfreesboro. Diamonds were once mined commercially there, although never successfully. Now it's open to tourists who can dig and keep what they find."

"Then Bill could have found the diamond in Murfreesboro?"

"Maybe. It's also possible your brother could have found it somewhere else in Arkansas."

I was suddenly all ears. "Please explain."

"The explanation requires a bit of scientific jargon."

"I'll stop you if you get too far over my head."

Quinn's expression changed slightly, and I wondered if it was his half-hearted attempt at a smile.

"Are you familiar with the term igneous?"

"Somewhat."

He took my answer as a no and began explaining. "Igneous rocks are formed by solidification from a molten or partially molten state and are either plutonic or volcanic. Volcanic rock pierces the earth's surface before hardening from its molten state. Plutonic rock hardened beneath the earth's surface, without penetration."

"What does that have to do with diamonds?"

"Diamonds are composed of the element carbon. Carbon transforms into diamonds when subjected to intense heat and pressure, such as found in an active volcano. The mine at Murfreesboro is an old volcanic plug that's been eroded to ground level."

I realized the old man was in the process of telling me something important and I nodded for him to continue.

"The Murfreesboro plug is but one of many extinct Cretaceous volcanoes extending south of Hot Springs through Texas and into Mexico. Are you familiar with the theory of plate tectonics or continental drift?"

"Just the snippet of conversation I caught earlier in the coffee room," I said.

"It's really a simple idea. Several concentric layers and a molten core comprise the earth. The crust is the top layer, very thin compared with the others, and is broken along planes of weakness like a cracked eggshell. These individual portions, or plates, are in constant motion. There is evidence they have moved or drifted throughout geologic time."

"If you say so."

"Look at a globe sometime. It's easy to imagine the east coast of South America once connected to the west coast of Africa."

"I follow what you're saying. What does it have to do with diamonds in Arkansas?"

"Let me finish and it'll begin to make more sense."

"Sorry," I said.

"Convection currents in the hotter layers of the earth cause these plates to move, thus the term continental drift. This movement is extremely slow, and it would likely go unnoticed during a person's lifetime. The movement of these plates has caused tremendous change through geologic time. Forces generated by plate interaction are more powerful than anything that is possible for a human to create, even a hydrogen bomb.

"Extinct volcanoes such as the Murfreesboro plug parallel the Ouachita Mountains, a range much older than the Rockies. These mountains are at the earth's surface in Arkansas and southwest Oklahoma but present only in the subsurface in Texas and Mexico.

"Everything north of the Ouachitas was part of the Continental Plate during the Cretaceous Period. The Gulf of Mexico Plate collided with it. Eroded Ouachitas and its associated volcanic plugs are the fossilized remnants of the collision of these two plates.

"And the diamonds?"

"Diamonds form under very specific conditions. Carbon, the allotrope of diamond, remains in a liquid state until conditions are favorable for the formation of diamonds. Because of the intense heat and pressure needed to cause this transformation, it must occur many miles beneath the earth's surface."

"How many miles?" I asked.

"Fifty to two-fifty," Quinn said. "The exact condition for the transformation of carbon into diamond exists within a tolerance of only several hundred feet. The temperature above a certain level would be too cool, conditions below too hot."

A light suddenly flickered in my brain. "You're saying conditions necessary for diamonds to form rarely occur?"

"That's exactly what I'm saying. Volcanic plugs exist throughout the world. Only a few contain diamonds. The reason is the zone was either never exposed or else eroded away. It is unusual and statistically rare to have the few hundred feet where diamonds occur preserved at the earth's surface."

"So what's your conclusion?" I said.

"I conclude the Murfreesboro plug is a rare occurrence. Still, the other plugs along the trend likely solidified at a similar depth. One of those plugs might very well contain diamonds."

I mulled his words. "Then why hasn't someone already found it?"

Quinn didn't immediately answer. Instead, he slowly shook his head, folded his short arms, and frowned.

"Did I say something wrong?" I asked, sensing a sudden chill in the book-crowded office.

"Just that you can't imagine, as a geologist, how many times someone has asked me that question."

"And what's the answer?"

"The answer is we discover new things every day. We call it technology. Do you think the Wright Brothers would have learned to fly if they had asked that same silly question? Just because no one has found it doesn't mean it doesn't exist."

"Then Bill's diamond could have come from another diamond-bearing plug and not from Murfreesboro."

Quinn continued to frown, tired of the conversation and conspicuously displeased with my skepticism.

"It's not that far-fetched, Mr. Logan."

Maybe the idea wasn't so far-fetched. I forced myself to consider the possibility. Perhaps Bill had located an undiscovered diamond-bearing plug and that knowledge was somehow responsible for his disappearance. Maybe even his death.

"You look pale, Mr. Logan. Would you like a glass of water?"

"I'm fine. If there is an undiscovered diamond deposit in Arkansas, is there something specific I should be looking for?"

"Igneous rock called kimberlite often forms in association with diamonds. When kimberlite erodes, it creates a soil with a unique blue color. Farmers sometimes find diamonds when they plant crops in this often very fertile blue earth."

"Then I'll find the diamond plug. . ."

"Where you find blue earth," Quinn said, completing my sentence.

"Where would I begin my search for this plug?"

"Your brother's thesis notes should give you the answer," Quinn said.

"I'm afraid all the work Bill did in southwest Arkansas has disappeared, along with him."

Quinn rubbed his chin and grunted.

"If I were beginning a search for this mythical plug I suspect I would start in Turkey Gap."

I sank back into the worn old chair, picturing an ancient, vanished coastline where giant volcanic cones abounded in a setting of long extinct, exotic vegetation. After visiting Professor

Fridel, I had already decided my next stop in Arkansas would be Turkey Gap. Now I knew what to look for when I got there.

"How do you know my godchild?" Quinn asked, interrupting my thoughts

"Your godchild?"

"Amber."

"She gave me a parking ticket," I said.

Quinn leaned back in his chair. For the first time since meeting him and smiled. This time, it was a real smile.

"Don't feel so bad. Amber has ticketed me twice. She makes no exceptions when it comes to her job."

"She said you were close friends with her father."

"Best friends," he said. "Amber's parents are deceased. They died in an auto accident while she was attending Berkeley."

"Berkeley seems an unlikely place to train to become a police officer."

"Poet," Quinn said.

"Amber is a poet?"

"One of the best," Quinn said.

"Then why is she directing traffic in Brannerville?"

"Ever try making a living as a poet, Mr. Logan?"

Chapter 4

I awoke with a start the following morning, a dull ache remaining from a remembered migraine and a forgotten nightmare. I wanted desperately to get in the rented convertible, return to Pineville and fade back into a familiar world of four bare walls and mind-numbing drugs. Instead, I slipped on my bathing suit and padded outside to the swimming pool.

The courtyard was deserted and the sun had just begun to emerge from behind distant tree-covered crests. Slipping up to my neck in cool water, I drew a deep breath of morning air and gazed across the hills. Sometime during the night, it had rained. Now, banks of dark cumulus clouds rimmed Brannerville. Along with colors of hazy morning gold, they painted the horizon with a wildly contrasting palette.

Ten laps of the small pool left me panting and wondering if I had the physical strength to continue my search. A familiar voice saved me from having to think about the mental energy that I would need to complete the task.

"Up early, aren't you?"

It was Amber, peering over the gate at me. She was dressed in revealing pink shorts and singlet for an early jog.

"Morning. You're up early yourself."

"I like to exercise before work. It invigorates me for the rest of the day."

"You look great. If I had legs like yours, I'd run ten miles every morning."

"You get legs like these by running ten miles every morning," she said, unabashed by my brazen compliment.

She did have great legs, long, tanned, and tapered; a dancer's legs without the emaciated look of some long distance runners.

"Slip on some shorts and come with me."

Amber's voice had a wonderful resonance. I found myself smiling with pleasure.

"I'd really like that, but I have no gear."

"Hey, that's a woman's excuse," she said. "Don't you at least have tennis shoes and shorts?"

I did. Five minutes later, I joined her, feeling slightly foolish in Bermuda shorts, dark socks, and worn-out tennis shoes. I followed her up a wooded trail, into the hills. After a mile, she slowed to a walk to let me catch my breath.

"You live around here?"

"Just over the ridge," she said.

"Hope I'm not holding you back. Run ahead if you'd like."

She laughed and shook blond hair out of her eyes.

"Don't worry about me. Are you all right?"

"A little winded."

"What about yesterday? Uncle Enos said you almost fainted outside his office."

"Must be the altitude," I said.

"It's only nine-hundred feet above sea level here."

I was strongly attracted to Amber and I felt she also liked me. I didn't want to spoil the moment by explaining my memory attacks.

"I'm fine. Let's run."

I sprinted up the path. When we reached the top of the distant hill, Amber grabbed my arm and stopped me, grinning as I doubled over and began to turn blue.

"Can you make it back to the motel?"

"Of course I can," I said.

"Sure?"

"I'm sure."

She patted my butt and said, "Take it easy. I'm leaving you here. I'll pick you up for dinner tonight at seven."

I watched as she hurried away over the rise at a rapid, lung-busting clip. She had barely disappeared from view when rampant greenery closed in around me, returning me to the jungles of Vietnam.

***

Jungle night, dark as a black glove cloaking a war waged on many fronts, mine fought along jungle trail systems, winding out of North Vietnam that skirted Laos and Cambodia. North Vietnamese regulars traveled in small convoys, always at night, always on trails that extended through the dark triple canopy.

We were on an ambush, lying in wait like stalking animals. My muscles ached from two days of disuse. My bladder was full, and I was almost blind from staring into the darkness. Our squad had placed three claymores on one end of the trail, three more on the other. Six weapons forming two claws of a deadly pincer as we flanked one side of the trail in a semi-circle.

The opposite flank encompassed thick jungle growth impossible to penetrate. At least as fast as hapless Vietnamese soldiers would have to exit the scene of impending carnage. I was lying on my stomach trying not to squeeze the trigger of my M-60 machine gun locked, loaded, and ready for blood.

I almost didn't believe it when I heard bamboo snapping beneath someone's foot followed by whispers that pealed like church bells. The sudden stench of their unwashed bodies was like a slap in the face as I began to see wraith-like movement along the trail. A row of single-file soldiers moved slowly past our position. My heart began to race, almost out of control.

Then it began. An exploding trip flare lighted the jungle with smoke and billowing crimson as our clacker man blew half the claymores. So close was I to the blast, I didn't hear the remaining weapons detonate. I did see the bloody result through dilated eyes suddenly awash in strobe-like eruptions of murderous light as bodies began dissolving in slow-motion explosions of flesh, blood, and bone.

Three North Vietnamese regulars somehow survived the blasts only to have us greet them with free fire from grenade launchers, M-16s, and the M-60. Realizing they couldn't escape through the thick jungle, they raised their weapons, opened fire and charged into our position.

Every third round from the M-60's muzzle was a tracer that continued lighting up the night until my bullets were exhausted. The semi-circle of flashing death had destroyed bamboo, trailing vines and any hapless creature caught in its deadly swath. A dying flare told me there was nothing left to shoot at though my twitching trigger finger kept trying.

One of the charging Vietnamese soldiers almost made it until taken out by a close-range gut shot. He died after thirty minutes of screaming agony. At first, there was silence, and then darkness. Left only was the stench of death, spent blood, and gunpowder and urine from a loosened bladder, maybe my own.

I opened my eyes on the hilly trail above the Holiday Inn. Someone was screaming. It was me.

Amber arrived at seven dressed in army-green shorts and a pink-flowered blouse that complemented her hair, eyes, and complexion. She was driving a topless Jeep complete with a roll bar.

"What do you do when it rains?" I said.

"Stay home."

"Then I'm glad it's not raining."

"So am I. I invited Uncle Enos to join us. He liked you a lot. Hope you don't mind."

"He told you he liked me?"

"Not in so many words."

"He only smiled once through our entire meeting."

Amber stifled a grin. "He comes across like a wounded bear, though he's really a pussycat."

"I'll take your word for it," I said.

When Amber turned off the blacktop road a mile from the motel, I realized her necessity for the Jeep. She lived in a mobile home at the end of a narrow dirt trail on a mountain overlooking Brannerville. Professor Quinn was waiting for us when we reached the trailer. I stepped out of the Jeep, gazing down the mountain at the vista behind me.

"This is beautiful," I said,

"My little acre of paradise," Amber said.

It was. Towering pines surrounded the trailer, and a giant hammock hung suspended from the trailer's patio beams. Mosquito mesh enclosed it, and I suspected Amber slept there when nights were warm. A flop-eared hound sauntered out from under the trailer, wagging its long tail and licking my hand with his warm tongue.

"Admiral's not dangerous," Amber said.

"Sure he won't lick me to death?"

She laughed. "I suspect he'd rather have your leftovers from dinner." She glanced at Professor Quinn and said, "We're here, Uncle Enos."

"About time. I'm starving."

Amber hugged the old man affectionately as a black cat slithered between her bare legs. I soon learned she had three more cats and a parrot named Bones. Other animals appeared as we sat on the ledge overlooking Brannerville: a possum, three raccoons, and a skunk. They ate cat food straight from Amber's palm. After washing up in the trailer, we returned outside to watch the dying sunset. Quinn uncorked a bottle of Arkansas red wine and offered me a glass.

"No thanks," I said.

"Sure?"

"I don't drink."

I was glad I couldn't see their reaction in the dim light of dusk. Amber was a vegetarian. She'd cooked a Chinese vegetable stir-fry. After eating, we watched the flickering lights of Brannerville. Quinn continued to grumble about his desire for a thick porterhouse and baked potato. Far away, a whippoorwill trilled.

"The moon will totally eclipse tonight," Amber said.

Old Man Moon had reached his apogee and was already yellow and full. As we watched, one of his edges began darkening slowly.

"What's your line of work?" Quinn said, breaking the darkened silence.

"I'm presently unemployed. Before that, I was a petroleum engineer."

Quinn was un-awed by my former profession. He only grunted, and his frown and headshake were apparent, even in the dark. Amber, sitting beside me in a canvas director's chair, surprised me.

"I'm impressed," she said, clasping my hand in an affectionate way I didn't expect.

"Professor Quinn tells me you're a poet."

I heard her sigh and could only imagine the expression on her pretty face.

"I'm a police officer," she said.

"Can't you be both?"

"Police work has changed my artistic perspective. Now I write Neo-Pop, and it's not exactly widely accepted by the American literary scene."

"Because Neo-Pop as you call it is total nonsense," Quinn said. "Major literary journals had published Amber's work before she. . ."

Amber finished his sentence. "Before I joined the Beat Revolution."

"At the risk of sounding stupid, what is Neo Pop?" I asked.

"It's short for New Populism. Field described it as the poetry of mass culture. At its best, it's brash, sexy, and loud. It makes a statement in an easy, unstuffy way."

"Poppycock," Quinn said.

Amber and I both looked at the old man and laughed. In forty-odd years I had never heard that word used in actual conversation. Our momentary levity was lost on the Professor who continued trying to out-glare the moon.

"You're a prude, Uncle Enos," Amber said.

"Maybe you should find a gentler profession, more compatible with poetry," Quinn said.

"You're very wrong," Amber said. "Creating poetry is the most violent profession. Even Frost said 'Poetry is a way of taking life by the throat.' It's real and visceral. Why shouldn't everyone, not just New York stuffed shirts, be able to enjoy it?"

When the old man grumbled, Amber hugged him, obviously incapable of sustaining any palpable anger.

"You understand, don't you Tom?"

"I think I do. You're talking about passion."

"Yes. Passion for life, and the written word."

After returning to her chair, she grasped my hand again. Above us, the moon stole away behind the earth's shadow leaving only a crescent of light, and then more. Feeling almost human, I squeezed her hand.

"Please recite a poem for us."

I could feel her hand tense as she began in whispered tones.

"If the Man in the Moon had a penis, someone would demand its nightly eclipse."

I waited for her to finish. When I realized the entire poem consisted of only two lines, I said, "Wonderful."

"And what are we supposed to make of that?" Quinn said.

"Whatever you like, Uncle Enos," Amber said.

We watched the moon become completely black. When it began to lighten Professor Quinn tried to make conversation, but soon lapsed into silence as the phenomenon continued to unfold above us.

"Early class tomorrow," he finally said. "And too much esoterica for this old man. Ready to go, Tom?"

I wasn't.

"This has been wonderful, Amber and I'm sorry it has to end. Maybe I'll see you again before I leave town?"

"Lunch tomorrow?" she said. "If so I'll pick you up at noon."

"Wouldn't miss it for the world," I said.

Admiral followed her into the trailer, wagging his tail and smacking his lips over an old bone he'd dug up from somewhere. I followed Professor Quinn to his old yellow Metropolitan.

The car started on the first turn of the key.

"Neo-Pop police poet, bah!" Then he said, "She likes you."

"How do you know?" I asked.

"I've never heard her recite before. Not even for me and I've known her for thirty-two years."

Chapter 5

I didn't have to wait until lunch to see Amber again because she stopped by the motel on her morning run. Having felt silly wearing Bermuda shorts and black socks during my jog with her, I'd visited an athletic store for shoes and running togs. Now, even though I didn't feel like a champion sprinter as we raced up the hill, I at least looked like one. When Amber left me, I made it back to the motel without suffering a flashback.

Just before noon, Amber picked me up in her police cruiser. Sitting in the front seat of the squad car returned me to earlier days in New Orleans when I sometimes rode shotgun with the beat cops. It felt good remembering a simpler time before my losing battle with rampant drinking and drugging had all but stewed my brain; a time before Vietnam.

Another glorious day adorned the Ozarks. A gentle breeze rustled golden leaves outside the restaurant. With autumn temperatures in the low seventies, we ate outside on the patio, watching leaves rustle, and college students, loaded down with bags of heavy textbooks, pass on the sidewalk. Both caught in the hypnotic moment, we stared at each other across the table as we sipped our tea.

"When are you going to Turkey Gap?" she finally asked.

"Tomorrow."

"I was hoping you'd stick around Brannerville a while."

"It's beautiful here in the hills. I'd like to stay longer but I have to finish what I came here to do."

"Maybe you can return for a visit after your investigation," she said.

"Maybe."

"Tell me about yourself."

"Not much to tell," I said.

"You're an engineer?"

"Not anymore."

Sensing my reticence, she let the subject drop. Instead, she grabbed my hand across the table.

"Tom, can I be direct with you?"

"I wouldn't have it any other way."

"Thirty days is a long time. Your brother's trail's a bit stale."

"It's the only trail I have."

Amber let go of my hand and squirmed in her seat. She frowned and glanced up at two squirrels quarreling over a nut on a tree limb above us.

"What do you expect to find in Turkey Gap the police haven't already uncovered?"

"All of Bill's thesis notes are missing. The police found nothing about his work, either at his apartment or his office at the university."

"Maybe he had them with him when he disappeared?"

"But why? His adviser said he had reams of information. What would possess him to take it with him?"

"I don't know. Maybe Bill didn't think his notes were safe in his apartment, or at the university."

"Maybe," I said.

Amber's thoughts haunted me. After lunch, we returned to the Holiday Inn. When I opened the door of the squad car, she pulled me close and kissed me.

"If I can't talk you out of leaving town tomorrow, then check out of the motel. Spend the night with me."

***

I felt free and alive, along with a shred of apprehension, as I maneuvered the red rental up the rutted dirt road to Amber's trailer. Above me, bordered by clear blue Arkansas sky, a phalanx of ducks was heading south. Admiral, wagging his tail and smiling a friendly doggy smile, licked my hand when I stepped out of the car.

Amber had not given me a key to her trailer, probably because she never bothered locking her door. I took my suitcase inside then sat on the covered patio, basking in the warm breeze and restful sounds. Soon I moved to the inviting caress of her hammock, falling quickly asleep.

***

I dreamed of jogging, this time alone, back home in Louisiana. There were no hills, only vast stretches of profuse vegetation and water. Clouds, filled to capacity with warm summer rain, darkened the sky. Misty haze rose off the dew-covered grass. Everywhere, water puddled in low spots on flat earth. A commotion caught my attention as I crossed a bridge over a high-water creek.

Stopping to look, I again heard something splashing in the pool below the bridge. Flooding caused by recent rain had left the creek littered with broken bottles, limbs, and other waterlogged debris. Now rain had abated, water finally receding. Only two or three inches of water remained in the shrinking creek and a fairly large fish, its body half exposed to shallow water, was causing the commotion. It strained and flailed against the current, trying in vain to swim upstream, back to the place it had lived before the storm dislodged it.

I wondered if I should help. After checking the water depth on the opposite side of the bridge, I decided that it was not appreciably deeper. There was little that I could do. The fish was a carp, the wild counterpart of a common goldfish. This fish wasn't used to living in a bowl.

As I watched, the big fish seemed to make a conscious decision. It could never return to its former home. As if it realized the futility of its endeavor, it turned and started downstream toward ever-shallower water. I hoped it would make it to a distant pond or drainage ditch before water in the creek dried up completely. I would never find out because gentle motion awakened me from the dream. It was Amber, smiling as she rocked the hammock.

"Nice nap?"

"Yes," I said.

"I have to change clothes. I can only take my cop uniform for just so long."

She returned in a flower-print cotton dress, the material so sheer that when she passed in front of the window, I could see she had on nothing underneath. In the trailer's tiny kitchen, she began slicing carrots and cucumbers. We were soon outside on the patio, feasting on the veggies and homemade dill dip.

Later, we had beans and rice cooked Cajun style though without andouille sausage. Amber even had a bottle of Tabasco and made a face when I doused my bowl of beans with hot pepper sauce. Much later, we sat on the ledge overlooking Brannerville, the stars seeming brighter than I'd ever noticed. One, cut loose from the Milky Way, shot past, leaving a trail in the sky.

As we enjoyed the peacefulness of separation from the rest of the world, Amber recited several poems written by an Italian poet. While she meditated, arms and legs folded in the lotus position, I pondered the enigma of this beautiful young woman with the body of a professional athlete who found no disparity between poetry and police work; someone who carried a deadly weapon but would not eat meat.

The night was ripe for a mystical experience, and I didn't have long to wait for one to occur. When Amber unwound herself from her meditative position, she drew closer and wrapped one willowy arm around my neck. With her free hand, she unbuttoned my shirt and began gently massaging my chest.

Finding my emotions torn between lust and fear, I said, "You should probably know I haven't been with a woman in several years."

She grinned and said, "You aren't gay, are you?"

"Wish it were that simple."

She snapped her fingers and said, "Veteran. Missing bodily parts?"

My own smile faded. "No missing parts."

"What then," she asked, inching her hand farther down my torso.

"Nothing physical, doctors tell me."

"You're impotent," she said without moving her hand from near my belt.

I was becoming used to Amber's directness and didn't take her words as an insult. From the tone of her voice, I realized they weren't meant to be.

"Yes, I'm sorry."

"No problem. Do you know what causes it?"

"Probably," I said. "At least subconsciously, anyway."

She drew close to me in the dark and spoke in her patented low, husky voice.

"I don't believe you're really impotent. I think it's just a shield you hide behind; a secret room you withdraw to when you feel threatened."

Although her words were direct, I again sensed it wasn't intended to hurt or disarm me. Instead, I felt as if I had known her forever and that she understood my innermost secrets. Maybe she did. With her fingers, she traced the circumference of the circular scar just below my scapula, then along the six-inch length of ribbed tissue beneath my right nipple.

"Your chest feels as if you spent serious time beneath a working combine."

"Yeah, but you ought to see the combine."

The exchange made us smile, and then laugh.

"Will you tell me about it sometime?" she said.

"I'm still trying to come to grips with what happened. I may have to make something up to tell you."

"I'm too old for fairy tales."

"Then how about horror stories?" I said.

"Darkness hasn't frightened me since I was three."

Staring into her eyes, expressive even in the dim starlight, I somehow doubted anything had ever frightened her. By now, the moon was yellow and full. Amber took my hand and led me down a winding path behind the trailer. The path ended abruptly at a cobble-bottomed pool fed by a crystal stream pouring from a ledge of solid rock. Slipping the yellow dress over her head, she let me admire her tanned, athletic figure in dim moonlight filtering through the trees before she waded into the waist-deep water.

"Join me?" she said.

She watched me strip and wade into the pool after her. It was early autumn, the water warm.

Still, ripples rose on the surface of the pond, and goosebumps on my skin as she slowly put her arms around my neck.

Sensual fireworks ignited just beneath my skin. It seemed like heat lightning flashing on some distant horizon. For what might have been forever though seemed like no time at all, we luxuriated in the feel of each other's bodies, groping like horny teenagers in the darkness of a movie theater. We ended in the grass, on the far bank of the pool. Suddenly overcome with feelings of inadequacy, I rolled over on my stomach in the grass.

"I didn't bring you here to perform for me," she said, rubbing my back.

Somehow, the moment was comical and slightly absurd. There was no malice in Amber's voice, and I knew she was telling the truth. Then she did something I didn't expect. Straddling the small of my back, she began massaging my shoulders with her supple hands.

As she worked my muscles, she moved her hips and thighs, slowly at first, and then faster. She continued with fingers trained to the task until I felt her soft brush of pubic hair as it rhythmically caressed a sensuous circle in the curve of my back. My loins stiffened, followed quickly by a full erection that stabbed soft grass, creating a complex union of pleasure and pain.

Amber remained straddled across my body as I flipped over. Draping herself across my chest, she excited the heated surface of my skin as our bodies joined and slowly began moving in a timeless, sexual dance. At the precise moment of climax, I issued a low moaning cry that escaped from far back in my throat.

In the distance, somewhere near the trailer, Admiral howled a mournful response as if he somehow understood.

Chapter 6

I awoke in a strange bed the following morning. Amber was crouching over me, looking concerned as she shook my shoulder. It took me a moment to realize where I was.

"You were moaning," she said.

"Sorry. Just a bad dream."

Slipping out of bed, she went to the bathroom, not bothering to close the door behind her.

When she returned, she said, "Sounded more like a nightmare to me."

Joining her by the window, I peeked out the curtain. It was still early morning. A fine mist was rising up off the grass behind the trailer as one of Amber's cats stalked a bird perched on a fallen tree. Winter weather was approaching, red and gold leaves already falling in the wake of a light breeze blowing up from the valley. Sensing my reticence to talk about the nightmare, Amber left me alone in the bedroom.

Curiosity drew me to the kitchen where I found her grilling pancakes. She was naked except for the innocent face of a little girl and the all-over tan of a dedicated nudist. Strangely, nudity highlighted her pear-shaped indigo eyes. As she stood at the stove stirring the mix, I studied her tapered legs and rounded rear unblemished by even a single dimple of fat. A quarter-sized birthmark emblazoned the back of her right knee. Despite her golden tan, she had pink nipples that revealed her skin type as naturally fair. She looked as lithe as her own stalking cat as she carried the plate of pancakes to the kitchen table.

"Impotent, huh?" she said.

"You never know if the plumbing works unless you try to use it once in a while."

Instead of laughing, Amber screamed, shaking as she pointed.

"Spider!" she said.

I quickly discovered the cause of her consternation.

A large spider, probably a harmless garden variety, was crawling across the floor. Realizing Amber's apparent aversion to the arachnid, I grabbed a paper towel from beneath a cabinet and scooped up the creature before it could scurry away into some dark recess. Taking it to the trailer's front door, I carefully unfolded the paper, watching as the spider hurried away before I could change my mind. Amber's nerves had calmed when I returned to the kitchen.

"Don't want to upset the balance of nature," I said. "They catch lots of varmints around the house."

Amber's only comment was an unbelieving headshake. Later, I watched as she slathered a copious quantity of syrup on her pancakes and ate them with gusto. I had trouble concentrating on my own breakfast. When she finished, she went to the bedroom, returning shortly in my shirt.

"Sudden attack of modesty?" I asked.

"There's something I have to discuss with you, and I want you to concentrate on my words and not my tits."

Her voice had grown suddenly serious.

"So discuss," I said.

"Tom, I did more than run the report on your brother's disappearance. I also pulled the sheet on you." She held up a palm to indicate she had more to say and didn't want me interrupting while she said it. "I don't make a habit of bringing men to my house that I've only known two days, even if I like them very much. Even though you are somehow different, I had to check you out first."

I stood up from the table, turned my back on her, and walked to the sink.

"You checked me out and still brought me here? Not a very good cop, Amber."

"I'm not just a cop. Remember?"

I grew up the son of a New Orleans cop; a third generation Irishman. I understood the nagging paranoia common to the profession. It left me with an uneasy feeling in the pit of my stomach. Amber sensed it immediately.

"Sorry, Tom," she said. "I just wanted to set the record straight."

Not knowing where the conversation was heading, I returned to the bedroom to get dressed, remembering that Amber was wearing my shirt as I pulled on my pants. Perched on the edge of the bed I tied my shoelaces instead, trying not to notice when she appeared in the doorway.

"Looking for this?" she said.

Slowly unbuttoning the shirt, she let it slip off her shoulders and settle into a seductive pile on the floor. I quickly felt my anger and frustration melt away and offered my hand in a gesture of reconciliation. It was unneeded as Amber lunged on top of me.

Much later, in the bedroom's cool darkness, we lay there. Amber didn't smoke, and I had buried my own destructive habit, along with several others, long ago. Didn't matter because the desire remained. Amber grinned as she watched me drum a staccato cadence on the bed's brass railing with nervous fingers.

"Forgive me?"

I squeezed her hand and stared into gorgeous eyes that mesmerized me more than Bill's diamond.

"I'm the luckiest man alive to find someone that can overlook my past. You don't need my forgiveness."

"No secrets?" she said.

"Never."

"Then tell me about yourself."

"It's a long story."

"I'm off today and I have no place to go."

Amber draped herself across my chest, close enough to kiss. She continued staring at me with eyes that would only take yes for an answer. I began slowly, and then warmed to the story.

"My mother was a nurse. She fell asleep driving home after pulling a double shift in the emergency room. Smacked the back of a semi parked on the side of the road. Daddy remarried when I was fourteen, Bill born a year later. Daddy and Betsy, Bill's mother, died when their plane went down on the way to a few days in Vegas. Quite a tragic coincidence between us, huh?"

Amber didn't comment. Instead, she drew closer and rested her head on my chest. Light through the curtain glinted in her eyes as I continued the story.

"I soon married Erin, my high school sweetheart; a horrible mistake I quickly learned. Erin and I had almost nothing in common, and we began fighting almost immediately. When I couldn't take it anymore, I lied about my age and joined the Army. I had graduated high school early and was in Vietnam before I turned eighteen."

"And Bill?"

"My Aunt Edna in Breaux Bridge raised him. Thank goodness because Erin and I were no more than kids ourselves."

"What did you do in Vietnam?"

"I was a grunt, an infantry foot soldier. We did helicopter missions toward the end of the war. First Cav. We called ourselves sky troopers."

"Is that when the dreams began?" Amber asked.

"No."

Amber squeezed my hand. "I'm listening."

"The dreams started when I got home. I enrolled at LSU on the G.I. bill. Erin and I had forgotten the hard times before the Army, so we stayed together. She worked in a factory at nights to support us. I finished my degree in less than four years."

"And then what?"

"I got a job with an oil company, mostly working on offshore drilling rigs. Twenty-one days on, seven days off. Our time apart was likely the only thing that kept our marriage together."

"But not permanently."

"I started drinking when I was young though I didn't learn about drugs until the army. I can't remember when I started taking prescription drugs for aches and pains or Valium to help me go to sleep and calm my nerves. Hell, before long I was snorting coke when I could make a score from anyone on the drilling rig that had some. During my bouts with drugs and alcohol, when I didn't pass out first, I often became abusive."

"You beat Erin?"

"Not with my fists. Sometimes mental abuse is just as pervasive. Guess it amounts to pretty much the same thing. I'm not proud of it. Fact is I think it stinks."

"She left you?"

"Our marriage had deteriorated to the point that I really don't know what was holding it together. One day Erin finally had enough. She'd packed her things and left. I was on a weekend drunk and didn't find out until I dragged myself home Monday morning."

"You didn't try to get her to come back to you?"

"Hell yes. I sat on her mother's doorstep and cried like a baby. She didn't need a baby. I lasted three years before the company I worked for fired me."

"Because?"

"Same old story. Drugs and alcohol. I opened my own little consulting firm and managed to make a living until a few years ago."

"What happened?"

"It got to where I couldn't get through the day without drinking a fifth of vodka. I got sentenced to a year in jail after my third DUI."

"Tom, I'm so sorry."

"Don't be. It probably prevented me from killing somebody. When I got out, I started going to AA and managed to quit drinking and using drugs, but then the dreams started. Eighteen months ago I checked myself into the mental ward in Pineville, and I feel fairly certain I would have spent the remainder of my days there if Bill hadn't sent me the diamond."

The sky had turned electric blue when we finally dragged ourselves out of bed. Dressed in army green shorts and a skimpy halter top Amber rested her hands on her hips, grinning as I lugged my suitcase to the red convertible.

"What's so funny?"

"City boy," she said. "You have no idea where you're heading, do you?"

"Turkey Gap."

"That red pussy wagon will get you to Turkey Gap, though not very far into the hills."

"And what do you suggest?"

"Take my Jeep. I have to work through the weekend and all day Monday. After that, I have some time off. If you like I could drive down Monday night." She didn't wait for an answer. Instead, she opened the door of her metal outbuilding and began rummaging through stacks of boxes. "You'll need a place to sleep," she said, dragging a folded tent from the shack.

We loaded the tent, a propane stove, lantern, one large sleeping bag and various other camping articles into the Jeep. Finally, she went inside the trailer and returned with an ice-packed red chest filled with fruit juice and vegetarian treats. Then we took a walk to the cobble-bottomed pool. The sun was already high in the cloudless sky as we entered the shade of towering oaks that guarded the path. A persistent woodpecker was pecking a hole in the tree above us.

"Tell me what you were dreaming about when I woke you this morning."

"Not sure I remember," I said.

"Yes, you do. No secrets. Remember?"

"I have lots of dreams, mostly about the past. Some are recurrent. Some aren't."

"Tell me."

The way she held my hand, I knew she did not intend to let me drive away in silence. Slowly, I found a way to verbalize something that had pained my psyche for so long.

"Dreams are supposed to be a compilation of random events that occur in a person's waking hours. This dream is a verbatim account of something that actually happened to me."

Her tone was insistent when she said, "Tell me."

"It started in Vietnam."

A soldier in an infantry line company, my job description was 11-Bravo. We called ourselves 11-bullet stoppers. We operated off a bald hillside protruding from the jungle called Firebase Betty. Fifteen days out, five days in. Delta Company had taken a hit from a regiment of NVA regulars near the Cambodian border. Our sister company had gone in to bail them out and had taken heavy casualties. By the time the rest of the battalion reached the battle, Charlie had already split up into small units and had disappeared into the jungle. HQ was pissed.

Our company was due for a five-day stand-down. Instead, support troops supplied us on the burned-out LZ and sent us back out. Part of the 1st Cavalry we rode choppers instead of horses. Our colonel who everyone called the Old Man was intent on evening the body count. Instead of securing an outpost in the jungle, we began circling over triple-canopy in our choppers, hoping to draw ground-to-air fire.

A pilot, copilot, and two side gunners worked the Hueys, the doors removed so that two grunts on either side of the open chopper could ride with their legs draped outside the bird. The jungle was a seamless sea of green as muzzle flashes began chasing up at us. The door gunner beside me returned fire with his M-60.

The whump-whump-whump of the rotor made communication, short of shouting, impossible and the gunner had no sack for his big gun. Shell casings began spraying across the open cabin, making me think for a moment that I had taken an enemy bullet. It sent my heart into my throat.

The chopper banked toward the AK flashes spitting at us from the trees. The pilots found a clearing and then descended, one-by-one, discharging their reluctant passengers weighted down with hundred-pound packs of weapons and supplies. The choppers hovered as we piled out and secured a perimeter near the tree line. When Charlie took out one of the departing Hueys with a Chicom claymore, the bird toppled into the trees like a pigeon with a wing shot off.

The NVA regulars had us flanked. When they began lobbing 60 MM mortar rounds on top of us, our Captain called in a fire-for-effect from the Howitzer battery on Betty. As the ground shook, and trees began exploding, flying shrapnel buzzed over our heads. Burying my face in damp earth, I held my ears as explosions of noise rocked the ground, digging craters every time a big shell connected. The place was a killing ground.

We had dead and wounded all along the perimeter, some from our own 105s. Even though the NVA had scattered as soon as the big guns began knocking down trees and digging craters, the choppers waited over an hour before returning. I was the last man to make it to a hovering chopper. At least that's what I'd thought.

My squad had just pulled me into the chopper when a lone grunt came running out of the jungle. A young soldier that had joined our company that very day. Our nervous pilot, unaware of the last minute passenger, lifted up under full power as I grabbed the grunt's arm. The chopper banked away from the firefight with me holding on to a slippery wrist and two other grunts hanging on to me. By now, everyone was shouting. The pilot couldn't hear, and the door gunners were busy strafing the hot AO we were rapidly forsaking.

I thought I had him but G-forces, the weight of his pack and my loose grip on his sweaty arm sealed his fate. As he slipped away from me and began his long slow-motion fall, I could see the terror glazing his eyes. I knew what he was thinking. He was hoping somehow would catch him before his body exploded against the earth like a melon on hot concrete.

Chapter 7

It was late afternoon when I started down the hill to Brannerville. Thanks to Amber, I had everything I needed to survive the wilds of southwestern Arkansas except for a pair of boots. Stopping in town, I remedied that little problem by buying hiking boots and some sturdier clothes than those I'd brought from Pineville. A flat tire altered my schedule as I motored out of town. My excursion to fix the tire took less than an hour. The same attendant in dirty overalls that I'd met my first day in town repaired it quickly. I finally began my journey to Turkey Gap.

Along with the Jeep and camping gear, I also had a road map from Amber and knowledge that Bill's three-carat black diamond could have come from a previously undiscovered source. Armed with this information and with my self-esteem unexpectedly bolstered, I headed south.

Though the weather was unseasonably warm, dark clouds warned of impending rain. The road, like so many rural Arkansas by-ways, was narrow and crooked with steep faces of solid rock jutting upwards on both sides. The scenery became so spectacular, I almost ran into the ditch gawking at it. When I reached the Ouachita National Forest, the highway grade steepened abruptly, and houses, stores, and billboards disappeared.

I followed the scenic route almost an hour before stopping at a spectacular road cut. A mountain stream flowed beside the road and I picked up a handful of rocks from the bank. One rounded stone fit my hand nicely, and I tossed it across the narrow stream littered with boulders. The moss-covered rocks set up opposing patterns of ripples and whitecaps in the rushing water.

Except for the stretch of roaring water exposed beside the road, the stream's origin and ultimate destination remained camouflaged by surrounding trees. Towering pines, growing almost to the stream's bank of rounded rocks, shrouded everything else. I noticed the sheer cliff lying opposite the stream.

The solid wall of rock looked like chocolate swirl cake, this particular road-cut sliced to the very core of the ancient Ouachita Mountain range. While the trees and stream imparted the feel of youth and vitality, the deformed rock radiated hoary antiquity. Now I saw what powerful force had drawn Bill to these mountains.

Down the road, a grinding noise beneath the front of the Jeep began grating on my nerves. I pulled the vehicle off to the side of the road for a look. Finding no apparent problem, I continued on my way. The wheel began singing immediately, the offending noise coming from the left front wheel well.

The driver of a passing semi waved and blew his horn when I stopped again. I wasn't feeling as friendly. Crawling beneath the Jeep, I rocked the wheel, realizing my favorite tobacco-stained filling station attendant had failed to tighten the lug nuts.

Friction had already chewed off two bolts, and two of the three remaining bolts appeared damaged beyond repair. One lone bolt tenuously secured the wheel on the Jeep. Glancing at the sky for divine intervention and seeing none, I kicked a rock instead.

Turkey Gap was nearby, maybe as close as ten miles. I could do nothing about the ruined wheel, and I had no better plan in mind than to limp as far as I could in the Jeep. If it failed me, I would walk the remaining distance for help.

Though the terrain had flattened, lessening the strain on the wheel, moisture-laden clouds darkened the sky. By the time I reached the base of a long grade, the grinding noise had become progressively worse. I glanced around for a place to abandon the Jeep. Seeing none, I continued up the next grade at a snail's pace. I saw my salvation at the crest of the hill.

Two gas stations, a roadside cafe, and several houses lay nestled in a sharp bend in the road. A nearby wood-railed fence surrounded a large clearing, its sign proclaiming that it was the Chaparral Camp Ground. A table stacked with bottles and mineral specimens sat just behind the fence, an old man tending the stand. I crept down the hill toward the campground.

The old man stopped what he was doing and watched me putter to a halt beside the bottle stand before sauntering over to the Jeep. He moved like an aged basketball player whose knees had undergone too many scopings. A worn hat topped his thin gray hair. Faded red suspenders held up his wrinkled brown pants. The bones in his back popped when he rested his forearms on the Jeep's open window.

"Looks like you got a problem, boy."

"Afraid so," I said. "I had a flat this morning and didn't get the lug nuts tight when I had it fixed. I didn't notice until it was too late."

I watched as he craned his neck to view the damage, wriggling the wheel as if he didn't believe the lone bolt was still holding it to the jeep.

"You're lucky you made it this far," he said.

I didn't feel particularly lucky.

"Mind if I leave it here while I walk to the station and see if someone can fix it?"

He scratched his head, as if the question required deep thought, before answering in a hillbilly twang far more pronounced than anyone I'd met in Brannerville. It sounded like cold molasses dripping from the lip of a mason jar.

"I don't mind. Don't matter none cause they won't have the part to fix it. Your wheel's ruined."

"Then how far is it to the nearest car dealership?"

"About twenty miles that way," he said, pointing to show me the direction.

"Can I use your phone?"

Grinning, he said, "Ain't got no phone. Not much use for one around here."

Glancing up at the clouding sky, I said, "Guess I'll worry about the wheel tomorrow. Can I rent a camping spot from you?"

"You bet you can," he said. "Two bucks a night."

"Not worried about the competition, are you?"

"Hope you got a tent," he said, ignoring my sarcasm. "Looks like rain."

"Wouldn't travel without one. It's in back of the Jeep."

"There are the bathroom and shower," he said, pointing down the hill at a cinder-block building. "Pull your Jeep by the cement table if it'll make it that far. It's the best spot I got."

"Thanks," I said, noting there were no other campers.

"I got some tools up at the house. I'll run them down in a little bit, and you can take that wheel off."

"And then what?"

"There's a junkyard down the road. It'll have a used wheel. Be right back."

The old man, leaving his bottle and mineral stand unattended, sauntered up the hill to an old wood-framed house. For the first time, I noticed how pristine and beautiful the campsite really was. Tall pines surrounded everything, engulfing the Jeep and cinder-block building beside it. He had equipped the little building with toilet, washbasin, shower stall, and even electricity. After a brief inspection, I unloaded the Jeep.

Twenty minutes later, following much fumbling with stakes and poles, I'd managed to raise Amber's tent. I unrolled the sleeping bag on its canvas floor and placed the ice chest in the opposite corner. After arranging the Coleman stove and lantern outside on the cement picnic table, I finished unpacking. The tent wasn't home but made me feel safe. I wondered if the feeling would remain when darkness came, and wolves began to howl.

Shortly the metallic groan of an old truck moving slowly down the hill riveted my attention. A battered old Ford whose engine continued running long after the old man switched it off. I helped him remove the heavy toolbox from the back of the truck.

"Take off the wheel," he said. "See how much damage there is."

We found a lone bolt hanging by no more than a single metal thread. I almost felt as if I were shooting a faithful horse with a broken leg when I finished it with the old man's hacksaw. Even though he and I were conversing as if we were old friends, I still didn't know his name and he didn't know mine. As I climbed into the front seat of his truck, I decided they probably handled things that way in these parts. Slowly. That is how he proceeded down the highway, never exceeding thirty miles an hour.

He finally said, "What's your name. son?"

"Tom Logan. And yours?"

"John Stewart," he said, shoveling his grizzled old hand across the cab. "Proud to meet you. Where you from?"

"Louisiana."

Stewart slowly removed a match and a corncob pipe from the pocket of his faded overalls and struck the match across the truck's grainy plastic seat cover. The scratching sound as the match raked across rough plastic filled the void of silence in the cab and the smell of burning sulfur mingled with the acrid odor of ancient upholstery. With one hand, he used it to light the pipe. He took two long puffs before speaking.

"Come a long way. Just here to camp?"

Instinct told me John Stewart had nothing to do with Brother Bill's disappearance. Still, I decided to feel him out a bit more before professing my real reason for visiting Turkey Gap and his campground.

"Something like that," I said.

As if he approved of my reluctance to pour forth my life's story to him, he simply nodded and continued down the deserted highway. His accent was markedly different from the common drawl of southern Oklahoma and Texas and bore the distinct nasal ring of hill-country Arkansas. It was almost like singsong. I remembered Professor Fridel's description of these hill people and decided that cowboy and carpetbagger had probably bastardized their old English accents. It added to my growing sense of visiting a place as different as a foreign country.

Stewart glanced out the window. "Rain again tonight. Wettest year we've had in ten years."

"Guess that's good for the crops."

Stewart nodded. "But not for selling rocks and bottles on the side of the road."

"How is your business?" I asked.

"With that new interstate up by Little Rock, we're lucky if we get six tourists passing down the road a day. Sometimes one or two carloads stop by."

"Sorry about that."

Seeing that his pipe had gone out, he dumped burned tobacco into the ashtray and chuckled, as if remembering a deep thought.

"I'm retired, my stand a pastime for an old man. Sometimes I even hide my best bottles to keep from having to sell them," his grin faded. "When we get to the yard, let me do the talking. If Sam thinks the wheel's for you, he'll try to charge you double."

"I won't say a word," I said, agreeing with the old man's logic.

Chapter 8

We finally arrived at Sam's junkyard by the side of the highway. The gate was open and we drove in, stopping beside a tin shack. Judging from the swirl of smoke coming from a pipe in back, it served as both Sam's office and his house. It also explained why the yard was still open after dark. We found Sam sitting in front of the shack in a faded lawn chair.

"We need a part," Stewart said. "Mind if we take a look around?"

Sam eased out of the lawn chair, moving even slower than did John Stewart. He was a skinny little man with one squinty eye and a suspicious frown. He watched us as if we were planning to shoplift an engine block. Also, he had an accent even more pronounced than John Stewart's was.

"Help yourself. What you looking for?"

"Wheel housing for a Jeep."

"Out behind that truck," Sam said, pointing.

Sam knew his junk. Behind the truck where he'd pointed rested the remains of several Jeeps of different vintages. The incomplete cars reminded me of animal carcasses, skeletal except for a few scraps of remaining hide and flesh. Several wheel housings rested beneath one of the vehicles up on blocks. Stewart pawed the stack until he found the one he wanted.

"This one will do. What you asking?"

"Five," Sam said.

When I reached for my wallet, Stewart elbowed me and shook his head.

"Sorta expensive for a rusty old wheel housing, ain't it Sam?"

"Depends on how much you need it, I guess."

"Give you three," the old man said.

"Take four."

"Three-fifty."

Sam didn't bother countering the last offer. Instead, he hefted the heavy wheel housing and headed back toward the shack. When he slid it across the truck bed, I reached for my wallet. Stewart's upraised palm halted me. Removing his own money clip, he paid for the part himself, putting the change in his coin purse and returning to the truck without saying goodbye to Sam.

"I appreciate your help," I said on the way back to the campgrounds.

Stewart reached over and shook my hand without taking his eyes from the road.

"Pleased to be of service," he said.

When we reached the campground, he dropped the wheel housing in front of the disabled Jeep.

"I owe you some money, Mr. Stewart, both for the wheel and the camping."

"We can divvy up when you finish with the tools. Be up at the house."

With that, the old man rattled away along the winding road to his house on the hill. By now, thick clouds cloaked the moon and stars, and damp darkness draped the campground. I lit Amber's lantern, placed it on the picnic table to illuminate the front hood of the Jeep, and began installing the rusty wheel housing. The job took an hour and left me smelling of grease and sweat and cursing over several badly scraped knuckles. When I finally finished, even the tepid water in the drafty washhouse felt wonderful.

I rested at the picnic table, suddenly hungry after a long day. Filling the coffee pot with water from the faucet beside the washhouse, I had hot coffee along with Amber's chilled vegetable slices. Despite how it sounded the simple fare tasted lots better than any meal that I had eaten in a while. Pulling a sweater over my tee shirt, I grabbed John Stewart's tool chest and started up the hilly dirt road to his house.

The house, a large, wood-framed structure, perched on cinder blocks. Stewart was waiting in a porch swing, the large hound beneath his feet oblivious to my approach.

"I'm returning your tools, Mr. Stewart."

"Get it fixed?"

"Yes."

"Good. Might as well sit a spell."

He motioned to a rustic rocking chair draped with a red and orange afghan, opposite the swing.

"Thanks. I also brought the money I owe you. Three-fifty for the wheel and four dollars for two nights camping."

Stewart was smoking his corncob pipe. He tapped it twice against the arm of the swing and shook his head. Even in the dark, he still wore his felt hat.

"Hold on to your money, son. You may decide to stay longer, and we'll divvy up before you leave."

For the third time that day, I took my hand off my wallet. By now, the moon had floated in and out of gray fluffy clouds, and there were no stars in sight. I took a deep breath and leaned back in the rocker. The soggy odor of distant rain played on the breeze blowing across the porch. Stewart was staring at me from the swing, a halo of flame from the pipe's bowl lighting his craggy face as he puffed snowballs of smoke into the air.

"You any kin to Bill Logan?" he asked. "You sorta look like him."

"Bill's my brother," I said, my pulse beginning to race. "Do you know him?"

"I knew the boy well. Bill was down here nearly every weekend for going on two years. He always camped in the same spot as you. Damn shame about him turning up missing."

Before he could continue his running monologue, a thump from the window behind me caused me to flinch. I turned in time to glimpse someone peeking through the blinds.

"Little jumpy, aren't you?" Stewart said.

"Old habit," I said. "Any idea what happened to Bill?"

"Sheriff seems to think he fell in a hole or something. Maybe broke his neck."

"What do you think?"

Stewart thought about the question before answering.

"Woods is so thick in them hills it's real likely they'd never found him if he'd gotten killed. Ain't many roads. Just some old logging trails and they ain't on any map."

"Is it possible he was a victim of foul play?"

"Son, they's wild hogs, rattlesnakes and every manner of critter you can imagine up in them hills. Anything could of happened to the boy."

"Where was he working when he disappeared?" I asked.

"He never told me much about what he was doing though he did say he was mapping something."

"Mapping? What was Bill mapping?"

"Quartz veins in the hills," he said, pulling out his gold pocket watch and glancing at it.

"Quartz veins? For what reason?"

"Was looking for something, I reckon."

Stewart looked again at his pocket watch and then glanced at the front door. As if an alarm had suddenly gone off in his brain, he began humming and thumping his shoe nervously against the porch. I inferred it must be past his bedtime.

"Thanks, Mr. Stewart. It's getting late. Think I'll turn in for the night."

"Better put the top up on that Jeep of yours," he said.

"It doesn't have a top," I said. "I have a tarp to put over it at night."

"Good," he said. "If you don't it'll be full of rainwater by morning."

John Stewart waved lazily as I strolled away down the hill along the winding dirt path. One question puzzled me. Why was Bill mapping quartz veins, and how did it relate to a cultural study of Arkansas hill people? Although bone-weary when I reached the tent, I found I couldn't sleep. Still wide-awake, I stretched out on the sleeping bag, my muscles rebelling against the hard earth. As I lay there, cradled against down-filled cotton, it began to rain.

The gentle drumming of raindrops on canvas soon relaxed me and my mind mulled the multitude of rural sounds; the rustling branches and a faraway nightbird singing the blues. As I listened, a cracking limb startled me back to full awareness. Long-dulled street senses told me it hadn't fallen from a tree in the wind.

I listened intently to the gentle movement of something approaching the tent. As it came closer, I sensed it was something large, perhaps the old man's dog. When it halted just outside the tent door my neck hair bristled, and a chill crept down my spine. I stared out the door flap and into the darkness, trying to divine what was out there. When something brushed the canvas door, I had to bite my lip to avert a blackout. A hand and then an arm appeared through the flap.

"Who is it?" I said.

"Hello," a female voice said. "You asleep?"

Relieved that it wasn't a bear, or maybe a wolf, I relaxed, my strained neck muscles slowly beginning to loosen.

"I'm awake. Who are you?"

Though I could see her shadow in the doorway, she didn't enter the tent. Instead, she stuck her head through the flap.

"Mary Ann Stewart," she said. "John Stewart's my grandpa."

I fumbled through the pile of equipment littering the floor, grabbed a fluorescent camping lamp, and flipped the switch. It filled the tent with soft light and revealed the shadowy figure of the girl standing in the doorway. In the distance an owl hooted, oblivious to the gentle pouring rain.

"Come in. You're getting wet out there."

She took my advice though continued standing in a bent over stance. She grinned when she saw my hatchet on the tent floor.

"You think I was a spook coming to get you?"

Her question, posed in the same twangy accent as her grandfather made me smile.

"Never know," I said.

"I was listening through the window while you was talking to Grandpa. You seen me, didn't you?"

"Yes. You can sit if you want."

After a quick glance around the tent, she plopped down, cross-legged, on the floor.

"What's your name?" she asked.

"Tom Logan. Nice meeting you, Mary Ann."

Still in her teens, Mary Ann's two ponytails bound her jet-black hair. A yellow bow held each in place. Her olive complexion sparkled with fire radiating from vivid green eyes. Her blouse was yellow and her faded jeans molded every tapered curve of her long legs.

Mary Ann must have noticed me looking. She smiled.

"I'm almost nineteen, a senior in high school. Got set back a year when my daddy got killed."

Ignoring the comment about her dead father, I asked, "What brings you out this time of night?"

"I heard you ask Grandpa about Bill."

"You knew him?"

"He is my friend. Is he really your little brother?"

"Yes."

Tears formed in her big green eyes and she began to weep. Her distress unnerved me, and I glanced away as she wiped her face with the yellow sleeve of her blouse. Amber had packed orange juice in the ice chest. When I poured us each a cup, Mary Ann drank hers with a grateful smile. The cold juice worked its magic, halting her tears.

"Does your grandpa know you're here?"

She grinned and said," he could sleep through a tornado."

I wanted to ask about Bill even though I feared it might cause her more stress. It soon became apparent that it was Bill whom she had come to discuss.

"Bill didn't fall in no hole, and no old snake bit him. Somebody might have killed him."

Mary Ann's words were surprisingly calm, following on the heels of her recent tears. They struck me like a sharp slap in the face.

"What makes you think that?"

"He told me someone was following him. Once he came back to camp with a black eye and a cut lip."

"Did he tell you what had happened?"

She shook her head and said, "He didn't do it bumping into a door, and he knew too much about the mountains to get trapped in a hole."

The girl I had just met was echoing my own sentiments.

"Mary Ann, just how well did you know Bill?"

She sipped the juice and stared at the tent floor. Again, tears appeared in her big puffy eyes. This time I handed her my handkerchief. When she stopped crying, she began telling me in disjointed sentences.

"Bill was mapping the veins in the hills. He always set up a tent here, just like you. Then he'd go up to the high forest and sometimes wouldn't come back until he was ready to leave. He collected pieces of the veins. Said it would tell him the age of the mountains and how they was made."

"Veins?"

"Quartz veins," she said. "Once he brought me a pretty piece of quartz that looked like nothing I'd ever seen before. It had a hundred tiny little crystals piercing right through one another. When he stayed here, I'd sneak down to see him. Grandpa didn't like me hanging round him cause he thought we might do something sexual." She paused, as if recalling a past moment, and crossed her long legs. "That's something we never did. Bill told me about college. He was so smart, seems like he knew the answer to most everything."

She stopped talking and wiped her eyes with the handkerchief.

"Part of your story confuses me," I said. "I thought Bill was doing an anthropological study of local hill folk. Why was he interested in quartz veins?" Again, she shook her head. "Any idea where he was working when he disappeared?"

She answered my question with a rambling, ambiguous explanation.

"Bill usually came down on Fridays after classes. When he first started coming down, he'd talk to the locals and use his machine to record what they said. Then he started going into the mountains to talk to people that lived there."

"Did you ever go with him?"

"Not at first. Then, he got real interested in the veins. He wanted Grandpa to show him some of the old workings in the hills. Grandpa's too old, so I showed him. After that, I'd usually go with him when he went up in the mountains."

"Why did his interests change? Was he still interviewing mountain people?"

Mary Ann's black hair flashed like broken graphite in the muted lantern light when she shook her head.

"Far as I know he stopped everything except studying the veins and old mines."

Although I didn't want to set off another crying jag, I had to ask her why she thought someone possibly killed him. She conveyed the story with amazing lucidity, considering her recent emotional outburst.

"Bill was working the south end of the mountain. He told me someone was following him. He didn't know who or why. He also told me he was on to something big. He didn't want to explain what it was till he knew for sure."

"Did he ever tell you?"

"No," she said, shaking her head. "Sometimes Bill slept in his truck. When he didn't come back for three days, I got plenty worried and told Grandpa. He called the police. They searched the hills. They never found him. He never came back."

Mary Ann's eyes filled with tears again and I poured more orange juice into her cup.

"What happened to his recordings and thesis material? Do you know?"

"Bill was worried someone would try to steal his work, so he kept them in his tent or in the pickup."

"Why would anyone want his thesis materials?"

"Don't know," she said. They weren't in his pickup when the police found it. Someone took everything in the truck. They didn't get his journal, though because he always kept it with him."

"Journal?"

Mary Ann's demeanor changed, and she said, "Bill had a little leather journal. It was like a diary."

It was then that I remembered that even as a youngster Bill had always kept daily notes. Once he'd gotten angry with me for thumbing through the worn yellow notepad he'd kept in his shirt pocket. I never understood why someone as secretive as Bill would want to keep his most personal thoughts on a pad of paper anyone might find and read. Maybe it was because he never let it out of his sight.

If we can't find Bill, how are we going to find the journal?" I said.

"It's on the mountain."

"Where on the mountain?"

She didn't answer. Tears had left her eyes, and she smiled when she turned and said, "See you tomorrow."

The young woman slipped back into darkness, silently as she had appeared. I waited a minute before turning off the light then reclined on my makeshift pillow, wondering about the significance of quartz veins and Bill's missing journal.

I decided to call Professor Quinn in the morning and question him about the veins. Like a powerful somnolent drug, the gentle thump of rain on canvas soon lulled me into a deep hypnotic sleep.

Chapter 9

A painful kink in my back from sleeping on the hard floor of the tent awakened me at dawn. Although I didn't relish rolling out of a warm bed, my spirits lifted once out of the bag. My muscles ached but gradually began to loosen as I stepped from the tent and saw the sun coming up over the treetops.

My legs were stiff and ankles popping like dry limbs as I hiked the short distance to the washroom. When I returned, I set the coffee pot and cast-iron skillet on the stove before remembering I had neither bacon nor eggs. I packed away the skillet and nibbled on a carrot slice instead.

After having found Bill's camping spot so easily, my discussion with Mary Ann became the second stroke of luck I'd had since arriving in Turkey Gap. As I crunched the last carrot slice, I heard the shuffling gait of someone coming down the hill behind me. I didn't have to look to know it was John Stewart.

"Morning," he said. "How'd you sleep?"

"The floor in that tent feels like a sack of potatoes."

Stewart winked and nibbled on the stem of his corncob pipe.

"There's a motel up the road about twenty miles or so."

"I'll tough it out. What I need is a good air mattress."

Stewart grinned and said, "I imagine you can get one at the hardware store in town."

"There's a town here?"

"Three-hundred people with Main Street and everything. Just over yonder," he said, pointing to the southeast.

"Thanks. Guess I'll test the wheel and drive over. What did you say you sell at your stand, Mr. Stewart?"

"Bottles, some old, some new. Dig them up all over the county. And a few mineral specimens Mary Ann finds or trades for me."

I watched as he sauntered away toward the bottle stand. Mary Ann soon followed him down the hill, her trademark yellow bow knotting her hair as schoolbooks loaded her arms.

"Morning. Need a ride?"

"Bus'll be here any minute. You can pick me up in front of the school around noon. Grandpa called and got permission for me to take most of the day off. I'll show you the veins where Bill was working."

"You sure?" I said. She continued walking out to the gate by the highway without stopping. "Wait. Where is the school?"

"First street past the cafe," she called over her shoulder. "Can't miss it. Meet you in front."

A yellow school bus screeched to a halt on the blacktop and picked her up. I policed the area and stowed the cooking gear in the tent, wondering why the old man had let his granddaughter skip classes to go into the hills with me. Finally finished, I headed to town to purchase an air mattress, quickly learning that Turkey Gap was bigger than the head of a pin, though not much.

There were no cars on the single street. Two old men were playing checkers in front of the local feed and seed. Lettered in faded gold paint, the words Bank of Turkey Gap emblazoned the time-silvered window of the building across the street. Beside it, a little man peered from the door of the clapboard hardware store. He met me with a mile-wide gap-toothed smile that highlighted dime-sized freckles on his moon face and red hair slicked back with a pint or two of Vitalis. He reeked of creosote and cow manure.

True to Stewart's prediction, the store did sell air mattresses. I returned to the Jeep with my purchase and a wheezy cough from layers of dust that coated the musty merchandise. Just before noon, I began looking for the schoolhouse, finding Mary Ann waiting at the door. With a wave of recognition, she crossed in front of the Jeep and climbed into the seat beside me.

"What now?" I said.

"That way," she said, pointing up the hill toward the mountains.

The road out of town quickly became crooked and narrow as it wound up the mountain. The few houses scattered on its outskirts soon disappeared, replaced by giant pines, and rolling foothills.

"Not exactly a super-highway," I said.

"Got four-wheel on this thing?" Mary Ann asked, glancing at the gearshift.

"Do we need it?"

"Rained pretty heavy in the hills last night."

"No worries," I said. "This baby will get us anyplace we need to go."

When Mary Ann tapped my shoulder, I took my foot off the gas.

"Guess you're wondering about my Ma and Pa, huh?"

"It crossed my mind."

"They're dead. Mama died when I was born, and Daddy was killed in Iraq."

"I'm sorry."

Mary Ann pivoted in the Jeep's bucket seat, wiped her eyes with the back of her hand, and stared out at the passing trees.

"You married?"

"Divorced," I said.

When she squirmed around in the seat, I could see her eyes were red, tears forming in their corners. After folding her arms tightly against her chest, she fidgeted until her knees were almost touching the gearshift. She began crying softly, her voice cracking when she spoke.

"You remind me so much of Bill."

"Why haven't you told someone about the journal before now?"

"Grandpa couldn't do anything, and there's no one else I could trust."

"What about the police?"

From her frown, I could tell she had little regard for the local constabulary.

"They's probably the ones that took Bill's papers and tapes."

"Why?"

She pointed to a clearing, surrounded by trees, beside the road, jagged stumps protruding from bare earth incised with deep ruts from logging truck tires. Someone had clear-cut a portion of the forest. It gaped like an open wound, still oozing fresh resin from its decimated remains.

Sun, reflecting off the Jeep's hood glittered in Mary Ann's green eyes, and she grew silent as the road narrowed and became progressively steeper. As we headed up the mountain, I glanced in the rear-view mirror. The rooftops of Turkey Gap were disappearing in the valley behind us. I quickly returned my attention to the road in front of me.

The thoroughfare had begun to wind, sometimes almost backing up on itself. Every hairpin turn required me to pump the brakes and wrestle the wheel. Finally, we reached the very top of the ancient mountain range. Mary Ann extended her hand. Signaling me to slow down, she pointed to a narrow dirt road jutting off the main blacktop. Pine trees growing to the very edge of the ditch virtually concealed it.

"Logging trail," she said.

"Trail is right. Can we use it?"

"If the big trucks can make it, then so can we."

Before proceeding into the trees, I stopped and locked the transmission into four-wheel drive. We were quickly out of sight of the highway though we continued climbing up a steep and narrow path. Ten minutes of washboard road set the Jeep's stiff suspension rocking and my bones aching again. An angular rock in the tent's floor had emblazoned itself in the nerve endings of my spine and my back kept letting me know about it as we reached a forest clearing

Terrain encompassing the clearing flattened abruptly and reminded me of a scene from Vietnam. Instead of Agent Orange, a timber company had deforested forty or fifty acres of trees with chainsaws. Someone had replanted the barren swaths on the highway with saplings that covered the ground like mats of tall grass. No such remedial measures were apparent in this clearing and eroded ditches, gaping like angry scars in the bare earth, had formed.

"Something doesn't look right about this clearing," I said. "Is someone cutting the forest illegally?"

Mary Ann nodded. "This is National Forest land. Bill said they are doing it all over the mountain."

"They?"

"BST, the big logging company. They have an office in Dill City. This is where the sheriff found Bill's pickup."

To our south, mountains overlooked a huge valley. Hazy clouds draped the forested indention hidden deep in the heart of the range. Like a lingering wraith, it imparted an ominous gloom to the rugged peaks. I took the binoculars from the back seat of the Jeep to get a better look at the wild valley. Before us, an endless stretch of rock and greenery lay shrouded by incessant cloud cover.

"This forest extends beyond visual limits."

"It's so big smart pilots won't even fly over it," Mary Ann said. "They're afraid of crashing and never being found."

"Sounds like the Devil's Triangle."

"Bill says the forest is just about the largest uninhabited area in southern North America - almost two million acres."

"Anyone live down there?"

"Timberwolves from Missouri, brown bears from Tennessee, and armadillos and bobcats from Texas. Bill said its one of the south forty-eight's largest game preserves. Some animals, he said, retreat mile after mile, year after year, until they find shelter in the big forest."

"Sounds like Bill knew a lot about the valley."

Mary Ann ignored my comment, more intent on picking red and yellow wildflowers that spread across the mountaintop. Picking a pair of bright flowers, she arranged them in her hair so that they resembled a Gauguin on black velvet.

"Bill reported the clear-cutting to the sheriff," she said. "He went to Dill City to talk to the BST people in person."

"What happened?"

"Don't know. The sheriff didn't help much."

Mary Ann started down the trail as I grabbed knapsack, canteen, and binoculars from the Jeep and chased her to the edge of the field. She stopped and pointed down the hill.

"Bill told me if anything ever happened to him he'd try to leave his journal in a cave or one of the mines along the trail for me to find."

We followed a logging road for three-quarters of a mile before reaching a winding trail that plunged toward the valley. Mary Ann and I bantered as we hiked. Soon, I found myself panting and out of breath as I attempted to match her rapid pace. After stopping several times for a drink, I quickly fell behind and soon lost sight of her in the trees. Finally, enchanted by forest sounds, I slackened my pace. Birds and insects echoed like instruments in a giant primitive orchestra. It was beautiful music, even to a city boy's ears. Wind playing through tree branches modulated the melody.

Forest sounds became white noise, omnipresent though unobtrusive as I chased after Mary Ann. Another sound had caught my ear. It was the bouncing rattle of a noisy old vehicle moving slowly toward us. Although seemingly distant, it was really very close and coming closer. When I bumped into Mary Ann, our collision startled me back to reality.

We had intersected another logging road and traversed it a hundred yards when an old pickup truck appeared from around a curve. Grabbing Mary Ann's elbow I pulled her off the grass-covered dirt road, waiting as the old truck screeched to a halt beside us. Two men occupied the cab of the pickup, a gun rack with two shotguns directly behind them. Bags of groceries completely filled the truck bed.

Grinning like a happy moron, the man who was riding shotgun had a sardonic smile that framed an almost toothless mouth. The driver was huge, his sweat-stained welder's cap brushing the truck's ceiling. His left arm, hanging from the window, was bigger than my own thigh. His empty eye socket winked at us through raw red lips. The muscles in Mary Ann's forearm flexed as she gripped her grandfather's pick hammer. One Eye studied us like someone shopping for a good steak in a meat locker.

"Lost?" he said, his twang drawing the word into two syllables.

"Hiking," I said.

Glancing around, he winked at his partner with his one good eye as if to share an inside joke.

"Looking for something special way out here?"

I glanced at my toes, and then at Mary Ann.

"We was looking for the mines," she said.

One Eye removed his cap and scratched his head with an index finger as big as a jumbo hot-link. His partner continued to grin, his face reminding me of a garishly painted Halloween mask.

"We know the whereabouts of a couple of mines that no one else knows about," One Eye said.

"Oh?"

"Want us to take you to them?"

"Maybe some other time," I said, finding my voice. "Thanks anyway."

One Eye replaced his cap and cocked his unshaven chin. Like his partner, he was also grinning as if his simian brain had suddenly conjured a humorous thought.

"How about us giving you a ride?"

"No thanks," I said. "We're not going much further."

I nudged Mary Ann's shoulder, directing her to start walking. She did, and I kept my fingers crossed that the two hermits wouldn't follow us. We were out of sight when the engine rumbled to a noisy start. I waited until I no longer heard the creak of its shock absorbers. Mary Ann hadn't stopped walking. Forgetting my fatigue, I hurried after her.

"About a quarter of the way down there's a vein Bill was studying," Mary Ann said. "We'll follow it till it saddles out."

"And how far is that?"

"Bout five miles west of here."

"And then?"

"Mostly an easy climb back to the top of the ridge."

I hurried down the slope, barely able to see the narrow trail. Grass, receiving maximum sunlight from the south-facing slope, grew knee-high. Almost immediately, I caught my foot and took a tumble, skinning my knees when I hit the ground. Exertion caused salty perspiration to form and drip down my legs, stinging the abrasions. Mary Ann gave me a hand before continuing down the trail, leaving me only enough time to wipe away blood with my shirt sleeve as I hurried to catch her.

Limestone boulders, having slumped down the hill through the ages, began to appear by the trail. Still centuries from their final destination, they guarded the valley like giant gray sentinels. I lost sight of Mary Ann when she went behind a large boulder. I found her kneeling in front of a wall of limestone.

"Here's the vein," she said.

A translucent vein, slicing across the wall of rock, reflected rays of direct sunlight. I recognized the mineral as quartz. There was also a dull black mineral, interspersed with reddish brown clay. With the pick, Mary Ann broke a large hunk of black ore. The heavy piece tumbled to the ground, shining like a new silver dollar.

"Manganese," she said. "Mingled with quartz. Clay shows it's a gouge zone or fault. Grandpa says the minerals was once liquid and moved up the fault till something caused them to harden."

Mary Ann dug through the underbrush, searching for Bill's journal. Twenty minutes of combined exertion produced nothing except a canteen. It was Bill's canteen. She leaned against a rock, distressed at discovering the ominous artifact.

"Why would he have left his canteen?"

I touched her shoulder. "At least we know he was here."

Mary Ann provided my aching muscles no respite. After springing to her feet, she started down the trail at a hurried trot.

"Let's keep going."

"Wait. Tell me how you know so much about geology."

"Grandpa was a prospector," she said as I caught up to her. "He had his own lead mine when he was younger."

High above us, buzzards circled in a hot current of air, far above the thick cloud cover shrouding the valley. From our vantage, it looked like a giant bowl of damp cotton balls. As the sun began its western descent, I suddenly felt tired and very hungry.

Chapter 10

When I could go no further, I persuaded Mary Ann to take a break. We sat on a flat rock by the trail, drinking water from the canteen and eating the remainder of Amber's carrot slices. The late afternoon sun had heated the terrain and sweat trickled down Mary Ann's tan neck as she lay with her hands behind her head.

"I wonder who those two men are," I asked.

"Hermits."

"Ever seen them before?"

The face Mary Ann made telegraphed her feelings on the subject long before she answered.

"No. They were kind of creepy, weren't they?"

"No kidding. Explain again why you didn't tell anyone about Bill's journal."

"I figured that if anyone could find it, it would be me and I haven't found a way to get up here yet. Until now," she said, staring into the hazy valley.

"How did you talk your grandfather into letting you skip class?"

Mary Ann squirmed and her face contorted into a silly grin.

"Didn't, really. Knew you wouldn't bring me otherwise, so I told a little fib. You're not mad, are you?"

"Only if your granddad calls the sheriff and has me arrested for kidnapping."

Mary Ann sat up and brushed nonexistent crumbs from her blouse and jeans.

"He won't, at least if we hurry and get back to our search. First I have to take a trip behind a rock."

"Not a bad idea," I said.

Mary Ann held out her hand for me to help her up and then strolled away up a trail. I went the other direction, stepping lightly through the thick growth of vines, briars and creeping trailers and trying not to imagine what creeping denizens resided beneath. Within ten feet of the trail, I was out of sight though I continued until I was far up the hill. There I relieved myself against a wall of rock. What I saw when I glanced up made me glad I had. I was staring directly into the cold eyes of a coiled rattlesnake.

Just as suddenly, I was back in Vietnam.

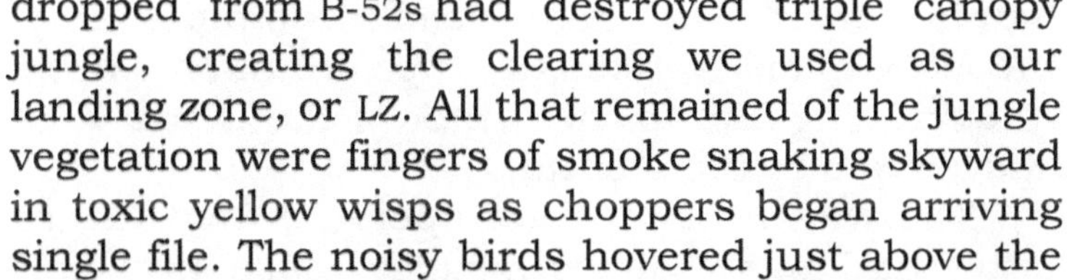

Incendiary bombs and thousand-pounders dropped from B-52s had destroyed triple canopy jungle, creating the clearing we used as our landing zone, or LZ. All that remained of the jungle vegetation were fingers of smoke snaking skyward in toxic yellow wisps as choppers began arriving single file. The noisy birds hovered just above the decimated earth, disgorging human cargo like bees from a hive. I climbed down onto the Huey's landing ramp and hung there a moment before jumping, rolling when I landed in the hot dirt.

Charred and broken stumps replaced jungle vegetation that had once covered the clearing. Its charcoal skeleton continued to burn in spots. Everywhere toxic smoke reeked of burned gasoline and destroyed vegetation. Craters big enough to swallow a house pitted the earth. Only brown and sickly yellow remained, along with the lingering stench of mass destruction.

Charlie Company spread out, forming a wide perimeter around the charred LZ. The stump on which I sat was still warm as we waited. The whump-whump-whump of a single helicopter, hovering a hundred feet above us, disturbed the pregnant silence. I glanced skyward in time to see a blindfolded person, clothed in black pajamas and with his hands tied behind his back, tumbling out the door. His body connected with unyielding earth in a sickening thud that sent a cloud of black soot into the air.

Moments later the lone bird landed beside the lifeless body. Two soldiers and another VC prisoner exited, bending low at the waist to avoid the whirling rotor blades. One of the soldiers accompanying the prisoner was South Vietnamese, the other an American. Sergeant Thompson, the black American, was a Vietnamese interpreter. The two men held their hands in front of their faces to circumvent toxic soot and smoke swirling all around them. The prisoner with bound hands gazed at his dead comrade until the ARVN soldier yanked the rope around his neck. After leading him to the center of the clearing, he shoved him to the ground.

The war in our area of operation had turned bitter and nasty as both sides made negligible progress. A firefight here, an ambush there. Most encounters lasted less than five minutes. About the time it took to call in a Cobra gunship or artillery barrage. Both sides played head games. VC and NVA regulars often tortured and killed soldiers they captured, leaving mutilated bodies for their friends to find. G.I.s were no better. Years of fighting had escalated these games into a brutal, often nonsensical contest.

Sergeant Thompson's fatigues were crisp and freshly pressed. Unlike the line company grunts, he looked as though he had just stepped out of an air-conditioned office building. He was handsome and clean cut and spoke six languages, including Chinese. He disliked whites, all whites, and had a streak of cruelty that transcended reason. He also had an ear collection. Unlike other collectors who extracted their trophies from the dead, Sergeant Johnny preferred taking his from living prisoners. It didn't matter much. Because we rarely took prisoners.

We'd lost one unlucky soldier, Private Jimmy Lee Tanner, an eighteen-year-old Alabama redneck, from our own company that week. Jimmy Lee had married his high school sweetheart shortly before shipping out for Vietnam. She called him Honeyboy, an endearment several of his friends had overheard. The name stuck.

Honeyboy had disappeared during a prolonged hump through the jungle. Usually, the company moved in single file, spread out in such a way that a well-placed mortar round or burst from a deadly RPG would only take out one or two grunts. During monsoon season, rain was incessant. Part of the year was dry, with little or no rain. The day Honeyboy disappeared this had become a problem.

Helicopters usually supplied our line company every third day. Each man received fresh rations, ammunition and two or more gallons of water to last until the next supply day. The eight pounds a gallon of water weighs restricted how much an individual could hump on his back and how often he needed new supplies. Three days was fine. Four wasn't. Following an unavoidable occurrence, we entered our fourth day without fresh supplies and our first full day with little or no water. Unlike the war, monsoon season had ended.

Echo, our sister company, had found an NVA bunker complex and a regiment of NVA regulars had engaged them, pinning them with mortar and small arms fire. This unexpected skirmish made necessary the use of every available chopper to assist in Echo's rescue. It had also left us with little remaining food or water. That morning we set out on a prolonged and unplanned hump to a distant river.

We rarely moved more than a kilometer at a time because of the debilitating tropical heat and humidity. We always cut our own paths through the undergrowth, forsaking jungle trails often booby-trapped or ripe for ambush. Thirst makes a man bold and sometimes crazy. That particular day the river was three clicks away.

We reached the river at dusk, and it was dark before anyone realized Honeyboy was missing. During the march, the single-file line of grunts had spread out further than normal, sometimes a hundred yards or more separating individuals. Honeyboy was drag gunner, the last man in line, and had fallen out of sight of the man in front of him.

A patrol found his boots and steel helmet but no Honeyboy. Now, we had captured our own prisoner, and Sergeant Thompson was questioning him with a straight razor in an attempt to learn what had happened to the soldier.

Thompson's razor didn't impress the prisoner, even after claiming an ear. Thompson was a pro and kept at it until he found something that did impress the young VC soldier. A sheath-like strip of rubber used to waterproof mortar rounds during transport did the trick. This strip of rubber looked like a giant balloon. Grunts collected these rubber devices from crates of ammo, using them to protect wallets, letters, and pictures from rain and rampant humidity. Because of their size and shape, we called them donkey dicks.

Sergeant Thompson noticed the prisoner wince when he removed his wallet from his own donkey dick. Recognition flashed in his brown eyes, his thin lips riding up in a cruel expression over his teeth when he grinned. Unrolling the rubber sheath from the wallet, he pulled it down slowly over the captured man's head, over his face and nose.

Blood and sweat caked the prisoner's neck and shoulder. His eyes were large, dark and filled with horror. Thompson had located the man's secret fear, and it had already loosened his bladder. Like impending death, a sickly fetid odor wafted through the humid LZ. Finally convinced by the good sergeant of his imminent damnation, the prisoner quickly confessed Honeyboy's fate and led us on a circuitous journey to a dark hole in the ground.

Tunnels, blind chutes, and spider holes laced the jungle. VC and NVA used them as shelter, command posts, and points of ambush and supply depots, among other things. This was different, a simple six-foot-wide hole plunging straight down into the ground that seemed to have no utilitarian purpose. According to the frightened prisoner, Honeyboy's body, thrown there after they had killed him, was in the hole. Our captain asked for a volunteer to go in after the body.

Never volunteer is the foot soldier's credo. I looked at my fellow troops, mostly city boys from northern climes, and saw the fear of the hole laced in their eyes. Crusty lesions caused by fungal growths and many tropical skin diseases proliferating in the incessant jungle heat and humidity scabbed their exposed arms, necks and faces. They were out of their element and knew it. Like an idiot, I raised my hand.

They tied a rope around my waist and lowered me into the hole. Five feet from the surface, I realized it was deeper than any of us had imagined. Though the jungle was hot, the temperature in the hole felt like the inside of a steam cabinet. Damp, musty, and acrid air assaulted my lungs like a full-strength shot of ammonia.

Soon the hole took an abrupt bend, blocking out most of the filtered light from above. My boots bumped against loose earth. Broken clods tumbled down into the bottom of the hole still far below. They lowered me through a huge spider web, elastic strands wrapping around my face and neck like a living hand. Tearing at it, I tried not to hyperventilate in the stygian darkness as cool air suddenly blasted up from the depths. It chilled the perspiration dripping down my face, neck, and damp palms clutching the rope.

Chilled air brought with it a different smell: the rotten odor of spoiled melon. Some forty feet below the jungle, my feet touched the bottom of the dank hole. I stood there, absorbing pitch-black silence with a noisy heart. When I probed with the toe of my boot, I connected almost instantly with something soft and squishy, the touch producing a low moan of escaping gas that sounded like the protest of a prodded spirit.

I heard and felt something else, knowing what it was without seeing it. When it slithered across my boot, I was certain. Yanking on the rope, I began to yell.

"Pull me up! Pull me the hell up!"

When I reached the surface, I had to shield my eyes from the muted glare reflecting through the trees. I must have had a look on my face because the soldiers were staring at me in silence as if I'd seen a ghost.

"Fix a torch," I said. "It's pitch black in that hole."

"Is Honeyboy down there?" the captain asked.

"Something is," I said, reattaching the rope around my waist.

My heart continued to race as they lowered me back into the entrance of what was apparently a cavern. This time I saw bats hanging upside down and huge rats turning away from the glare of the burning torch. I reached the bottom of the cavern and located Honeyboy in the glow of the torch. The body was lying on its back, its arms outstretched, staring at me through eyeless sockets.

Honeyboy wasn't alone. Hundreds of snakes, both large and small, matted the floor of the circular cavern like a living carpet. Their bodies pumped and pulsated, one of the viperous beasts twining itself around my ankle and another started up my leg. A hooded viper dropped from a ledge above me, landing on my shoulders. As if in a nightmare, I found I couldn't move, my arms frozen in place and a scream stifled in my throat.

I somehow managed to brush the snake off my shoulder and thrust the torch at the pulsating mass of reptiles. Courage trickled down my leg, and only a sudden surge of straight adrenaline saved me. Tossing the torch at the angry mass of reptiles, I wrapped my arms around Honeyboy's chest, not wanting to wait alone in the viper pit while the grunts pulled his body to the surface. With a desperate yank on the rope, I closed my eyes to the darkness clutched Honeyboy's putrefying body to my chest, trying not to breathe but knowing I would remember the pungent smell of his rotting flesh until the very day I died.

"Tom, you okay?"

I stared up into Mary Ann's eyes, and the clear blue Arkansas sky.

Chapter 11

"What happened?" Mary Ann asked again.

"Saw a snake and lost my footing," I said.

"Rattlesnake?"

"A big one. Scared the daylights out of me."

Mary Ann giggled, put her hand over her mouth, and turned away, trying not to laugh though without success.

Finding little humor in waking up flat on my back in a pile of brush, I wasted little time descending the slope and returning to the large flat rock. There I sat, despite Mary Ann's protests, stubbornly refusing to move until my temples quit pounding. When my blood pressure finally returned to normal, I was left with a tremendous headache. Mary Ann shook her head and disappeared down the trail, returning with a wild yellow rose she had found growing somewhere on the slope. Smiling, she handed it to me.

"Thanks, but what's it for."

"Make you feel better. My daddy would always give me one when I was sad or hurt."

"Your father?"

"Yeah," she said in a suddenly dreamy voice. "Yellow is my favorite color. When I was real little, I fell and skinned my knee. That was the first time he gave me a rose. He said, Mary Ann, everything's okay. He would always be there with a rose and a smile when I needed one. It always made me feel better."

"Your old man must have been a thoughtful person."

"He was. I cried all night before he went away to the war. Grandpa and I drove him to the bus station the next day, and I cried again before he left."

She paused, and a tear appeared in the corner of her eye. This time I didn't wait for the inevitable result.

"Let's move on," I said.

Mary Ann dabbed at her eyes with the back of her hand and followed me down the trail. Soon we reached the saddle, tan as bleached leather against blue afternoon sky. Wind and rain had sculpted it from solid rock, and a small stream that followed its surface poured over the ledge into the valley. Mary Ann pointed up the hill to the east.

"That's the way back to the Jeep. We're almost there. I want to check a little cave in the cliff first, though."

Mary Ann pointed up the hill to the dark entrance of the cave. Without waiting for me, she raced up the trail and disappeared into its mouth. When I reached the natural hole in the wall, I took a deep breath, ducked through its tiny aperture, and followed her.

Cool air washed over my face and arms, and muted light swathed the opening of the silent cave. We weren't alone. In a corner was a pile of droppings left by some small animal. Above us, a lone bat hung from the ceiling. Amazingly, the cave caused me no adverse reaction. After finding nothing of interest, we started back to the Jeep. Feeling remarkably relieved to be in sunlight again I fished in the ice chest for the carton of orange juice.

"Sorry about the snake deal back there," I said, handing it to Mary Ann.

Some of the juice dribbled down her chin when she smiled. After brushing it away with her fingertips, she climbed into the passenger seat of the Jeep.

"If it had been me I'd have probably wet my pants," she said.

"So would I," I said. "Except I'd just gone."

We both laughed.

It was late afternoon when we reached the campgrounds. I was happy to see that John Stewart had already shut down his bottle stand for the day. Though a hot shower sounded like heaven, I had something else on my mind I needed to do first.

Mary Ann gave me directions to the county seat some twenty miles away. I dropped her off and returned to the highway, hoping to visit with Sheriff Amos Bonner before he went home for the night.

"Tomorrow's Saturday," she said before starting up the hill.

"So?"

"So there's no school and Grandpa will let me go back up in the hills with you."

"Then I'll see you tomorrow," I said, waving as I drove away down the dirt path to the highway.

It was late and the eastern range of hills already formed purple outlines against a pink and ocher horizon. Out of the north, damp gray clouds had begun rolling in. Purple martins darted overhead, feeding on gnats and mosquitoes stirred up by the approaching front. It looked like the beginning of another rainy night.

I found the road to Dill City deserted and reached the little town in less than twenty minutes. Fast food restaurants, used car lots, and cheap motels marked the county seat that was a city in name only. I found the courthouse, just like so many other small southern towns, in the square. It took me five minutes to find the jail and another five to locate Sheriff Bonner. He didn't bother getting up when I entered his office.

Bonner looked like a pro linebacker that had gone to flab. His skin was as pale as a flipped pile of manure, and his pasty complexion accentuated a somber face once ravaged by teenage acne. When I explained who I was, he told me to sit a spell. Stretching out his arms, he clasped his hands in front of his expansive gut and popped all ten of his fingers.

"Just what can I do for you, Mr. Logan?"

"I'm looking for my brother."

"Son, you come a day late and a dollar short. We done covered the whole county looking for the boy."

"Mary Ann Stewart says Bill told her that someone had followed him, perhaps intending to do him harm."

Sheriff Bonner's homey grin disappeared. Leaning forward in his chair, he rested his elbows on the desk. His pockmarked jowls formed a frown, and I could see something ignite in his watery gray eyes. He pointed out the window, toward the mountain front.

"You know what them woods is like out there? They's miles and miles of nothing but brush, rattlesnakes and razorback hogs. You break a leg, and you don't come out. Am I making myself clear?"

"Bill was an expert woodsman. He hiked, camped and rock-climbed for sport."

"Don't square by me if he was an Eagle Scout. Makes no never mind if you get yourself in trouble up in them hills."

Despite his explanation, Bonner seemed disturbed by my visit. He raised his substantial bulk from the chair and poured himself some very black coffee from the pot in the corner. He didn't offer me a cup.

"You don't think foul play is a possibility?"

Bonner stared at me as if I were a mosquito he was preparing to swat. He blinked, shook his head, and said, "Rattlesnake, maybe, but not the human kind."

"My brother kept his thesis notes and recordings in his truck. According to your report, they weren't found. Any idea what happened to them?"

"There wasn't nothing in the boy's pickup I didn't report. Now, this case is closed and there ain't no ifs, and, or buts about it."

"Did you ever talk with Bill? Mary Ann says he complained to you about BST."

"You and me are speaking on different wavelengths," he said, leaning even further over the desk. So close, I could smell coffee and nicotine on his breath and the aromatic oil in his stringy hair.

"I was up in the mountains today near the place you found Bill's truck. Someone's clear-cutting the forest. The National Forest. Does the government give permits to cut National Forest land?"

"Ain't nobody clear-cutting illegal in my county," Sheriff Bonner said. "What makes you think you can come in here and accuse the biggest employer in these parts of doing something you don't know shit from Shinola about?"

"I'm not accusing anyone of anything. I just thought that maybe some of the loggers might have met Bill from time to time. Maybe there is a lead there. I don't know."

"Son," he said, popping his fingers again. "I don't guess you know there was a warrant out for your brother's arrest when he turned up missing."

Bonner's statement caught me like a lead pipe to the back of the head. I blinked and said, "Mind telling me what the charge was?"

"Breaking and entering."

"My brother was no thief. What proof do you have?"

"Don't make no never mind now. BST dropped the charges after your brother disappeared."

"Maybe they trumped up the charges to discredit him for blowing the whistle on them. Maybe after they took care of him on the mountain, they didn't need to worry about setting him up any longer."

"Now you look here," Bonner said, his face turning dangerously red as he pointed his crooked index finger at me. "BST don't have nothing to do with your brother's disappearance, and I don't want you flagging around town spouting it. You hear me?"

"Fine," I said, standing up from the chair. "I'll just go over to BST and get the facts myself."

"You leave them people over there alone," he said, practically coming over the desk at me. "Get my drift?"

He was standing in my face when I said, "Loud and clear."

I backed out the door, finding a pay phone outside a café on the main street of town. After I had eaten my first hot meal in two days, I made a long distance call to Professor Fridel. Just as I had hoped, I located him in his campus office putting the final changes on some research paper. As I suspected he knew nothing about why Bill was mapping quartz veins. Finally, I called Amber.

"You didn't tell me about the bumps in the floor of the tent," I said.

"Buy an air mattress."

"I did."

"Is this a social call?"

"I wanted to hear your pleasant voice, and I also have a favor to ask."

"Shoot, Troop," she said.

"It seems someone is illegally clear-cutting National Forest land down here on a large scale. Can you check out BST Corporation for me? I think they may be involved."

"Are you on to something already?"

"Don't know yet."

"I'll see what I can turn up," she said. "Anything else you'd like me to check?"

"Yes. Ask Professor Quinn what he knows about the significance of quartz veins."

"Is that all?"

"Nope," I said. "I wanted to make sure you were still planning to join me Monday."

"Wouldn't miss it for the world," she said.

When I returned to the Jeep, the rain had just begun spotting its dusty windshield. Before I reached Turkey Gap, the sky had turned pitch black, except for ribbons of lightning lacing the horizon with remnant flashes of electric color. After parking the open Jeep beneath the washhouse overhang, I rushed inside the tent, just as dark clouds opened up and began dumping their noisy torrent on my shoulders.

That night I blew up the air mattress and draped the sleeping bag over it. I closed my eyes a few minutes before my plan to scurry to the washhouse to brush my teeth and wash my face. The rain had stopped when I opened them again. It was morning, sunlight shining through the window of Amber's tent.

Chapter 12

After crawling out of my tent the next morning, I rubbed my sore back as I inhaled crisp mountain air. A slight breeze rustled the pines. The sky was blue with no sign of rain. I ate breakfast, stowed my gear in the tent and glanced at my watch. It was almost seven when I heard Mary Ann, chattering as she strolled down the hill with her grandfather. When they reached me, John Stewart grinned, showing lines in his wrinkled face.

"Morning," he said. "Sleep any better last night?"

He gave me a backward wave and continued down the hill to the bottle stand without waiting for my answer.

Mary Ann's face bore its own mischievous grin, and she said, "Dream about snakes last night?"

"I shook out my sleeping bag before I went to sleep."

"What about your boots?"

I glanced nervously at my feet, then back at Mary Ann. She was laughing, and I made a mental note to check my boots next time before putting them on.

"Ready?"

"Is it all right with your grandfather?"

"It's Saturday. He lets me do what I want."

"Then let's go."

This time we stopped at the cafe in town, Mary Ann waiting in the Jeep while I bought sandwiches and potato chips for lunch. We were on our way back to the mountains, Mary Ann looking radiant in faded blue jeans and her patented bright yellow blouse.

"I visited Sheriff Bonner in Dill City yesterday. He said there was a warrant for Bill's arrest. Bonner says Bill broke into the BST office."

"Bill wouldn't have done that," she said.

"I don't think so either. It's probably just a smoke screen to discredit Bill and circumvent his finger pointing."

Mary Ann was silent for a moment. "You think they could have done something to Bill?"

"Don't know yet but I'm going to check it out. First things first. Where are we going today?"

"East along the vein," she said. "There are some old mines on the trail no one's worked in fifty years."

"Did the ore play out?"

"The veins are real narrow and get hard to follow. There wasn't an easy way to bring the ore down the mountain once you dug it out so I guess they just finally gave up."

"You're planning on crawling around inside a deserted mine?"

"Yep." She took two miner's lamps from her daypack and grinned when she saw my expression. "If you're afraid, you can wait outside while I go in."

I didn't answer. Mary Ann misjudged my reticence as disinterest. She folded her arms and crossed her long legs, remaining silent the rest of the drive up the mountain. When we reached the summit, I turned off the highway and followed the dirt road to the clearing. Without waiting for me, she started down the winding trail. So rapid was her departure from the Jeep she forgot her daypack. Grabbing it, I hurried after her just as the sun disappeared behind a cloud.

Before long, the sky grew darkly overcast. Within minutes, rain began to fall, first in large lazy drops and then in a heavy downpour that soaked my clothes as I hurried down the path after Mary Ann. Earth, already damp from last night's rain, quickly became muddy and slick.

Mary Ann finally stopped on the trail, cupped her hands, and shouted above the torrent.

"There's a mine just ahead. It's covered with a brush so I don't know exactly where." I almost bumped into her as she slowed to a stop and pointed down the hill. "There. A talus pile."

The heavy downpour all but masked a pile of rubble and rock dug up from a mine. I followed Mary Ann off the trail, trudging after her through wet, shoulder-high vegetation. We found the conical mound of debris adjacent to a water-filled open hole.

"That's the shaft," she said. "We won't be looking around down there today."

"Not unless you brought along an Aqualung," I said.

Mary Ann took the daypack from me, removed her grandfather's hammer, and began banging on the pile of tailings. A broken cantaloupe-sized rock revealed solid metallic ore that glinted in a flash of lightning.

"Let's get back on the trail," she said.

I followed her through the undergrowth to the path, and we continued down the slope. The rain was falling in sheets and my shirt molded to my shoulders as water poured down my neck and back. Mary Ann didn't slow down for ten long minutes. At times, I completely lost sight of her through the deluge. When I finally caught her, she was standing on the trail, staring at a clump of undergrowth.

"There's an adit below us."

"How do you know?" I said wiping soaked hair away from my eyes.

"Don't know. Feels like the right place, though."

She left the trail again, this time heading straight down the mountainside. I followed, groping my way through brush, briars and who knows what else.

"Found it," I heard her call.

I pushed away a branch and saw her standing at the mouth of a timbered opening in the mountain. She fumbled in the daypack for the miner's lamps.

"Get out of the rain," she said, motioning me to join her.

The entrance to the mine was barely four feet high. The crowning timber had fallen, partially blocking the opening. Red filigree fern cloaked the collapsed access making it impossible to see more than ten feet into the mouth of the old mine. I nudged a rock with my foot.

"You shouldn't go in there. Too dangerous."

Mary Ann continued attaching the lantern to the metal clamp on the front of her cap. She added carbide and water from her canteen before screwing the cap back on. When she finished, she wiped her face with the back of her hand and gave me a glance.

"This is carbide. When you add water, it gives off acetylene gas. You coming with me?"

"Are you serious?"

"As a heart attack. Well?"

"You're really crazy, you know it?"

Mary Ann read something in my expression that told her more than my reply.

"It's all right if you're scared. Lots of people are scared of holes in the ground. You stay here. I'll look."

"It has nothing to do with being frightened. This place is dangerous."

She ignored me as she removed a ball of twine from her pack. "I'll tie this at the entrance and unwind it as I go. Unless it breaks, it'll keep me from getting lost."

My heart had begun to thump above the sound of thunder. My throbbing temples signaled an approaching migraine. Moisture, along with rainwater, dripped from my forehead as I shrugged and frowned at the angry clouds, blinking away water from my eyes.

"I'm going with you," I said.

"You sure?"

"Just don't leave me in there by myself."

Mary Ann grinned and handed me the other miner's cap, lighting the burner for me as she shielded the match from the gusting wind with her cupped hand. Opening its valve, she twirled the striker with her thumb until a small flame curled from the aperture. Handing it back to me, she repeated the process with her own lamp.

I stared into the black hole in the ground. "This isn't enough light."

"It'll be plenty once your eyes adjust."

Mary Ann attached twine to an entrance timber and crawled into the black gaping mouth of the old mine. I crawled after her, brushing the top beam and feeling it shudder. When my eyes adjusted to the gloom, I gulped musty air that quickly replaced the fetid odor of dust-filled rain.

In minutes, our eyes dilated. Once they did, the carbide lamp's dim light illuminated the muddy path. I followed her with little difficulty. The floor of the old workings was slick, and fallen timbers lay strewn in our path. Perspiration caused by claustrophobia induced anxiety soaked my palms. I gripped the twine so tightly it cut into my fingers and caused them to burn when I wiped my sweaty forehead. Her words echoed like a hollow recording she called to me.

"Careful," she said. "It's getting real slick up here."

The tunnel grew increasingly narrower as I crawled on my hands and knees, the walls seeming to close around me. I realized it wasn't my imagination. The walls were closer. I had to slither on my stomach through the mud to follow the path of twine before finally reaching a tunnel intersection.

One path went right, the other left. Twine lay crumpled in the mud on the mine floor and the word, severed, ignited like an alarm in my brain. Darkness had engulfed us, and I knew it wasn't just from the tunnel. I took three deep breaths in rapid succession and started to scream. Mary Ann's voice echoed through the blackness of the tunnel, preventing me from blacking out.

"Where are you?"

"Right here. Where are you?"

"Just in front of you. You all right?" Mary Ann said, hearing the panic in my voice. "Want me to come back for you?"

"No. I'm coming."

I turned right, soon bumping into Mary Ann who was on her knees, staring at something on the wall of the mine.

"The ore vein," she said. "Miners must have followed it straight into the side of the mountain. Looks like it cut another fault cause they had to branch the tunnel until they found it again." She grabbed my forearm and squeezed. "You're shaking."

I took a deep breath of the musty air and almost fainted. Mary Ann grabbed my shoulders and shook me back to reality. My eyes popped open when she slapped me hard across the face. I took another deep breath.

"I'm okay," I said. "I got a little light-headed."

"Sorry I hit you," she said. "I thought you were going to pass out and I didn't know anything else to do."

"I'm okay now," I said as I regained my senses and glanced at the two tunnels. "Are you sure you're not a mining engineer?"

Darkness and solid rock amplified Mary Ann's giggle. "Don't take a genius to see what they did, just common sense."

"Then explain it to me."

By the dull light of the carbide lamp, I concentrated on the ore vein, trying to follow her analysis.

"They started losing ore." She pointed to a spot high above us on the wall. "When they did, they opened up a tunnel for another hundred feet. But then they must have lost it for good beyond that."

Both Mary Ann and I were on our knees in the narrow tunnel, the air becoming increasingly stale. Now I knew we were near the farthest point from the entrance. Mary Ann put a hand on my shoulder. Her eyes flashed vivid green in the light from the flickering carbide lamp.

"I'm going to the end of the tunnel. You stay here in case I get stuck."

She moved away on her hands and knees. I sat motionless, waiting to hear sounds of her return. Instead, her scream, echoing against the walls of the narrow passage, caused an instant rise in my blood pressure.

"Mary Ann. Are you all right? Mary Ann?"

I inched forward on my hands and knees until I heard her angry voice about ten feet in front of me. With my fingers, I felt the rounded edge of an apparently shallow hole. Mary Ann had fallen into it.

"Shit!"

"Are you all right?"

"Fell in a damn pit."

A dark hole plunged deeper into the earth. I saw it as I tilted my head so the light from the lamp could provide illumination. Mary Ann's lower lip protruded in an angry pout as she lay mired in a foot of sticky mud. Her icy stare silenced my relieved laughter as I helped her from the hole. Even though she looked like the loser in a mud-wrestling contest, she finally chuckled as she scraped thick ooze out of her long hair.

"Pretty silly, huh?"

"Let's get out of here," I said, trying hard not to comment.

"Yeah, guess we've seen it all."

"I'd say you got a rat's eye view," I said, receiving a punch in the chest for my levity.

As I crawled out of the pit behind Mary Ann, my first sensation was the fantastic smell of fresh air. Above us, the sky was robin's egg blue. Rain and dark rolling clouds had moved away. Slimy mud with a distinctively rotten odor coated Mary Ann like a second suit of clothes. Relieved at being out of the pit I found myself unexpectedly jovial and incapable of suppressing laughter that washed over me much like the recent torrent of rain. Mary Ann laughed with me.

When we were both too numb to smile, I said, "Now what?"

Chapter 13

Mary Ann lifted the pack and started down the trail.

"Quit your grinning and follow me," she said.

I chased after her until the terrain began to flatten. We followed a mountain stream that gushed over a base of solid bedrock, its crystal water pouring down the steep incline into the valley below. Abrasive rocks carried by fast-moving water had hollowed circular potholes into solid rock. They looked like pristine mirrors of shimmering sunlight trapped within the turbulent rivulet.

To avoid thick vines and trailers, Mary Ann used the streambed as a path up the hill. She moved quickly, jumping from rock to rock to stay out of the water. I found it impossible to match her pace and quickly lost sight of her muddy yellow blouse. The terrain became so steep I was panting from exertion when I reached the top of the hill.

Over the rise lay a large clearing. Behind it, sheer cliffs of solid rock jutted steeply into cottony clouds. A horsetail waterfall plummeted from the summit creating a pristine pool at the base of the cliff. Water pouring from the pool formed the stream we had followed up the hill. Trees as large as I'd ever seen formed giant clusters in the clearing. It was too steep and remote, even for high country loggers. Mary Ann broke the spell, calling to me from the pool. She was floating on her back in the rippling water, her clothes spread along the bank, freshly washed and drying in the sun.

"What took you so long? Come on in. Water's perfect."

My face flushed and I said, "That's all right. I didn't get as muddy as you did. I'll look around while you swim."

Mary Ann fanned me away with an impish grin and said, "Suit yourself."

Quickly doing an about-face, I hurried back to where the stream began its descent to the base of the mountain. Clear azure sky reflected direct sunlight. Amazing, I thought, considering the recent downpour. The panorama unfolded before me for miles. Like a giant multi-colored banner, a distant rainbow spanned the horizon.

As I wandered toward the western edge of the hidden mountain grotto, I imagined myself as the first human to have ever visited the place. After the sordid halls and somber expressions of Pineville, I marveled that such a beautiful place even existed. Something disturbed my thoughts, jostling the vegetation in front of me. Rounding the boulder, I tiptoed quietly in hopes of glimpsing the creature.

Instead of one animal, it was many; a litter of hairy piglets rooting at the base of a tree digging morels with their hoofs and snouts. I watched until another anomalous sound caused me to stand up board straight. Something snorted and pawed the ground behind me, sounding very much like an angry bull. I knew without looking that it was the piglet's mother.

After quickly scoping my field of view, I realized the rock wall was too steep to scale. The piglets were in front of me, their mother behind. With no better avenue of escape, I wheeled to my right, sprinting toward the trees without looking back.

Trampled underbrush crashed behind me as I zigged and zagged, searching for a place to hide. Every tree was a giant, only one with even a single limb low enough for me to reach. It was my only chance.

Wind or disease had contorted its trunk until it lay almost parallel to the earth. I ran up its woody incline, climbing ten feet off the ground before realizing the enraged sow was right behind me. Having climbed high enough to reach the lowest branch of a neighboring tree, I bent my knees, took a deep breath, and dove for it.

Years had passed since I had attempted such a leap and my momentum swung me when I grasped the branch. When my weight broke my grip at the far point of the arc, I tumbled ten feet to the ground, dazed as I landed flat on my back. Stunned by the fall and unable to move, I waited for the enraged sow to tear into me and rip me to shreds.

The inevitable failed to happen. Something distracted the huge animal. Someone had come to my rescue, diverting the sow with noise and bluster. It was a stark-naked Mary Ann, waving a broken branch in the face of the infuriated Arkansas razorback.

"Haaah, pig! Haaah!"

The animal was monstrous, its thick shoulders rising above Mary Ann's waist. I had seen large domestic hogs before. This beast was wild, all muscle, without an ounce of fat. Its snout was much longer than a normal pig and two ivory tusks curved from either side of its mouth. Black bristles protruded from its head and muscular back.

The razorback snorted, pawing with its hooves, but Mary Ann held her ground, waving the branch and yelling as I raised myself into a painful sitting position.

"Can you move?"

"Yes," I said, probing sore ribs with shaky fingertips.

"Stay between me and the pig," she said. "Back up till you're in the water. She won't come in after you."

"What about you?"

"She don't want me. If you make it to the water, she'll leave me alone."

I pulled myself off the ground and did as she commanded, my movement bringing an angry shift of the razorback's gaze from Mary Ann to me. Lifting its head, it started forward as Mary Ann yelled furiously, trying to distract it. Screaming like a banshee, she slapped the ground, directly in the pig's path, with the broken tree branch.

"Move it! Can't hold her much longer."

I inched backward, still facing Mary Ann and the enraged hog. When the beast head-faked, skirting around her, I knew for sure the animal wanted me and not Mary Ann. Not waiting to see if my bruised muscles would obey, I whirled around and raced toward the pool. A waist-high boulder stood between the water and me, and I had no time to run around it.

Hoping my out-of-shape legs could make the jump I leaped to the top of the rock then dove into the crystal water. I didn't stop stroking until I'd reached the center of the pool.

The razorback halted at the edge of the water, shaking her big hairy head, snorting and pawing the dirt. After a suitable show of aggression, she turned and trotted away.

Mary Ann remained in place, waiting until mama porker cocked her head and trotted past her, eager to retrieve her piglets. Instantly a big grin swept over Mary Ann's face. Dropping the limb, she broke into a run. After repeating my dive into the pool, she surfaced with water rippling off her shoulders and raven hair. She swam to meet me near the center of the pool. Encircling my neck with her arms, she squeezed me like a comforting teddy bear.

"Doesn't anything frighten you?" I asked.

Remembering her nudity, I attempted calmly to disengage her arms. My actions sent her into a giggling convulsion, and all I could do was wait red-faced until her laughter ceased.

"You're wet now. Might as well wash the mud out of your clothes and set them in the sun to dry," she said.

Mary Ann released her grip and swam to the far side of the pool, seemingly uninterested in what I might do. She was correct about the mud, so I swam to shore and stripped. After washing my filthy clothes, I draped them on a rock to dry.

I joined Mary Ann under the waterfall as she washed dirt from her hair beneath foaming spray. The sun-bronzed body of a beautiful young woman overshadowed her innocent teenage face, falling water revealing a lithe female, graceful as Venus rising from the foam. It reminded me of my own nudity.

Mary Ann could have cared less. After washing her hair, she climbed to a rocky ledge and did a graceful swan dive, begging me to watch as she splashed and then cavorted in the water like a playful sea otter. I swam a few slow laps, trying hard not to notice.

The waterfall was quite spectacular and plummeted a hundred feet from the gray limestone cliff into the deepest part of the pool, falling water obscuring the rock face behind it. Soon, Mary Ann plunged beneath the downpour and disappeared.

I waited for five minutes. When she didn't reappear, I swam into the torrent, holding my breath and swimming with broad strokes as the glimmering blue light began to fade into the shadows. When I surfaced behind falling water, I found I could touch bottom, but just barely. It took a moment for my eyes to adjust to dim light filtering through the wall of water. When they did, I marveled at a gaping grotto hollowed into a rugged wall of solid rock.

"Mary Ann. Where are you?"

Nothing but droning water answered and creeping fear that she may have drowned gripped my neck with cold fingers. She soon relieved my fear, calling to me from the limestone cavern.

"Over here."

As I climbed from the pool to the cavern's entrance, my eyes continued adjusting to the filtered light.

"Where are you?"

"Here."

"Where?

"In the back of the cave."

Mary Ann's shadows danced across broken limestone as she bent over something on the ground. Quickly I padded over to see what she was looking at.

"What is it?"

"Bill must have camped here. Had a fire built."

"You think it was Bill?" How do you know?"

"He was the only person that would have had this."

She held out her hand and opened it, revealing a shiny object.

"What is it?"

"Bill's hand lens."

Mary Ann handed the tiny magnifying glass to me.

"How do you know it's his?" I asked.

"Cause I gave it to him. It's got his initials engraved on it."

The hand lens bore the initials B.F.T. My curiosity excited, I began searching the floor of the grotto. So did Mary Ann.

"Here's his pack," she said.

Scattered contents lay strewn on the cave floor beside the open knapsack. Mary Ann dug through the pack, not finding what she was looking for. She sat on the cave's muddy floor and began to sob.

"It's gone. It's just gone."

"It must be here," I said. "Why wouldn't it be with the rest of his things?"

"Don't know," she said, rubbing her eyes. "But it's not."

"It has to be. We just haven't looked in the right place."

Mary Ann stopped crying, wiped her eyes, and resumed her search. This time we combed every foot of the cavern floor. The result remained the same.

"It just has to be here," Mary Ann said, still very much distressed.

"Let's get our clothes," I said. "It's a long way back to the Jeep, and it'll be dark before we get there if we don't start now."

Chapter 14

We were near the top of the trail before either of us said anything. A northerly wind was blowing, golden leaves wafting in a warm thermal high above us. Far away, lightning struck a tree. Thunder reverberated in the valley, sounding like a firecracker in a can. Another storm was fast approaching. This time it brought with it the first chill of fall.

Muscles in my legs ached as I followed Mary Ann up the last rise before reaching the Jeep. When we crested the hill, I saw we weren't alone. Two stretch-bed pickups and at least six men, loggers from the appearance of their work clothes and steel helmets, awaited us. Sullen expressions masked their weather-beaten faces as we approached.

One of the men was sitting on the hood of the Jeep, and I discerned a difference between him and the others. Although they were all large men who obviously earned their wages with their hands, this man was even bigger. Tattoos covered his huge arms and buzz cut red hair matted his massive head. Unlike the others dressed in overalls, he wore black biker leather. Even though I'd never seen him before that moment, I guessed he was a biker. Mary Ann dropped behind me, nervously touching my shoulder.

When I reached the Jeep, I nodded to the tattooed man and said. "Can I help you?"

His answer was a meaty forefinger stabbing into my breastbone. "You the fellow trying to put us out of work?"

"You're confusing me with someone else," I said.

My response satisfied neither him nor the others. They crowded around us in a semi-circle, so close that I could smell the strong odor of men who worked for a living beneath the hot sun. Buzz Cut stood in my face, smelling more like stale beer and bad breath than he did hard work. Without warning, he crooked his foot behind my ankle and pushed. It sent me tumbling backward, brushing the sweaty men grouped around us as I fell.

"Leave him alone," Mary Ann said, rushing to my side.

"Better get home to your mama before you get yourself hurt, little girl," Buzz Cut said.

He didn't wait for her to take him up on his proposition. Instead, he kicked me in the groin with the steel toe of his motorcycle boot. I recoiled instantly and convulsed on the ground, trying to will away the pain from his attack.

"Stop it," Mary Ann said, her voice animated as she tried to impose herself between the man and me.

Two of the loggers grabbed Mary Ann's arms and shoved her against the Jeep. Paying no attention, Buzz Cut grabbed my shirt and the hair on my head, yanking me to my feet and slamming me into the Jeep. By now, Mary Ann was struggling and screaming obscenities. As my head crashed against the hood, I glimpsed her vain attempt to wrench loose from the grasp of her captors.

Buzz Cut twisted my arm behind my back and bent me over the hood of the Jeep, again slamming my face into unyielding metal. My lips were swollen and bleeding, and I had bitten my tongue. Somehow, I managed to croak out a pitiful threat.

"Hurt the girl, and you'll be sorry."

"What are you going to do? Piss on my foot?"

His Neanderthal witticism brought a few nervous chuckles from the loggers. When he twisted my wrist while pulling on my thumb and little finger, I braced myself for another vicious slam into the hood. This time it didn't come. Instead, one of the loggers stepped forward.

Buzz Cut turned to face him without releasing my wrist. Mary Ann was still struggling but now had a red bandanna stuffed in her mouth. The logger, an older man with ruddy skin and thin graying hair kept his somber gaze averted to something at our feet, refusing to look me directly in the eye.

"Whatever's happening on this mountain ain't no concern of yours," he said. "Best just pack up and get on out of the county."

"Check out the Jeep," Buzz Cut said.

The loggers bent to the task, tearing into our possessions, dumping the ice chest and rifling through Mary Ann's daypack. Mary Ann pulled away from the two loggers and flailed with both hands against Buzz Cut's chest. Blood and sweat dripping from the wound in my forehead filled my eyes and my right arm throbbed from the savage attack. Still, I twisted my body and managed to get between Mary Ann and the brutish man, remaining there until the two loggers regained their grip on her arms. My action earned immediate reprisal. Buzz Cut grabbed my hair and wrist and slammed me into the Jeep's hood again.

The first thing I saw as I regained consciousness was Mary Ann kneeling over me.

Her eyes were red, and tears streaked her olive skin. The loggers had littered our possessions across the ground before leaving.

"Why didn't you do something?" she said. "Least you could have kicked him in the shin."

"Guess I could have pissed on his foot," I said, swollen lips distorting the words as they crept from my mouth in a garbled mumble.

Mary Ann grinned, despite herself, at my mumbled retort. "You all right?" she said.

"Nothing that a team of dentists and neurosurgeons can't fix," I said. "Now at least we know what probably happened to Bill's tapes and thesis material."

Levity shattered the tension. The reason behind the attack remained imprinted in my brain. Mary Ann helped me into the Jeep. Even though she had no driver's license, she got behind the wheel and headed for Turkey Gap.

She cut short a few corners as she raced down the mountain. My vision was too blurry and brain too muddled to help or to care. I could barely bend my right arm as she hurried me to a doctor in Turkey Gap. Unlike in any city, this doctor had an office in his house. He asked no questions as he cleaned and bandaged my wounds. No bones were broken. Except for many scrapes and bruises and a splitting headache, I was okay.

That night rain returned along with the darkness. Violent memories accompanying the rain colored my fitful dreams, returning me to Vietnam.

During monsoon season, our clothes stayed constantly damp. Each of us had a sheet of plastic liberated from packaging used for waterproofing boxes of ammunition. When it rained, we used our plastic sheets to shield ourselves from the downpour. During monsoon season, they got lots of use.

We were operating in a free-fire zone. According to Intelligence, there are no friendlies in a free-fire zone. This meant that we could open fire on any human we encountered without calling back to Headquarters to ask for permission. Headquarters apparently didn't consider members of the Montagnard tribe human.

The area where we were working was the ancestral home of one of the many tribes loosely lumped into a group called Montagnards or "mountain people" by the French. Damp from incessant rain and tired from an all-day hump, we came upon an unexpected clearing in the jungle. It was a Montagnard village, and that set off a primordial alarm ringing in my ears.

The tribes that comprise the Montagnards occupied Vietnam long before the ethnic group that most now think of as traditional Vietnamese. To say that the two groups of people disliked each other would be understating the issue. They hated each other. Because of this hatred, Montagnards fought on the side of the Americans during the Vietnamese War. This act of defiance had earned them relentless retribution.

We found the small village eerily quiet and apparently recently abandoned. The fire pits looked fresh, the half-dozen longhouses recently constructed. There were also broken cooking utensils and other personal objects that spoke of a rapid exit from the premises. This did not seem that unusual, as approaching NVA soldiers had likely prompted the villagers to make a hasty exit and seek a more secure hiding place in the jungle.

That night, the torrential rain returned. Most of us kept our personal belongings in waterproof ammo boxes. It was raining so hard that my air mattress and ammo box both floated out from under my poncho liner, taking me with it. I spent the remainder of the night dripping wet.

Morning brought a temporary end of the rain, along with the return of extreme temperature and humidity. The village occupied a bit of ground adjacent to a mountain stream. The villagers had dammed the stream to form a small pond. After ten days, our clothes were as filthy as we were. We took the opportunity to wash our clothes and bodies in the pond.

Our clothes, left beside the pond to dry, felt wonderfully clean when we finally tired of frolicking in the water and got out to dress. Answering the call of nature, Lenny Dotson disappeared into the jungle in search of a little privacy. When he didn't return after ten minutes, I followed his path into the snarl of vegetation to check on him.

I found Lenny not far away, standing with his back to me and staring at something on the ground. It's not a smart thing to disturb someone with a gun. Not even your best friend. Instead, I called to him gently.

"Lenny, what's the matter?"

Lenny didn't answer. He just continued standing there, catatonic. When I approached, I saw that he was staring down into a crater, a bomb crater, created by a large explosion. The Montagnard villagers had used it as a refuse hole to discard their trash and whatever they could no longer use. NVA soldiers had apparently found a more nefarious use for the hole in the ground.

Lenny's mouth gaped in a silent scream as he stared down into the pit. When I joined him, I realized why. The massacred remains of the Montagnard villagers, three men, five women, and six children, littered the killing hole. A swarm of rats and maggots were feasting on the mutilated bodies.

Chapter 15

"You awake in there?"

Mary Ann shook the tent, awakening me. The moment I moved, I remembered the meeting with the loggers and biker.

"What time is it?" I said, crawling out of the sleeping bag and slipping on my pants.

"Seven. You all right?"

"Sore all over," I said, sticking my head through the tent flap and squinting into bright sunlight.

"Ohhh!" She touched my swollen forehead with her finger. "You don't look in any shape for a hike in the mountains."

"I'm fine though I'm not sure we should go back up today."

"Why not?"

"Because I still don't understand why Bill was mapping quartz veins. What significance do they have? Maybe I'll pay a visit to the BST office in Dill City instead."

"You think those loggers had something to do with Bill's disappearance?"

"Maybe. Besides, where else is there to look on the mountain?"

Mary Ann didn't answer. Biting one of her nails, she prodded a rock with her toe, not seeming to hear my question. She glanced at her grandfather, already at work at the bottle stand, and nodded as if she had suddenly determined the solution to the problem.

"Remember me telling you Grandpa used to be a prospector? Let's ask him about the veins."

She started toward the bottle stand without waiting for me. With painful stiffness in my joints, I wriggled my shoulders and neck. When I reached the stand, I found John Stewart busily dusting a bottle the sun had varnished an opaque green. He blinked in surprise when he noticed my swollen face and black eyes.

"Been tangling with a mountain lion, boy?"

"More like a bear," I said.

The old man let the subject drop and returned to dusting the bottle. Mary Ann braced herself against the trunk of a giant pine, listening to our conversation. Behind us, a semi droned by on the highway. The sky was blue, and a nip of autumn had chilled the air.

"Mary Ann tells me you were once a prospector."

"Yup," he said, not elaborating.

"Well, I have a question."

He glanced up from the bottle, briefly rubbing his large hooked nose and said, "Shoot, Luke."

"What's the significance of quartz veins?"

Stewart didn't immediately answer. For a moment, I thought it was because he didn't know. I was wrong. In his slow hillbilly drawl, he explained while making slow-motion gestures with his long skinny arms.

"Panned for gold once in Colorado. Set up camp at a crook in a river. Know why?"

I shook my head.

"Cause when the river takes a bend the current slows down, and heavy minerals drop out and settle in the bank of sand. That's where you find the gold."

"Because it's too heavy to go any further?"

"Son, you hit the nail on the head. Gold don't come from the river. Comes from somewhere upstream."

Slower than a napping tortoise, he reached across the table crammed with bottles and mineral specimens and handed me a beautiful crystalline mass of raw metal.

"This is sphalerite and galena which is zinc and lead ore. But you see what it's mingled with?"

I did, and could plainly see the metallic crystals embedded in a milky matrix of quartz.

"Gold, like zinc and lead, comes up in veins of quartz. When the placer deposits played out we prospectors moved upstream until someone found the quartz veins. They's the source."

I tapped my toe against the leg of the table, letting my mushy brain absorb the old man's words. Mary Ann had deserted her post beneath the pine tree. She took the ore specimen from me, staring at it reflectively as she turned it in her hand. When I reached into my pocket for the black diamond and dumped it into John Stewart's hand his pale eyes bugged.

"Ever seen anything like this before?" I asked.

"You find this over in Murfreesboro?" he asked.

"Bill sent it to me. I thought you might know where he got it."

"Nope," he said, his gaze unwavering from the crystal. "I never seen a black diamond like this one."

Light reflected through the diamond like a broken prism, and Stewart turned it in his hand, touching every edge and studying every reflection. His next statement caught me quite by surprise.

"But I do know where that pouch come from," he said.

I glanced at the brown leather pouch in my hand and asked, "Where?"

"The Conjure Man. On Lacy Mountain," he said, pointing toward the east.

Another semi sped down the hill, honking its horn as it passed. John Stewart waved as the mournful whistle echoed through the hollow. When he handed the diamond to Mary Ann, she grinned and placed it on her ring finger.

"Tell me about the Conjure Man," I said.

"Name's Zekiel. He's old. Been old long as I can remember," he removed his wide-brimmed hat and scratched his snow-white hair. "Performs spells, mixes potions, things like that."

"Voodoo?"

Stewart grinned and said, "Don't know about that. The story goes he once tranced a man into a mule cause he stole a bottle of his shine."

"And you think he made this pouch," I said, ignoring his tall tale as I fingered the cracked leather pouch.

"Sure as I'm sitting here," Stewart said.

"Thanks, Mr. Stewart. By the way, did Bill ever ask you about quartz veins?"

"He was as curious about prospecting as you are. I told him to chase the quartz, and he'd find the ore."

"Thanks," I said over my shoulder as I hurried back to my campsite.

Mary Ann followed me into the tent and handed me the diamond. The large black crystal had a greasy feel and left a lingering sensation on my fingertips long after I had dropped it into the pouch.

"You know where the Conjure Man lives?" I asked.

"I never been to see him myself. Girls at school say he can turn you into a frog."

As I slid the red ice chest into the Jeep, I said, "If he does be sure to kiss me when I return."

Mary Ann made a face at my bad joke and jumped into the passenger seat of the Jeep.

"You'll never find him without me," she said.

"You're not frightened?"

"Maybe just a little." We both smiled when she added, "Though not enough to wet my pants."

We ate breakfast at the cafe in town, listening to two old men in an adjacent booth bantering about the qualities of their respective coonhounds. An unattended infant in a bassinet by the cash register cried for its mother. After bacon, eggs, and half a pot of coffee we started up the mountain to find the Conjure Man.

"There's a liquor store just outside of town," Mary Ann said. "Might oughta stop and buy him a bottle of whiskey."

"An offering," I said. "Good idea."

A sea of broken rock, the parking lot for customers yet to arrive, surrounded the tiny liquor store by the highway. Mary Ann waited in the Jeep. When the bell on the door signaled my entrance, it left me in a peculiar state of uneasiness.

"Help you find something?" asked the skinny man behind the cash register.

His expression bordered on constipation. His toothbrush mustache twitched when I declined his offer. He rang up the fifth of Jack Daniel's, and then watched me exit without saying thanks. Armed with a suitable gift, we started up the mountain road.

The path to the Conjure Man's house was unpaved. It was also steep, narrow and rough and even the Jeep rebelled against the grade until I switched it into four-wheel drive. By now, the sky was clear and azure blue, and we could see for miles down the slope. Far below, the highway wound a circuitous route through steep hills. The rumbling of big trucks and the distant drone of occasional passing cars wafted up the hill. We found the Conjure Man's house around an abrupt bend in the dirt path. It was more shack than a house.

The tarpaper shack centered in a tiny clearing on a hill overlooking the highway. An old black man occupied an antique rocking chair on its rickety front porch. He didn't attempt to rise when he saw us round the bend. Like John Stewart, he had a large, lop-eared hound at his feet.

He also had cats. The most spectacular cat was a solid black tom with a long tail that looped like a question mark over its back. As I parked the Jeep, the black tom wove a sinuous path between the old man's legs and slow-moving rockers of his chair. The friendly hound walked out to meet us, wagging its bony tail in easy swipes. When I patted its large head, it gave my hand a warm lick with its tongue.

"Morning," I said. "I'm Tom Logan, and this is Mary Ann Stewart."

He caught me by surprise when he said, "Been expecting you. Sit a spell, and we'll talk."

He motioned to two crates on the ramshackle porch. Mary Ann sat on one, and I turned the other around to face him. It was readily apparent that he was very old.

"You knew we were coming?" I said.

He pulled himself up from the rocker and crossed the porch with the help of a cane. Stooped with age, he had no meat on his little body, just ropy sinew, and furrowed skin stretched tightly over ancient bone.

"Been waiting for you for weeks."

The old man's accent was straight from the bayous of south Louisiana though imprinted softly with a hillbilly twang. Despite his obvious years, his voice was deep and clear, as were his eyes.

"You know about the diamond?" I said, unable to mask my surprise.

Completely white was the color of what little hair remained on his head. It was feathery fine as the underside of a snowy egret. He nodded an affirmative to my question.

"Then you know my brother, Bill?"

He nodded again, touching my shoulder to signal me to make room for him on the crate. He took my hand and said, "I'm Zekiel. I knew your brother well."

"Is he...?"

Zekiel raised his palm and shook his head ever so slightly.

"Bill recorded my voice with his machine. Asked me questions about these mountains and people that live here. He came back many times after that. He told me all about himself and about you."

"Did you give him the diamond?"

"He found the stone on the mountain and brought it to me, wondering what to make of it. I don't know where it came from. I do know it was a gift to him; a powerful gift."

"I don't understand."

"It was stuck to the flesh of a rabbit carcass. A hawk dropped it in front of Bill on the mountain."

"Why did he send it to me?"

As an answer, he quoted a poem:
The Evil Eye shall have no power to harm
  Him that shall wear the diamond as a charm,
    No monarch shall attempt to thwart his will,
      And e'en the gods his wishes shall fulfill.
"Zekiel, I still don't understand," I said.
"A diamond has powerful magic. It attracts planetary influences so strong it renders its owner invincible, brings him spiritual peace, and chases

away his demons. The black diamond is rare and its powers even stronger. That's why Bill sent it to you."

"But Bill wouldn't have believed that malarkey."

Zekiel glanced at the dirt floor of the porch as if my words were blasphemous. To him they probably were. He began to chuckle, and the hoarse sound rose out of his sunken chest like a scratched record.

"It did work," he said. "You're here."

"I got better because it was what I had to do to find my brother."

"The black stone gave you the strength."

I could see there was no use arguing with the old man. He evidently knew many things about Bill, and I intended to find out what they were.

"Where is Bill?"

The old man shook his head and turned away from my stare. "Bill is dead," he said. "But I think you already know that."

Chapter 16

The old man's words struck me like a sledgehammer to my chest.

"Dead? How do you know?"

"I scryed it," he said.

"Scryed it?"

"Gazed it in the crystal ball."

Zekiel was talking gibberish. Now, I didn't know what to believe. I must have looked dejected because Mary Ann stood behind me and placed a consoling hand on my shoulder.

Zekiel glanced up at the cloudless sky and said, "Mighty fine weather we're having lately."

"Lovely," I said, by now sure he was completely senile.

He chuckled again and used my shoulder to brace himself off the crate.

"Son, I'm sorry about your brother. Come inside," he said as he opened the door of the shack. "I'll get you something to drink."

I looked at Mary Ann and then at a hawk soaring high above us. Except for the wind whistling through the pine boughs, big trucks on the highway far in the distance made the only noticeable sound. As we followed the old man into his shack, the black tom rushed between my feet, slipping through the screen door before I could close it.

The shack was small and dark inside. Weathered cardboard papered its thin walls. A flowered curtain, suspended from a wire, quartered the single room. An old army green cot marked the spot where Zekiel slept. There was no indoor plumbing.

A stained oak table occupied the center of the room. On the table, a coal oil lantern glowed, lighting cave-like darkness with a flickering flame. Scattered papers, various gemstones, and an antique microscope littered the table. Boxes of old newspapers and magazines lay strewn on the floor. Various bottles containing who-knows-what lined the walls in homemade shelves.

Zekiel motioned us to have a seat then ambled over to a squatty icebox in the corner. It was a real icebox of white porcelain, chipped and yellowed with time and rust showing through flaking paint. He returned with a cold drink for Mary Ann and a ceramic jug. Removing the cork from the jug, he tipped it over his scrawny old shoulder, pouring clear liquid into his toothless mouth. He held it there until liquid dribbled down his face before handing the jug to me.

"I know you're teetotaling. This time it's all right. I'm here to guide you, and you'll need a dose of shine for what we're about to do."

Something in his words persuaded me, and I tipped back the jug, drinking some of the fiery liquor. Zekiel gripped the jug in his gnarled hand, holding it to my mouth until a nearly lethal amount had sloshed down my throat. He took two dark stones from a cigar box on the table.

"I want to show you something."

After clearing a spot in front of him with his forearm, he held the two stones about six inches apart. They clashed together with a loud click when he released them.

"Lodestones?" I said.

He nodded. "Powerful attraction. Agree?"

"Yes, but there's a scientific explanation."

Ignoring my skepticism, he said, "They have the same powerful attraction as between planets and stars."

"Maybe."

"Same powerful attraction the moon has on tides."

"I don't see what all this has to do with the diamond."

"You believe lodestones have power. You believe in the attraction of stars and planets and moon and tide. Why not believe in the power of the king of gems, a stone that takes its strength straight from the sun?"

"You're trying to compare a precious gem with metallic minerals. Diamonds have no such power. Neither does any other stone."

"Oh yes they do," Zekiel said. "So does every stone."

He reached into his cigar box, this time removing a blood red gem. By the coal oil lamp sat a glass of water. The red stone plunked when he dropped it into the glass.

"Bloodstone," he said. "It gains power from water. Together they can suck a hurricane from desert sky."

"Get serious," I said.

Distant thunder sounded outside the shack.

"Storm's coming," Zekiel said.

Within seconds, heavy raindrops began pelting the shack's tin roof as lightning flashed across the dirty windowpane. Fetid odor of damp soil and crackling ozone flushed like a wave through cracks in the wall.

"Coincidence," I said. "It has rained every day this week."

Zekiel reached across the table and clasped my clenched fist in his gnarled old palm.

"Son, I know you got more than your share of pain. It sticks out like a red flush on your face. You wouldn't be here now if it wasn't for Bill and the diamond."

Mary Ann seemed to agree because she leaned closer and rested her hand on my shoulder.

"You say Bill is dead. How did he die?"

"Don't know," he said. "I tried to see. My old eyes gave out on me."

"Can you tell us where his journal is?" asked Mary Ann, speaking for the first time.

When Zekiel took a deep breath, the dark skin visible through the vee in his shirt stretched across his bird-like ribs. This time, he extracted a three-inch crystal ball from the cigar box. Metallic needles pierced its transparent thickness. He placed it on an ebony stand in front of us then took another drink from the moonshine jug. After a second drink, he handed it back to me.

"I need your help," he said. "We got to help each other to make this work."

"Tell us what to do, Zekiel," Mary Ann said, drawing closer to the table.

The old man cocked his head and stared at me, waiting for an answer to his unspoken question. Red light from the bloodstone in the glass of water danced on the shack's dark wall. Outside, the storm raged, rain pummeling windows and tin roof.

"Let's do it," I said, showing him a thumb up.

"Lock your gaze on the crystal. Won't nothing work till your eyes start to dim. Don't blink. Don't do nothing 'cept gaze at the crystal."

Zekiel kept up a low-voiced banter, imploring us to stare at the finely polished crystal ball. Soon, his words became a subliminal message, directed to some remote portion of my brain usually familiar only in my deepest dreams. Zekiel's banter continued until my vision began to dim. Or was it the crystal ball? It seemed to turn black and become fluid. Clouds parted and my gaze penetrated the sphere, opening a vivid panorama into another place and time.

Though my vision was gone, I could see Bill. He was alone, draped in darkness, water cascading behind him as he stood on his tiptoes. As I watched he reached for a ledge nestled in a wall of rock and placed something on it. An explosion of noise jolted me back to reality. Nearby lightning had struck a tall pine, thunder sounding just outside the window. As I shook cobwebs from my head, Mary Ann and Zekiel attempted to do likewise.

"Bill's journal," Mary Ann said. "It's in the waterfall cave."

The storm had passed when we exited the shack's dark interior. Azure again dominated the sky. The grass was wet, and crystal drops of water hung from their blades. It reminded me of what I had just seen.

"Thanks, Zekiel," I said, handing him the bottle of Jack Daniel's.

Zekiel extended his closed hand. I opened my own, waiting until he dropped a misshapen object into it. It was a pearl.

"Diamond brought you here," he said. "Pearl go with you to complete the journey. Diamond is the king of gems, pearl the queen. You got yourself beaucoup dragons, and you're going to need all your powers to conquer them. Give this to your queen when she comes tomorrow."

The rain had soaked the Jeep's bucket seats, and I squirmed behind the wheel as we negotiated the washboard road, back to the highway.

"Who was he talking about?" Mary Ann asked.

"Tell you tomorrow," I said.

My answer seemed to satisfy Mary Ann as we waited in silence at the intersection for a car to pass before turning up the highway toward the clearing at the top of the mountain. We found no loggers or bikers and parked the Jeep beside a pile of brush.

It took us more than an hour to retrace our steps down the mountain on the winding path to the stream pouring from the ledge high above us. Mary Ann scurried up the steep grade, and I followed, jumping from rock to rock, trying to keep my feet out of the water. When the grade finally flattened my labored breath came in wheezing bursts. Then I saw it, cloaked in the clearing by a cloudy mist was the waterfall pool.

Mary Ann didn't wait for me, quickly shedding her clothes on the bank and diving in. As I crested the last rise, she had already reached the middle of the large pool, churning water and leaving a wake as she swam with powerful strokes toward the waterfall. No longer worrying about my modesty, or Mary Ann's, I stripped, dived in, and chased after her.

I caught a glimpse of Mary Ann as she disappeared into murky dimness. I followed her up the rounded limestone rise as wet clay oozed between my toes and sent sensual messages to my brain. Mary Ann had begun her search in earnest, this time along the walls of the grotto. I joined her.

"It's got to be up on a ledge," she said. "I saw it in the crystal ball."

So had I, although I could still barely believe what I had seen. For ten long minutes dim shadows, masking cave walls with silence and darkness, defied our search. Along with shadows, the walls cast doubts on what we thought we had seen in Zekiel's magic crystal. Before long, doubt began to linger.

Suddenly, Mary Ann's excited shout echoed through the chamber.

"I see it sticking out over that ledge."

Though Mary Ann's eyes were better than mine were, I could see the metal corners glinting in the muted light flooding through the mouth of the cave.

"Give me a boost," Mary Ann said. "I can't reach it."

Mary Ann put her barefoot in my cupped hand and stretched to reach the ledge. Finally, she pivoted in my grasp and dropped into my arms, a smile of pure joy lighting her pretty face.

"We did it," she said, squealing with delight. "We found Bill's journal."

Chapter 17

The discovery of Bill's lost journal lifted a heavy weight off my shoulders. It had the same effect on Mary Ann. When we left the grotto, she clutched the treasure above her head, pointing it toward the sky to keep it from getting wet. Because of her lop-sided stroke, I reached shore first and dressed as she made slow progress with one hand. When she reached shallow water near the gravel-strewn bank, she looked like a mermaid rising out of the surf.

"Here," she said, tossing the journal. "Don't drop it or I'll murder you."

I grabbed the journal, flipping it into the pile of clothes behind me before extending my hand to help her out of the water. Standing naked beneath direct sunlight, Mary Ann didn't reveal even the slightest pang of modesty. Nor did she bother dressing before she grabbed her pack and began digging through it.

"I'm starved," she finally said. "Let's eat these sandwiches we been toting all day."

"Great," I said. "Crystal gazing really works up an appetite."

My flippant comment brought a grimace to Mary Ann's pretty face.

"We have ham or turkey. Which do you want?" she asked.

"Turkey," I said. "I had enough ham the other day."

"You're hopeless," she said, smiling as she tossed me a sandwich.

I caught it in midair and searched for a place out of the sun to sit. I found a little shade beneath a nearby pine tree. Mary Ann stuffed the journal carefully into her pack before joining me. Her olive skin, still wet from the swim, glistened in the muted light reflecting through the overhead greenery. I could see she had an all-over tan. She smiled, sensing my question.

"I don't like wearing clothes much and take them off whenever I can." I grinned at her honesty as she continued to explain. "When I was little, I used to explore the woods behind the house and pretend I was a mountain lion. I'd take off my clothes and wander around, swimming and climbing trees. Bet you think I'm crazy, don't you?"

"Nope. It's the way you express your feelings."

She sat beside me in the soft pile of pine straw. Crushed needles filled the air with a piquant fragrance that rippled through the warm air on a gentle breeze and sent the branches above us into a timeless dance. After eating, Mary Ann strolled to the water's edge and washed her face. She finally dressed and gave me a wordless signal that we should start back to the Jeep. When we crested the last hill, my legs felt as if they had survived a squeeze in a vice.

"What now?" Mary Ann asked.

"Go back to camp and study the journal. See if Bill left any clues."

"And then?"

"Don't know yet."

As we followed the winding mountain road back to town, the setting sun cast a pink glow on the valley below. The next day was Monday. Mary Ann was spending the night with a friend in anticipation of school. I stopped in front of her friend's house and watched as she grabbed her pack and hurried toward the front door.

"Can I keep the journal tonight?" I asked.

With narrowed eyes, she said, "You're not leaving town are you?"

"No way, I promise."

She opened the pack and removed the journal. With a winsome smile, she tossed it to me. "You lose it, and I'll burn your house down."

"I don't have a house," I said with a wink. "See you tomorrow."

There was a pay phone outside the cafe on Main Street. It was only seven, but the streets were already dark and the cafe closed. Swallows, chasing mosquitoes, circled overhead. Somewhere in the distance, a dog howled. I dropped coins in the slot and dialed Amber's number, hoping to catch her at home. She answered on the second ring.

"Tom, I hoped you'd call. Is everything going okay?"

I told her about Zekiel, crystal gazing and finding Bill's journal.

"You've been busy," she said. "So have I."

"What's up?"

"I have some preliminary information on BST."

"Tell me."

"Big Sky Timber is one of the largest private corporations in America, and it's owned by the Townsend family. Gerald Gray Townsend is president. He lives in Dill City."

"I've heard of him," I said.

"In addition to timber BST is into mining, manufacturing, and chemicals. The EPA has cited them for violations ranging from illegal clear-cutting to dumping toxic waste into rivers.

Little has ever come of the charges because it seems they have powerful friends in Washington."

"Interesting," I said.

"One more thing. I also learned that Bill reported BST's illicit cutting to a higher authority."

"Higher authority?"

"A senator, clearly one that Townsend doesn't own, in Washington. Caused quite a stir and I'm still checking into the ramifications." When I didn't immediately respond to her information, she said, "Tom, what are you thinking?"

"That I may have a motive for Bill's murder."

"Murder?"

"I'll explain tomorrow. Can you still make it down?"

"Wouldn't miss it," she said.

"What else have you got on BST?"

"I'll tell you everything tomorrow."

"Good," I said.

"And Tom, I'm the cop. Don't do anything until I get there."

"I'll be fine," I said, evading her innuendo. "Did you ask Professor Quinn about the quartz veins?"

"He's here. Why don't you ask him yourself?"

I could hear Professor Quinn clearing his throat in the background. Amber said good-bye and handed him the phone. I quickly explained what John Stewart had told me about quartz veins and mentioned Zekiel's story about how Bill had found the diamond stuck to the carcass of a rabbit. I waited while the Professor digested the information I had given him.

"Your brother had no expert to ask about the origin of diamonds," he finally said. "Like you, he consulted the camp owner, a former prospector. Unfortunately, Mr. Stewart only has experience with metallic ores. Not diamonds."

"Sort of my impression, too," I said.

"Bill must have suspected a diamond source was somewhere nearby. He was looking for it in the wrong place."

"What about the rabbit story?"

"Plausible," Quinn said. "Diamonds do adhere to fat. The hawk could have killed the rabbit almost anywhere, and the gem could have stuck to the carcass when he flew away with it."

"Almost anywhere?"

"Well, anywhere in the area in which the hawk lives and hunts."

"And how far is that?"

"I don't know, maybe within a hundred miles or so."

It was dark when I reached the campground. I went into the tent, switched on the camp light, and opened Bill's journal. The leather-bound notebook contained about a hundred loose-leaf pages of hand-written notes. Bill's handwriting ranged from barely readable to indecipherable. Mud and coffee stains on the pages made interpretation doubly difficult. After an hour of diligent study, I still had found no reference to diamonds or demons. Only work notes on Arkansas hill people.

Disappointed and dog-tired I dragged myself to the washhouse where I remained beneath the showerhead's tepid water until it became frigid. Feeling much better, I pulled a long-sleeved turtleneck over my head and returned to the tent.

That night it rained again, this time bringing with it an early winter chill. I huddled inside the sleeping bag for warmth, tenuously balanced between fitful sleep and mental awareness.
In the eastern mountains, a wolf or maybe a coyote howled at wandering clouds. Much closer, an owl keeping time with a freight train passing in the distance, hooted. Both animals seemed oblivious to gentle drizzle that kept up a constant timpani on

the tent's canvas roof. Far away, in a dream-like mist, a light glowed and then flickered.

❖

My stay at the sanitarium in Pineville had taught me all I ever needed to know about lucid dreams. Now, I was in the middle of one although I had no idea where I was, or even who I was.

This dream was so real that when I coughed I could feel the burn of stomach acid rushing up my throat. As I clawed my way out of thick underbrush, my shirt in tatters, the blood-red moon above me poked through a cottony-cover of remnant clouds.

Multiple cuts and abrasions stung from acres of sharp briars through which I had fought. Warm blood, along with the perspiration, trickled down my arm. Moonlight revealed a puddle gouged in the muddy dirt road. I collapsed into the mud, exhausted, pain searing my left shoulder. Dried mud and coagulated blood crusted the open wound.

I struggled back into the underbrush as something that stank of filth and pestilence chased after me, ripping my back with steel talons. A comforting hand encircled my chest and spoke in a familiar voice. A voice I recognized.

"Hang in there Buddy. I won't let you die."

"That you, Lenny?"

"Who'd you think it was?"

I had little time to answer.

Something terrible and unspeakable lay behind me. Explosions of noise rocked the forest. Strong hands dragged my broken body toward a distant light bursting through the clouds.

"Hang in there, Buddy. I won't let you die," Lenny said as he pulled me toward the light.

Directly behind us a wraith, its claws extended, grabbed him by the neck. I tried to

133

scream. Only a hoarse whisper rolled from my bloody lips as I watched the beast devour its hapless victim. I kicked at the creature and struggled toward the light as it ripped at my neck with claws of steel.

Somehow, I managed to pull away as I crawled across the fetid forest earth, grasping with desperate hands, reaching for the light.

❦

My sleeping bag was in tangles when I awoke with a start a few hours later. I took a drink of water from my canteen, still shaking from the lucid dream I'd had as I wondered what it meant.

The rain had ceased. Yellow moonlight bursting through seams in cottony clouds shined through the open door of the tent. Only a gentle breeze remained. It continued blowing the tent flap and letting moonlight flood through the opening.

In my hand was the open diamond pouch. Bill's diamond lay spilled on the tent floor, the blue light radiating from it dancing across the canvas wall to the beat of my racing heart.

Chapter 18

Next morning I started a small fire in the camp grill warming my chilled limbs as I stood in front of it. I was still mulling what Amber and Professor Quinn had said. Despite Amber's warning, I had already decided to visit BST's office in Dill City. I also had reason to believe I knew why Bill had searched the veins before his disappearance and why he had sent me the diamond.

Like a thorn in the side of corporate BST, Bill had placed himself at risk when he publicly criticized the company. From my own experience with the loggers on the mountain, I knew someone in the company possessed the necessary means to extract worrisome thorns. Circumstances had persuaded me that BST had trumped up the breaking and entering charges against Bill to undermine his accusations. My question was, why had he become involved in the first place?

Trying to forget the nagging inconsistency and keep my anger from erupting into something I couldn't control, I drank instant coffee from a tin mug and forced myself to concentrate on the noisy mockingbird on a limb above me. Within the hour, I left the campground to two busy chipmunks and started toward Dill City.

Indian summer had run its course and a chill wind forced me to raise the Jeep's canvas roof. Last night's rain had left tranquil puddles, some still capped with thin sheets of ice, on the blacktop. Overhead, a solitary mallard circled a farm pond. Seeing none of its brethren, it headed south alone. As I traversed the lonely road, I felt a strange kinship with the wandering duck.

Loggers and farmers in pickup trucks, having begun their daily commerce well before dawn, crowded the highway into Dill City. For the last ten miles of my trip, I followed a cattle truck, watching hapless frightened eyes peer back at me through wooden slats. Jammed together, the cattle slipped on manure-slick wood and tossed and bumped into each other as the truck swayed. Unlike convicts approaching the gallows they were unaware of their imminent fate, though obviously no less fearful.

Near the city limits, I took a side road that led through the little town's industrial section where bars, liquor stores, and warehouses crowded both sides of the street. A large neon beer sign bearing the name Pancho's topped one of the bars, and a chopped Harley with a dented gas tank lay on its side in the gravel parking lot. I wondered if it was a hangout of the big biker.

Dirt replaced blacktop near the murky river that coursed through town. I soon reached train tracks that lay three abreast. Beside the tracks, I found the Sunrise Cafe and stopped for breakfast and the answers to a few questions.

A nearby crew loaded cargo with a forklift. Behind the little white roadside diner, the metallic clank of freight cars connecting echoed like the dull ring of a broken bell. Nearly eight, most of the customers had already come and gone. The place was empty except for two old men in a corner booth. I found a spot on a red revolving stool facing the front counter and smiled at the woman leaning against the wall.

"Coffee?" she asked already tipping the lip of the pot toward the white mug in front of me.

"Please. Still serving breakfast?"

"You bet," she said, her voice a husky imitation of Mae West.

Vera was the name on her tag, pea green the color of her rumpled uniform. She was plump probably mid-fifties and the color of her hair matched the mustard stains on her blouse. She handed me a dog-eared menu individually typed on a machine badly in need of a new ribbon.

"Bacon and two eggs. Over easy," I said after a brief glance.

"Not from around here, are you?" she said, not bothering to record my order on her pad.

"New Orleans."

"Visiting relatives?"

"Sightseeing," I said. "Guess I got off the beaten path a little."

Her throaty laugh came from deep within her big bosom. One of her front teeth was missing, the others black around the edges.

"Just a little," she said.

Vera called my order to the unseen cook in the kitchen before bending over the counter and staring at me as I sipped hot coffee.

"So what's happening in Dill City?" I said.

"Rent and taxes. Just like every place else."

"Too bad. Thought I might stay awhile and soak up a little local color."

"Honey, you're close as you are ever gonna get to any of that right here," she said, pointing at the counter.

We both grinned at her little joke. When she returned with breakfast, I said, "Gas station attendant down the road told me you have a local celebrity in town."

"You bet we do. G. Gray Townsend. We had a senator straight from Washington D.C. visit him just yesterday. Served him apple pie myself, right there in that booth," she said, pointing.

"Townsend has quite a reputation," I said, not knowing exactly what my wild stab might produce.

"Honey, you don't know the half of it. That man has had every woman in Dill City. Present company excepted of course," she said, cupping her hand to her mouth and bending closer as she confided the last sentence in a near whisper.

"Playboy, huh?"

"Ain't the half of it. Townsend owns Dill City and thinks every woman in it is his personal property; at least every attractive woman."

From beneath the counter, Vera removed a timeworn photo album and flipped it open to the first page. Gray Townsend's life unfolded before me, documented by old Polaroids and yellowed newspaper clippings lovingly kept by one of the women in Dill City he supposedly never had. The pale skin of Vera's plump neck tinted noticeably pink when her fingers paused near the photo of Townsend and a young woman. They were standing arm-in-arm, the skyline of a large city behind them.

It was obviously a much younger Vera. She quickly flipped the page when she caught me studying her melancholy expression. Closing the album, she shoved it back under the counter.

"A real bastard," she said as she hurried into the kitchen.

Five minutes later the short order cook, wearing a grease-stained apron over his jeans and tee shirt and sporting a day-old growth of beard, sauntered out of the kitchen to refill my cup from the half-empty pot of coffee. Ash from the cigarette Bogarted between his lips dropped to the counter beside my plate. He didn't seem to notice.

"Don't pay no attention to Vera," he said. "She ain't never going to get over what Townsend did to her."

"Sorry," I said, hearing the concern in his voice.

"Earl," he said, shaking my hand. Without waiting for me to introduce myself, he said, "You'd think a woman would forget about something happened twenty years ago."

I was dying to ask what Townsend had done to Vera. After seeing Earl's own morose expression, I decided to refrain. Without prodding, he poured forth the story, and it was more than I really wanted to hear.

"Townsend owns this town, the bank, the old folk's home, feedlots, paper mill, everything. Want a job in Dill City you get it from Townsend. And, he likes his girls. Still keeps a few on the line. Sets them up with a car, job, and a nice place to live," he chuckled as if remembering something humorous. "Visits maybe once a month and don't care what they do when he ain't around."

"Cozy arrangement," I said.

Earl nodded and said. "He knows how to manage his women. Vera's my old lady. Guess she found out first hand."

"Does Townsend live around here?"

"Straight up the road about ten miles. Has a fancy estate on the mountain," Earl said.

"Seems likely a powerful man like Townsend could have done lots of good for Dill City."

Earl's reply was sarcastic and bitter. "A lot of good all right, 'specially if you like the stench coming from the smokestacks across the river or eating fish from the river after the crap the mill dumps into it stews them like so many prunes."

"Maybe it's the only way to create jobs."

"Jobs my ass. Townsend could clean it up if he wanted. He'd feed his old widowed mother raw chicken shit if he thought it would save him a nickel."

"Sounds like a man that would murder for a buck."

Earl flicked an ash on the floor and glanced up from the counter. For a moment, he stared at me, assessing my use of the word murder.

"Wouldn't put it past him," he finally said, dusting off his apron with both hands before folding them tightly against his chest.

I paid the breakfast tab and started for the door. With my hand on the knob, I said, "Thanks, Earl. Tell Vera I enjoyed talking with her."

With a sullen nod, he lit another cigarette from the glowing butt in his hand and returned to the kitchen.

Before leaving Turkey Gap, I'd already decided to confront Gray Townsend. I knew the only thing to gain by such a visit was the guilt. If it were there, I might see it in his eyes. After talking with Earl and Vera, I had a feeling it would be.

Across the river, a paper mill's twin stacks belched yellow smoke into the sky. Its fetid odor hit me like a kick in the chest. With burning eyes, I continued through town, hoping the wind was blowing in the opposite direction. Near the city limits, I started up a winding mountain road and found Townsend's estate near the top.

Acres of the manicured yard and native stonework surrounded the large English Tudor mansion. A black Rolls Royce convertible occupied the circular driveway. Shouts and laughter coming from the back of the house attracted my attention. I parked and got out, not bothering to knock on the front door.

An eight-foot stone fence bordered the huge backyard. Climbing over the fence, I found myself staring at a huge pool sparkling with rippling water the color of Aqua Velva. It occupied, along with cabana and redwood deck, much of the backyard. Two attractive young women clad in matching bikini bottoms and nothing else were shouting, and splashing in the pool. Wisps of steam rose up from the heated water. Someone grasped my shoulders and wheeled me violently around.

"What the hell you think you're doing here?"

I stared up into a man's coal black eyes. Dressed in white linen pants and black pullover shirt, he looked at least six inches taller than I was. His build complemented his height and a matching temper from the scowl on his face. Black hair pulled into a little pigtail imparted a somewhat prissy look to the large angry man. He shoved me back against the stone fence.

"I asked a question. You a peeping tom? Getting your rocks off?"

"I'm looking for Mr. Townsend."

"Then why didn't you try the front door?"

"Mistake I guess. Thought I heard him back here."

Pigtail blinked, considering if I really did have an appointment with Townsend. Grabbing my shoulders, he shoved me toward the house. The near-naked girls in the pool continued their noisy antics, unmindful of my confrontation with Townsend's tough.

We entered the house through a sliding glass door overlooking the back patio. Oriental rugs draped the polished wood floors. Vaulted ceilings with rough-hewn beams and knotty pine paneling dominated the architecture of the large house. Pigtail directed me up a massive stairway to an upstairs corridor. After following him down the hall to a double-doorway, I watched as he knocked. He entered without waiting for an answer.

It was an office with bookshelves on three walls and a giant desk in front of a wall-sized picture window overlooking the backyard pool. Someone sat behind the desk with his chair turned toward the window. He was staring at the girls swimming in the pool below.

"Mr. Townsend. I caught this creep in the backyard." Pigtail said. "Looks like he was trying to get a better look at the girls. What do you want me to do with him?"

The man, still with his back to us, didn't answer. Unlike the young man in Vera's picture, his hair was iron gray. When he turned around, I saw the chair in which he sat was not an office chair at all. It was a wheelchair. Snowy sideburns extended below fleshy earlobes and a twisted grin locked his portly face. Little eyes, the color of lime green Jell-O, glared at me.

He said, "Get lost, Breck. I'll take care of Mr. Logan."

Chapter 19

Pigtail glared at me as he left the room, shutting the heavy door behind him. Townsend's baby blue silk jacket stretched tightly across his broad shoulders. The top two buttons of his starched white shirt were open and exposed a bush of gray hair on his chest as he grinned at me.

"Welcome to Townsend Mountain, Mr. Logan. You look as if you were expecting someone else." When he saw me glancing at the wheelchair, he smiled and said, "Degenerative muscle disease. Doctors don't know quite what to make of it. Personally, I think I went skinny dipping in the sump pond behind the mill once too often."

I ignored his cynical comment. "I've seen your picture in magazines. I had no idea."

"Company publicists keep it a secret. Don't want to lose market shares now do we?"

Despite the house in which he lived and the trappings of wealth all around us, Townsend's accent was like a southern sharecropper's. If I'd closed my eyes, I could easily have imagined I was talking to Vera's husband back at the diner. There was an underlying tone of cruelty in his raspy baritone voice, and I had little doubt he knew all the moves of a Wall Street power broker.

"Now what exactly can I do for you?" Townsend asked spreading his palms and leaning his big head back against them.

"Maybe you should tell me."

He laughed, and it drew into a hacking cough. From a box on his desk, he fumbled for a cigar. After lighting it, he expelled a plume of smoke toward the ceiling. All this he did before answering my question.

"I'm not responsible for your brother's death," he finally said.

"Then how do you know he's dead?"

Townsend's piggish eyes narrowed even further, and he said, "Seems likely, don't it?"

"You tell me."

"Your brother's disappearance is as much a mystery to me as it is to you."

"And I suppose you're not the least bit happy to see him go?"

"I think you're overestimating your brother's ability to influence anyone important. Do-gooders have pointed fingers at BST for years, both at my father, my grandfather, and now me. Nothing came of it then, and nothing would have come of your brother's finger-pointing. Why?" He didn't wait for me to answer. "Because BST is synonymous with commerce. That means jobs and taxes paid. Maybe even a few kickbacks," he said with a chuckle.

Ignoring his insinuation, I changed the subject and said, "Maybe your men aren't as secure about that as you are."

"People around here don't cotton to strangers poking around in their business."

"I think people around here do what you tell them to do."

Townsend thumped the cigar into an ashtray. "Your brother was a troublemaker. He broke into our headquarters in Dill City."

"Look, Townsend," I said, pointing an accusing finger. "I don't believe that story for a minute. What's the motive?"

"You tell me. Fact is he did. We caught him in the act, on video. Be happy to show you the tape if you'd like."

"I don't believe you."

Townsend touched a button on his desk intercom and said, "Breck, bring the tape of that fellow that broke in downtown."

Pigtail quickly appeared through the door, his scowl intact. After opening a large oak cabinet containing a television and stereo, he placed a cassette in the VCR and switched it on. Within seconds, the shadowy picture of a lone man rifling through a desk appeared on the screen. It was Bill without a doubt. For a moment I couldn't speak.

"What did he steal?" I finally asked.

"Nothing. Didn't even mess up the place. Don't matter though. Your brother Bill was there. Now I think you should just get the hell out of my house and go back where you come from."

"Not before you explain why your men attacked me up on the mountain."

Townsend didn't deny the attack. Instead, he said, "I told you they just don't like strangers around here."

"Maybe it's you that doesn't like strangers."

Townsend laughed again and puffed the aromatic cigar. "I didn't order them to do what they did. Fact is I didn't even know about it until after the fact. It was Bear's own idea, and I guess he got a mite overzealous."

"Bear?"

Townsend scratched his fleshy nose and said, "My ne'er-do-well first cousin. We both got the same granddaddy, but Bear never did a lick of work in his sorry-ass life. Never did anything except ride that funny looking motorcycle of his and terrorize the county."

"Your story doesn't add up. I think you put Bear up to it."

"Maybe he thought you were a threat to his inheritance. It would have taken something special for him to leave Pancho's right in the middle of happy hour."

I'd seen my share of people that could lie with a straight face, some on both sides of the law. Even a few guilty ones along the way had managed to convince me of their innocence. Despite my suspicions, I somehow felt Townsend was telling the truth. Didn't matter because I wasn't about to let him off the proverbial hook.

"You're trying to shift the blame," I said.

When Townsend grinned, I saw no humor in his green eyes. "You're barking up the wrong tree, Logan. I'm a goner, and sure as shit, I won't be here much longer. Maybe I should put a sign on that pond."

"You callous son-of-a-bitch. If you don't care about your own health, you should at least consider the safety and well-being of your children and grandchildren."

"There's screwing, and there's reproduction. I did a lot of the former but none of the latter. Know why, Logan?" I shook my head, not bothering to answer. "Because this planet's already a shithole and there's nothing anyone can do to make it better. The reason is population. It just won't stop growing, and all those people need food to eat and a place to live, and all that takes money."

"But you have the power to make things better. Right here in Dill City, for instance."

"Make things better," he said in a mocking tone. "You know who the worst polluter is? You," he said, pointing his finger at me. "You dumb assholes dump tons of fertilizer and insecticides on your own front lawns. Where do you think it goes? When it rains, it washes off the lawn into the gutter. From there it flows into rivers and streams and goes straight to the ocean. There's nothing I could ever do that could harm your precious ecology more than that."

Townsend's emotional outburst brought with it another hacking cough. This time it emanated from deep within his phlegm-filled lungs. Red-faced and gasping for breath he reached for a buzzer on the desk. Before I could react, Pigtail burst through the door. He wrapped one arm around Townsend's shoulders and tipped back his head toward the wastebasket. Immediately Townsend vomited foul-smelling fluid into the basket.

"Call an ambulance," Pigtail said. "Can't you see he's dying?"

I called the county hospital from the phone on Townsend's desk and almost immediately heard distant sirens far down the mountain begin their wail. I found a washcloth in the bathroom adjoining the office, wet it beneath the faucet and handed it to Pigtail. Ten minutes later the ambulance arrived, and two paramedics placed Townsend on a stretcher, administering an IV as they carted him downstairs.

I followed them outside to the circle driveway in the front yard. The day had grown late, the temperature warm. Now, without a seam in sight, the turquoise sky melded with mountain greenery poking through it. The girls in the pool were still frolicking, apparently unaware of the crisis inside the house. Unsure of what I had managed to accomplish I followed the ambulance down the hill.

Because of my visit to Townsend's home, I had missed lunch. Now I found I had an overwhelming desire for a giant chocolate milkshake. Finding a

Dairy Queen in Dill City, I ordered the shake and drank it in the Jeep as I watched local teenagers circulate through the parking lot. I remembered the rite of passage from my own adolescence as I pondered my visit.

When I finished the shake, I drove around town, searching for a grocery store. Not knowing exactly what a vegetarian might like, I chose a variety of fresh fruits and vegetables, a box of rice, some pasta, and an apple pie. Still wondering about Townsend's cousin, I returned to the main highway by way of the back road through town. The parking lot of Pancho's was already crammed with chopped Harleys and beer-drinking, leather-clad bikers. I caught a possible glimpse of Bear's buzz cut as I passed.

Late afternoon shadows had begun covering the highway as I left Dill City and retraced my steps to Turkey Gap. As I neared the campground, my thoughts returned to my conversation with Amber, and I wondered if she would be waiting for me when I arrived. I had my answer when I rounded the last curve and saw her at John Stewart's roadside stand. She recognized the Jeep as I turned off the highway and smiled when I pulled beside them.

Following a prolonged hug and kiss, I held her at arm's length, contemplating my luck. She wore beige hiking shorts that looked freshly pressed and a Grateful Dead tee shirt. Because of her tiny frame, all-over tan and surfer-blond hair, she seemed no older than did a teenager. She was anything but, with the sharp mind of a college professor, the stamina of a professional athlete and the resolve of an attacking grizzly bear.

"You made it okay?"

"Fine," she said, smiling.

I looked around for the red rental car I had left with her, and said, "Where's the car?"

"I turned it in last week. No use wasting money."

"Then how did you get here?"

"I hitchhiked," she said.

I laughed, realizing I still knew very little about a beautiful young woman that would lend someone her car then hitchhike to where she needed to go.

"Amber, Amber, Amber," I said. "I'm glad you made it."

"I was talking with Mr. Stewart, and it seems we have a common interest."

The old man smiled blithely, his arms folded.

"Miss Armstrong collects old bottles. I already sold her one."

Amber smiled, pointing to a lone bottle on the edge of Stewart's table. "We've had an interesting discussion."

"Oh?"

"About bottles," Amber said with a grin. Looping her arm through Stewart's, she asked, "Is there someplace I can wash off the trail dust?"

Stewart smiled, pointing proudly to the washhouse. "Right there, Missy. All the hot and cold water you'll need."

"Thank you, Mr. Stewart," she said, lavishing her arms around his bony old shoulders as if they were old friends.

Stewart's ruddy face blushed bright red, and he said, "Don't forget your bottle, Missy."

He handed her the bottle she had purchased then reached beneath the table and extracted another old bottle. Long exposure to the sun had turned it a deep aqua blue.

"Been saving this one for some pretty lady," he said, grinning broadly, as he handed it to her and pressed it gently into her hands.

"It's beautiful. Thank you so much."

"Thanks, Mr. Stewart," I said, leading Amber to the Jeep. "See you later."

I didn't explain our sleeping arrangements to John Stewart and felt relieved he didn't ask.

"Nice old man," Amber said as we climbed into the Jeep.

"I believe he likes you too."

We parked by the tent. Amber's only luggage was her heavy knapsack, and I quickly transferred it to the tent.

"I'm glad you came," I said again. "I need someone with a mind for police procedure."

"Is that the only reason?"

I had almost forgotten the softness of her shoulders, the gentle curve in the small of her back and the hint of perfume just behind her right earlobe. I remembered with blazing recall when she draped her arms around my neck and drew closer.

"The least of two. The very least," I said.

With a cautious finger, Amber touched my cheek, slight pressure reminding me of my black eye and busted lip.

"What happened to your face?"

"Met some loggers on the mountain that thought I might be responsible for trying to put them out of work."

"They did this?"

"Gray Townsend's cousin, actually - prehistoric throwback masquerading as a biker."

Without commenting, she frowned and glanced up at a squirrel on a branch above us. Leaving the question of my bruised face for another time, she changed the subject. As my thoughts had focused on something other than Big Sky Timber, I was more than happy to oblige.

"I wasn't supposed to get off work until five but nothing much happened at the station today, and the Chief pushed me out the door. He said he was tired of seeing me staring at my watch."

"Remind me to thank him," I said.

"I'm pooped," she said. "How well does the shower work?"

"Water's slightly tepid, and the pressure isn't great. Other than that, the cracks in the wall don't let in too much cold air."

"Faint praise," she said.

Amber pulled away and rummaged through the knapsack on the tent floor until she found a towel and bag of toiletries. She patted my behind, winked, and headed for the little building.

"Looks interesting, Troop," she said. "But a girl might need a little company."

I didn't wait for a written invitation. Feeling more than slightly soiled after my visit with Townsend, I grabbed a towel and hurried after her. For the first time in several days, I completely forgot about Brother Bill and his black diamond.

Chapter 20

Dancing moonlight guided our path through the trees and bounced golden beams off Amber's flaxen hair as we returned to the tent wrapped in moonlight and bath towels. By a flickering lantern, we cooked tomato sauce on the propane stove and served it over pasta. With clean bodies and satisfied appetites, we grabbed a blanket and went for a walk in the woods. Amber stopped on a hill overlooking the camp and spread the blanket in a soft bed of fallen pine straw.

"It's beautiful here," she said.

"I thought you'd like it."

She snuggled against me and said, "There's nothing quite like the forest at night. So much sound, yet soothing. Rain on a tin roof." She touched my bruised cheek again. "Tomorrow, I want you to tell me everything."

Much later, feeling Amber's warm body beside me in the sleeping bag, I drifted away into an incandescent dream.

Sunlight glaring through the open flap of the tent awakened me the next morning, Amber already up and dressed for a morning jog. After a brief visit to the washhouse, I put on my own outfit and chased her up a narrow trail, into the hills behind the campground.

With my own muscles strengthened by several days of mountain hiking, I surprised even myself by keeping up with her for the first two miles. When she continued up the trail, I had to stop. Out of breath, I hiked slowly back to camp.

When Amber returned, her complexion flushed from exertion. Her pink shorts and singlet were damp with perspiration, and she looked as happy as if she had just won the lottery.

We had melon and fruit juice for breakfast. Finally, I recounted to Amber everything that had happened since I'd arrived in Turkey Gap. She howled with laughter when I told her about my encounter with the angry razorback and how it had resulted in a skinny dip with Mary Ann. It was something I didn't expect.

With freckled cleavage peaking from the top of Amber's frilly blouse and tanned legs revealing just a hint of creamy white beneath the cuff of green hiking shorts, she looked radiantly healthy. As if her touch might somehow help her divine an unwritten message, she stroked the rippled leather on Bill's journal sitting beside us on the concrete picnic table.

Up the hill, a screen door slammed. Mary Ann hurried down the path, a sullen expression framing her face when she reached us. I could see the confusion in her big green eyes, and maybe just a hint of jealousy.

"Mary Ann, this is Amber Armstrong. She's a policeman from Brannerville and a close friend of mine."

Amber also noticed Mary Ann's confusion because she stood from the concrete plank and hugged her.

"Tom told me all about you," she said.

"He never told me about you," Mary Ann said, her arms at her side.

When Amber rested her hands on Mary Ann's shoulders and stared into her eyes, something noticeable transpired between the two.

"You're every bit as pretty as Tom said you were. I think I can help you find out what happened to Bill. Do you mind if I try?"

"You a real policeman?" Mary Ann said. When Amber nodded, she smiled and said, "Guess it won't hurt nothing."

Up the hill, the screen door slammed again. Boots shuffled against gravel as John Stewart plodded in our direction on his morning journey to the bottle stand.

"I have to go," Mary Ann said. "Grandpa will skin my head if I miss the bus."

"She's so pretty," Amber said as Mary Ann hurried away.

Mary Ann boarded the yellow school bus waiting on the highway and waved to us through an open window. With a clunk of shifting gears, it eased back on the road and slowly disappeared into the distance.

"Morning," John Stewart said, saluting as he walked past. "Sleep well?"

"Like a top," Amber said.

The old man didn't stop for a conversation. Amber waited until he reached the bottle stand before returning to the bench and squeezing me into a comforting embrace.

"You seem so sure your brother is dead," she said. "Pardon my skepticism. An image you thought you saw in a crystal ball hardly seems like much evidence to me."

"Zekiel's no New Age psycho-maven," I said. "Something else compels me to believe it's true. I also had a dream."

"Like the one you had in Brannerville?"

"No. Most of my dreams are repeats of events in my life. Sort of like a broken record. This one was different."

"How so?" Amber asked.

I recounted the dream for her. "Something was pursuing me through the forest, beneath the light of a full moon. There were hunting dogs baying in the distance. Nothing like that has ever happened to me. I believe I was dreaming of Bill."

"Tom, that's so unbelievable," Amber said.

Still, she took my hand and clutched it tightly as if she had suddenly felt the cold chill of a midnight breeze caress the back of her neck.

"Whoever or whatever was chasing me drew very near. I sensed something just behind me and felt an evil presence. My fatigue was almost unbearable as I clawed through vines and briars, my arms and chest lacerated and bleeding."

"Why do you think the dream was about Bill?" Amber asked, interrupting me.

"Because when I reached a dirt road and fell on my face in a muddy puddle, I saw the back of my hand in the moonlight."

"And?"

"There was a birthmark there. Heart-shaped, the size of a half dollar. It was Bill's birthmark."

"Dreams don't necessarily reflect reality."

"That's what the shrinks at Pineville kept telling me. I'm not so sure Zekiel would agree with them. He thinks Bill sent me the diamond as a talisman; something to chase away my demons. He also gave me this to give to you."

I dropped the pearl into her palm.

"What's this?"

"Juju," I said. "Keep it in here and wear it around your neck."

I handed her the pouch, explaining how diamond and pearl combine to give their owners power. Though Amber seemed unconvinced, she dropped the pearl into the pouch and secured its thong around her neck. Shaking her head ever so slightly, she began drumming pink-glossed fingernails against the concrete tabletop.

"Maybe Bill sent you the diamond for another reason."

"Such as?"

"From the way you've described him to me, he doesn't sound like a person that coveted wealth. Maybe he found something else; something so extraordinary he didn't know who else to trust with the information."

Amber's speculation raised more questions at least for the moment then I cared to consider. On the highway, an eighteen-wheeler passed, John Stewart waving at the driver when he blasted the horn. I got up from the table, still deep in thought, and began putting away breakfast dishes.

"I'd like to talk to your so-called conjure man," Amber said. "Maybe I'll see something in that crystal ball of his."

"There's something else about the dream I didn't tell you," I said.

"What?"

"Part of what happened in the dream is from my past. Something that happened in Vietnam."

"Tell me."

"I can't."

"Is it that bad?"

When I nodded, Amber stepped behind me, extended her hand beneath my arm, and touched my cheek. My bruised face drew her attention from my dream. Swelling had diminished, though a thin crescent of blackness still rimmed the base of my right eye.

"I think we should have another talk with the sheriff. I want to hear what he has to say about the attack."

"He didn't help much the first time we talked."

"I'd like to speak to him. Maybe he'll feel more comfortable talking with a fellow lawman."

"Yeah, and he may be working for the other side. He's the only person that could have tipped off my attackers. No one else except Mary Ann and her grandfather even know who I am."

Amber pondered this thought a moment. "I have new information since we talked Sunday. A Senate subcommittee is investigating BST. A favoritism scheme that goes back a decade or more implicates seven senators. It doesn't leave many motives for Townsend to have harmed Bill."

"What about Bear?"

"I want to talk to him," she said.

"He probably has his own agenda," I said.

So far, my time in Turkey Gap seemed somehow ill-conceived. Nothing I'd learned disputed the facts of Bill's disappearance as reported by Sheriff Bonner. They only raised more questions, each one increasingly more complex. Every lead so far had dead-ended.

"Too bad there's nothing in here," she said, fingering Bill's journal."Especially after what you and Mary Ann went through to find it."

"I've read every word at least twice."

Amber tossed the journal on the concrete picnic table and started for the Jeep.

"Let's ride over to Dill City," she said. "I think it's time we visited Sheriff Bonner and have another look around."

Chapter 21

Content to relax and let Amber drive, I enjoyed the cool breeze as we tooled along the road to Dill City. We found Sheriff Amos Bonner perched behind his desk, pouring over uneven stacks of paperwork. He frowned, rotated his shoulders and slouched back into his chair when he saw us.

"Sheriff Bonner, I'm Amber Armstrong," she said, extending her badge for his inspection.

"Am I supposed to be impressed?" he said, scratching the gray stubble shadowing his fleshy jowl.

"We're not here to waste your time, Sheriff. I have just one question."

Bonner glanced at the cracked crystal of his old Timex.

"Better take about thirty seconds. That's all I have to waste before heading out on my rounds."

Bonner hoisted himself out of his chair, smoothing an imaginary wrinkle in his khaki shirt before moving slowly across the room. When he reached the door, he removed his worn Stetson from a peg on the wall and adjusted it on his large head.

"What's the story on Bear Townsend," Amber asked.

Bonner didn't bother turning around. "A low life, drug using, knuckleheaded troublemaker. Now you've asked your question. I answered it. Time's up."

"You think he could have murdered Bill Logan?"

Amber's blunt question stopped Bonner in his tracks. Turning slowly, he removed his hat and rubbed the bald spot on his head.

"Who the hell said anything about murder?"

"Mr. Logan is convinced his brother is the victim of foul play. Frankly, Sheriff Bonner, so am I."

"Well, you just take your beliefs back to wherever you come here from. I'm the sheriff of this county," he said, stabbing his index finger into his sternum for effect. "Ain't no indication the boy's disappearance is anything other than accidental."

"New information, Sheriff. Bear Townsend assaulted Mr. Logan and implied he'd done the same to his brother. There were witnesses. If you ignore this the Attorney General might have reason to suspect you're covering something up."

"And just how's the Attorney General going to get wind of this new information?" Bonner asked, his cheeks growing redder.

"If I have to, I'll file a report through my office in Brannerville."

"You got no jurisdiction."

"Brannerville is Bill Logan's home of record. I have a perfect right."

"Then you just do that little girl," Bonner said. "Sheriff Tate, your superior officer, is a friend of mine. We'll see who he believes and what he thinks about you digging through someone else's dirty laundry."

"If you'd do your own wash, I wouldn't have to. Let's go, Tom," Amber said, brushing past the rotund Sheriff before he could reply.

Sheriff Bonner shouted something at us as we traced the fluorescent-lighted hallway to the parking lot. We just kept walking, passing two police officers as we did. They stared at us as if we might be escaping criminals. When I opened the door for Amber, I glanced back down the hall. Bonner's face was flame red, his legs spread in a shooter's stance. Instead of a pistol, his index finger was pointing at a spot between my eyes.

"Son, you so much as spit on the sidewalk and I'll have you seining shit in a state-owned rice paddy. Understand me?"

I gave him a backward wave and exited the basement of the county courthouse to the parking lot. Outside the sky was dark blue and completely free of clouds. From the industrial part of town down by the river, a fast-moving freight train whistled a mournful signal to the motorists waiting at an intersection for it to pass. I had to put my hands on Amber's shoulders to calm her shuddering anger.

"He shouldn't have treated me like that," she said.

"He doesn't strike me as the type that worries much about political correctness."

"I'm sorry, Tom. I made a fool of myself in there."

"The hell you did. I don't know about your career as a poet, but you'd have made a dandy prosecuting attorney."

Amber blinked, and the flush slowly abated from her neck. "Think so?"

"Absolutely. You instilled in Bonner just a hint of doubt. If he's somehow involved in a cover-up, you made it impossible for him to let it rest."

She stood on her tiptoes and kissed me. "Thanks. Even a hell-raising poet needs occasional reassurance."

By now, the sun was high overhead and our breakfast melon already long forgotten by my growling stomach. The keys to the Jeep were in Amber's hand. I took them from her and climbed behind the wheel.

"I'm hungry. We can discuss Sheriff Bonner over lunch."

Amber didn't argue. Not knowing the location of any vegetarian restaurants in town, I made a beeline to the Sunrise Cafe. Vera, still dressed in her pea green uniform, met us at the door. She remembered me. Grinning broadly, she slapped my back and escorted us to a table by an open window. Somewhere outside someone was mowing grass, probably for the last time of the season, and the wall behind me vibrated with the high-pitched drone of a two-cycle engine.

"Honey," Vera said. "You still visiting our little town?"

"I'm starting to like it here," I said.

"Oh, it'll grow on you all right. Like mold on an old loaf of bread."

Vera's deep voice resonated against the walls and melded with the drone of the lawn mower as she laughed at her own little joke.

"Who's this pretty little thing you got with you?" she asked when her laughter abated.

"This is Amber. She's a friend of mine."

As if she knew no strangers, Vera measured Amber's arm between her thumb and forefinger.

"Your mama must have known how to hide the grits," she said. "Don't worry, Honey. Earl's chicken fry'll put some fat on your fanny."

"Amber's a vegetarian," I said, holding up my hand to stop her. Vera stared at me as if I had just informed her that Ronald Reagan was a Communist. In case she didn't understand, I added, "She doesn't eat meat."

"Well, it ain't no wonder she's so skinny. You just sit tight, Honey. I will have Earl fix you up a fried veggie plate that'll make your mouth water. And fatten you up, too," she added, winking at me before hurrying to the kitchen.

I expected to find Amber upset by Vera's blatant assessment of her slim figure. Instead, she was grinning.

"It's really a tragedy to visit a place where no one has an opinion."

When I stopped laughing, I said, "I met Vera and her husband Earl yesterday. They filled me in on some of Gray Townsend's proclivities."

"I'll bet your ears are still burning," she said.

Shortly, Vera returned with two steaming plates heaped with food. I ate my chicken fry with gusto, albeit some guilt as I sat across the table from Amber. She didn't seem to notice. Steamed zucchini, fried okra, green tomatoes, and an appetizing assortment of other vegetables cooked in vegetable oil occupied her attention.

As we worked on our meals, the cafe filled with noontime customers. The person outside the window finally finished mowing, and the hum of patrons and rattle of plates replaced the little engine's throaty drone. When we finished lunch, Amber and I sipped hot coffee and discussed our next step.

"What now?" I asked.

"Check out every place in town Bill may have visited. Ask questions. Try to dig up a lead."

"You don't sound confident."

"Like I said in Brannerville, the trail's stale."

Her pronouncement cast a gray pall on my morning optimism. The remainder of the afternoon was spent visiting libraries, courthouses, paper mills and every cranny Bill might have frequented. As Amber had predicted, our search proved fruitless. When we called it quits cottony clouds were forming above us, a cuticle of crimson and pink rimming the western horizon. Instead of returning to Turkey Gap, Amber headed for the town's industrial district.

We followed the dusty back road through Dill City's seamier side, past bars, used car lots, and slaughterhouses. It also led to Pancho's. Amber parked the Jeep in a graveled parking lot littered with chopped Harleys and bikers already celebrating approaching sundown.

"What do you think you're doing?" I asked.

"One more person I need to talk to," Amber said.

I noticed she said I and not we. An evening chill had replaced cool afternoon as Amber grabbed her black nylon jacket from the back seat and slipped it over her shoulders.

"This place could be dangerous," I said. "Bear's a borderline psycho. He'll never admit to harming Bill."

"Probably not," she said.

"Then what do we have to gain by being here?"

"Stay in the Jeep. I'll take care of it."

"Take care of what?" I said, hurrying after her across the parking lot.

She didn't bother answering my question, sprinting instead up the stairs and entering the front door. I took a deep breath and followed her.

A single large room encompassed the bulk of Pancho's, dark paneling doing little to offset its cave-like feel. Darkness was awash in neon light, crowd noise and a Neil Young psycho-melody blaring from the corner jukebox. Fifty or so leather-clad bikers looked us over closely when we entered the front door.

"What'll it be?" the stringy-haired bartender asked.

"Draw and a Coke," I said.

I noticed the heart tattoo on his hand as he stared at me. He was probably trying to decide which of us wanted the Coke. When he nodded and moved away to complete our order, Amber sat on one of the tall stools and turned her back to the counter.

"Two bucks," the man said when he returned with our drinks.

I paid him and took the stool next to Amber. A young woman with unwashed hair and a frown on her acne-ravaged face sat at the far end of the Formica counter. Dressed in worn blue jeans and a black tee shirt, her elbows were on the bar, her nose in a warm mug of beer.

Two men wearing earrings and leather were shooting pool at a table in the back. An eight ball slammed against the rack, and an indecipherable hum of muffled obscenities accompanied the clatter. Someone was talking to himself as he beat on an old mechanical pinball machine.

One thing struck me. Unlike New Orleans or most places in the Deep South, there wasn't a black face in the place. Thinking back, the only black person I'd seen since arriving in Sheriff Bonner's county was Zekiel. I didn't have long to reflect on the thought.

"See Townsend?" Amber said.

"Nope, though you can bet we will if he's anywhere around."

Despite crowd noise and a room that reeked of stale smoke, body odor, and urine, the cool soda tasted good after a day spent mostly in the sun. Someone approached us through the room's smoky confines as I savored it.

"You Logan?"

The breath of the young man standing in my face made Pancho's bar smell like rose petals. The amateur tattoo on the back of his hand said, Clint. Little more than a gawky adolescent, Clint had shaved his head on one side. Long greasy hair touched his shoulder on the other. His eyes were red and watery, the soft skin around them swollen like overripe plums. A skull and crossbones painted on his black tee shirt said 'Ded Head.' I nodded in answer to his belligerent question.

"Bear's outside. Wants to see you."

He stumbled out the front door, and half of Pancho's frowning patrons followed him.

"I think the shit's about to hit the fan," I said.

Without replying to my remark or waiting for me to react, Amber followed the skinny youth to the front door. Suddenly my neck grew red hot, and explosions began reverberating in my brain, along with flashes of blinding electrical static. What remained of the patrons in the once-crowded bar parted before Amber and me.

When I stepped through the door, the acne-scarred woman from the end of the bar appeared through the crowd and took a drunken slap at me. Because of the bombs exploding in my brain, I was only vaguely aware of her shouted obscenities or the saliva dripping down my neck when she spat in my face. Ignoring her, I caught up with Amber as she reached the Jeep where we found Bear Townsend leaning against the hood.

The late afternoon sun was low on the horizon and muted crimson filtered through Townsend's red hair. His Hitler mustache twisted into an amused grin as he watched us approach through the throng of smelly bikers. His right hand was resting on the hilt of a long-handled ax. From the looks of the Jeep's mangled right front fender, he'd already made use of it.

"Bring your cunt along to hide behind?" he said, looking over Amber's shoulder at me.

"He doesn't need anyone to hide behind," Amber said. "I'm the one looking for you."

Lightning flashed in the distance, followed by the rumble of thunder. Only silence issued from the bloodthirsty spectators drawn into a tight semi-circle around us.

"Did your pansy boyfriend tell you I got a big set, Baby Cakes."

"He told me you're a sadistic monster. I thought I'd just give you some of your own medicine."

"I think he must have told you about my giant schlong. Why don't you just kneel down and check it out for yourself?"

With his left hand, Townsend reached for Amber's head. Amber, although eighteen inches shorter and almost two hundred pounds lighter than her assailant, reacted immediately, blocking the big man's hand with her own forearm. Even faster, she reached into the flap of her nylon jacket and whipped out a .38 caliber police special. With the full weight of her diminutive body, she swung the pistol like a battle-ax, catching Bear Townsend across the base of the nose.

Townsend's eyes crossed, and he sank to his knees, blood gushing from the cut as he grasped his nose and leaned forward. Amber gave him no time to react, her knee exploding upward into his chin. As Townsend fell forward, she kicked him in the head for good measure and then wheeled around, brandishing the pistol, forcing the stunned crowd to back away from the fray. Clint, the greasy youth that had summoned us from the bar was standing beside me. Before he could step away, Amber grabbed his shirt collar and rammed the pistol into his mouth.

"Which one's Bear's?" she said, glancing with angry eyes at the row of choppers. When Clint didn't immediately respond she shoved the pistol deeper down his throat until his watery eyes grew round and glistened with fear. "Which one? And you better not lie to me."

Clint pointed to a chopped Harley and fell backward in the gravel when Amber gave him a push. She lurched through the mob to Bear Townsend's awaiting motorcycle. Aware of what she was about to do, everyone backed away and watched her empty the pistol into the black chopped hog.

That was her first mistake of the night. Everyone, including myself, counted each report from the pistol. As they closed in around her, I grabbed the man in front of me, trying desperately to bull my way through the crowd. I managed to reach her but not before half a dozen angry bikers got there first.

Chapter 22

Police sirens suddenly began to blare as red flashing lights swathed the parking lot of Pancho's. With one hand, I held on to Amber's shoulder. The other was in an assailant's face when the white beam of a powerful floodlight raked the mob, and a familiar voice boomed at the crowd through a megaphone—Sheriff Amos Bonner's voice.

"You've had your fun for the night now back away from the girl. Now!"

Slowly, the crowd pulled away from Amber and me. Three police cars had cordoned the parking lot. At least six khaki-clad troopers were facing us, their riot guns poised and ready. Bonner, his corpulent frame backlighted by the rising moon, was standing on the hood of his own car. Bear Townsend was still sitting in the gravel beside the Jeep, holding his chin, and massaging his swollen nose. One of the police officers took a white towel from the back seat of a squad car and tossed it to him.

"Party's over," Bonner said. "Now go back inside or go home."

The mob, voicing more than a few muffled obscenities and cries of police brutality began to disperse. Clint was the most vocal.

"Stop that little weasel right there," Bonner said, pointing.

A deputy grabbed Clint's collar and hustled him away to a squad car as Bonner climbed down from the hood of his own car and sauntered over to where we were waiting. Expecting handcuffs, we received only gentle nudges from his meaty hand in the direction of his awaiting vehicle.

"Get in," he said, holding the front door open for Amber. "You," he said to me. "Backseat."

He gunned the engine, spraying gravel as he tore out of Pancho's parking lot. As we raced along the dirt thoroughfare at almost sixty miles per hour, static and broken police reports from his radio blended with silence and darkness. My head ached, and a brass bell was ringing in my left ear.

"If you're going to arrest us, Sheriff, I suggest you read us our rights," I said from the back seat.

What followed surprised me more than Amber's fighting prowess. Bonner giggled like a schoolgirl, leaning his head back until his neck popped. Resting his right arm on the back of the bench seat, he slowed the car as laughter rocked his large body.

Finally, he said, "I ain't seen the Bear get the hell kicked out of him like that since we was in eighth-grade football. Little lady, I sure got to hand it to you."

"You're not taking us in?" I said.

"Why hell no! I ain't ate since breakfast, and I'm about half starved to death. Thought since the little lady here so kindly provided me with such fine entertainment I'd take you two good people to supper."

Amber glanced back at me and dark concern in her indigo eyes reflected from the dashboard lights. Sheriff Bonner continued to giggle though he remained silent until we had gone twenty miles down the road. He pulled into the well-lighted parking lot of an all-night truck stop.

The place was alive with truckers and eighteen-wheelers. Bonner got out of the car and motioned us to follow him, leading us to a cafe nestled within the large building.

"Just across the county line," Bonner explained. "I come here when I want a little privacy." We seated ourselves at a booth in the back and waited until a saturnine waitress filled the coffee cups already on the table. Bonner returned the menu. "All night breakfast buffet is what I'm having. You two get what you want."

"I'll have the buffet," I said.

"Salad bar," Amber said.

The mousy waitress left with our orders, and we went through the buffet and salad bar lines. Bonner quickly heaped his plate. When Amber and I returned to the table, he had already buttered three biscuits and was dousing them with redeye gravy.

"Did some checking today after you left my office," he said, his cheeks pouched with half-chewed food. "Bear Townsend was in California when your brother disappeared. Biker's convention," he chuckled again and said, "Those boys like their little conventions more than old maid Southern Baptists."

Amber blinked and started to say something. Thinking better of it, she nibbled on her lettuce and remained silent instead.

"But I got to admit," he said, looking at Amber. "You got my attention today. I pulled out my report and read it again. Still, nothing and that's with a capital N. You're welcome to try your hand if you want to come to the office tomorrow."

Bonner's sudden sincerity left me doubtful. I said so, fearing only a full frontal lobotomy could have provoked such a rapid personality swing.

"What made you change your mind about us, Sheriff?"

"Hell, I told you Sheriff Tate's a friend of mine. I see him all the time at Arkansas Sheriff's Association meetings. I called and asked him about the little woman here. He told me clearly that she is the best man on his force. Threatened to come down and kick my butt if I didn't help. Ol' Tater'd do just that, too."

"How'd you find us?" I said.

"After my little talk with Tater, I had a hunch Miz Amber Armstrong here wouldn't let sleeping dogs lie. Sure enough, I was right."

"Thank heaven for your hunches," I said. "We were slightly outnumbered."

Laughter rose up from Sheriff Bonner's lungs until he almost choked on his buttered grits. "Hell, I think the little lady would have done just fine."

Bonner's eating habits were like that of most overweight people—frenetic. Shortly, he excused himself to return to the buffet line for a refill.

"Well, little lady, I think the sheriff likes you," I said, trying to emulate Bonner's cornpone accent.

Amber rewarded my effort with an elbow in the ribs.

When Bonner returned, he said, "Something I have to confess. Because of what your brother did over at BST, I called over there after your first visit to my office. Told them to be on the lookout for you. Guess that's how Bear knew you was up on the mountain. Mighty sorry for the problem it caused you."

His apology sounded sincere. "You made up for it tonight by saving our necks, Sheriff. I probably would have done the same, in your position," I said.

"One thing bothers me," he said. "What blessed reason have you got for still believing somebody murdered your brother?"

I told him about my visit to Zekiel's, refraining from mentioning my dream. When I finished the story, Bonner sprawled back against the plastic-covered booth, spread his arms across the back rim, and belched. He didn't bother excusing himself.

"Known ol' Zekiel all my life," he said. "Maybe there's something to your thinking."

"Really?" Amber said.

Even with his cheeks puffed with biscuits and gravy, Bonner continued to espouse. Bits of food sprayed from the corners of his mouth as he waved his knife and fork like semaphore flags.

"In case you hadn't noticed, they ain't many black folks in these parts. Ain't many outsiders, period. But the mountain people trust Zekiel cause he treats what ails them and seems to do a pretty good job of it."

"Could someone on the mountain have killed Bill," I asked.

"Could of. They're a tight-knit bunch," he began to chuckle, sending his big belly into a paroxysm of rubbery motion. "They think we are big city folk here in Dill City."

"Then they'd be really lost in Little Rock." Missing Amber's sarcasm, Sheriff Bonner nodded and returned to his eggs and sausage. "Tom tells me Bill had a rapport with most of the hill families."

"Maybe he got too close to one of their stills. They're mighty particular about that. Anyway, your brother ain't the first to disappear without a trace around here," he said, shaking his fork at me.

Amber and I had both finished eating, and Bonner's sudden tidbit of information came as a surprise to us. Amber pushed her salad plate aside, leaning forward on her elbows.

"There was nothing in the report to connect Mr. Logan's disappearance with similar situations. How many other cases are we talking about?"

"Hell, for years we've had revenue agents, loggers and hunters disappear up near the Big Valley. Started before I became sheriff. Probably ten or more, I'd guess."

"Ten disappearances without a clue? And you didn't think to mention it in your report?"

"Now wait just a cotton-picking minute, little lady. Ain't nothing about his brother's case here to link it to the others."

"Except location and circumstance," she said. "It could be a serial killer."

"And you have no suspects?" I added.

"I said they're a tight-knit bunch up there. I don't buy into any serial killer nonsense. Too many things can happen in them hills for that. Snakes, holes, wild pigs, moonshiners. Hell, maybe the Valley Monster got him."

Amber and I waited for him to laugh. He didn't. "Valley Monster?" she said. "Is that a joke?"

"Hell, sure it's a joke. It's one every school kid in the county has heard since before they're knee-high to a toadstool. Whenever anyone turns up missing around here, the Valley Monster gets the blame."

"And what's the basis for this story?" Amber asked.

Sheriff Bonner stopped eating. With a delicate touch for such a large man, he placed his knife and fork on the edge of his plate.

"You've seen the Big Valley," he spread his arms to show us just how big. "It's like a giant soup bowl with mountains all around. Stretches fifty miles across and the bottom of the valley is nearly a half mile from the top of the peaks. And, it ain't barren. There are trees down there that ain't never been cut."

Glancing at Amber, I could see she was as curious about Sheriff Bonner's tale as I was.

"What's the access to the valley?" I said.

"Ain't none. No roads, no trails, just miles of neck-high briars, vines, and undergrowth. Hell, there's always thick clouds over the valley that even masks the trees. Because of the clouds, you can't see into the valley from an airplane. You get lost in there, ain't nobody ever going to get you out."

Amber pushed her half-finished glass of tea aside and said, "Can anyone at all tell us more about this valley?"

"Just the hill folk," he said. "And I can tell you right now you won't get a blessed thing out of any of them."

Though the conversation was near an end, Sheriff Bonner still hadn't finished eating. I sipped coffee and drummed the cup as he consumed another heaping plate from the breakfast bar. When he finally finished he returned us to Dill City, at a much slower speed this time. We found the Jeep in the parking lot of Pancho's. After a quick examination of the ruined fender, we decided most of the damage was cosmetic.

"Take it to Jake's Body Shop on Main and get an estimate," Sheriff Bonner said. "I'll see Bear cuts you a check to get it fixed."

He opened the door of his squad car and started to get in. Then, as if remembering something he had forgotten to tell us, he slammed the door and returned to the Jeep.

"I think you folks ain't going to let this disappearance lie," he said, leaning with an elbow on the window. "That's all right by me. Just remember one thing. Those mountains are dangerous. Get yourself in trouble, and it'll be too far for me to bail you out again." After removing his hat, he handed Amber a business card. "Most hill folks are decent people. They don't cotton to strangers, but they keep tabs on each another. Something happens, news travels faster than an Apache smoke signal. Just get me a message, and I'll beat a path up the hill faster than you can say scat."

"Thanks, Sheriff," Amber said.

When Amber kissed his forehead, I could see a red flush spread over Sheriff Amos Bonner's big face.

"Sheriff Tate would kick my butt if I let anything happen to you," he said, backing away from the Jeep. "You two take care, you hear?"

Bonner put his hat back on his head and returned to his car. After racing the engine, he sprayed gravel across the parking lot and hurried away into the night.

Amber saw me looking at her and said, "What are you staring at?"

"You."

"Stop it. You're making me nervous."

I turned away with a grin as she cranked the engine and pointed the Jeep back toward Turkey Gap. Stars were out and the night air crisp. A cool breeze, bathing my face with a frosty chill, whistled through the Jeep's loose canvas top.

"What now?" I asked as we approached the campground.

"Tomorrow, we find out more about the Big Valley from the only person I know that might actually tell us something we don't already know."

"And who is that?"

"Zekiel," she said.

Chapter 23

Sweat beaded my forehead as Amber, concern apparent in her eyes, knelt beside me. The tent door was flapping in a cool breeze as moonlight flooded through the opening.

"Tom, you were having another nightmare."

Our silhouettes formed dancing shadows on the canvas. Outside an owl in a nearby tree filled the darkness with its hoots. In pursuit of some hapless tiny creature, it flew away leaving only silence in the wake of a lusty rush of beating wings. Without replying to her concern, I crawled out of the sleeping bag and walked to the washhouse.

With the campground swathed in darkness, I didn't bother dressing. A chill breeze and damp grass between my toes quickly made me regret that decision. When I reentered the tent's catalytic warmth, I found Amber bathed in the fluorescent glow of her battery-powered lantern. She shivered when I opened the door and the loose weave of the orange Afghan draping her shoulders revealed goose bumps rising on her breasts.

Trying desperately to forget the dull ache behind my left eye, I shook away the chill. Instead of the shot of whiskey my body craved, I poured us each a glass of orange juice from the jar in the cooler, hoping to quell a racing heart caused by my nightmare.

"What were you dreaming about?" she said.

"Nothing," I said, shaking off her insistent tone.

"Sometimes it helps to talk about it."

"Just a nightmare."

"But you just can't keep having them forever. Was it the war again?"

When I nodded, Amber squeezed my hand and moved closer. "It's over now. Let's get back to sleep."

Amber let the Afghan slide off her shoulders. Crawling back into the sleeping bag, she opened the flap for me to join her.

"I'm wide awake," I said. "I have too many things on my mind. Think I'll just sit awhile."

"I'll stay up with you."

"I'm fine. Go back to sleep."

Amber leaned on her elbow, propping her head against her palm.

"My college minor was psychology, you know?"

"Then you may as well try your hand at analyzing me, Dr. Armstrong. Everyone else has."

"No analysis. I'm guessing your problem has a lot to do with guilt. That's just a guess."

"Maybe not such a bad guess. Even now I rarely tell anyone I served in Vietnam."

"Why?"

"Maybe because lots of people still believe soldiers that served there are all drug-using, homicidal maniacs."

"Not anymore. Besides, don't lump me into that category. Why do you feel that way?"

"It started with my ex-brother-in-law the night after I returned from Nam. He and his wife invited Erin and me to dinner. Bobby got a little looped on his own scotch. During dessert, he asked me how many babies I had killed. Later he wanted to know how many mama sans I had raped. He tried to act as if it was a joke though he said it in front of his two kids."

"Your own brother-in-law? What a jerk."

"He was that all right, exceeding the normal limits of obnoxious, even for a brother-in-law."

Amber giggled, and I allowed her to pull me down beside her in the sleeping bag.

"I'm sorry," I said.

"About what?"

"Dragging you into this mess and exposing you to danger."

"Hey, Troop," she said. "I'm enjoying every minute of it. If I weren't here with you, I'd be chasing drunken college students in Brannerville."

"It doesn't seem like we're making much progress."

When she propped herself on one elbow, I noticed her goosebumps had disappeared. A warm pink flush just below her neck replaced them.

"We probably already have the pieces of the puzzle in our hands. Professor Quinn says the simpler a possible solution, the more likely that it's correct."

"Yeah, well where is he when we need him?"

This time Amber didn't answer. Instead, she pulled the folds of the sleeping bag around her neck and closed her eyes. I reached over and turned off the fluorescent lantern. Neither of us heard the owl returning from his hunt. With devils intact, I slipped back into the same dream as before.

Near dark, forty miles from Phuoc Vinh, flying low over triple canopy jungle. In the distance, a cloud of black smoke hung just above the treetops as a line of tracers chased up through the vegetation. That morning, Bravo Company had strolled into an NVA bunker complex and taken multiple casualties. Now they were disengaging from the enemy, and we were arriving to take their place.

I sat beside the door gunner, my legs draped outside the chopper, hanging on to the vibrating bird. The chopper ahead of us nosed into a jungle clearing, quickly disgorging its passengers. Our Huey followed.

Grunts were already spreading out along the perimeter when I jumped from the landing rail and tumbled into the damp earth. Two medics bearing a wounded soldier on a litter rushed from the trees. They bent at the waists to avoid the chopper's whirling rotor. After depositing their bloody charge into the bird, they returned to the jungle for more casualties.

One at a time, exhausted grunts began emerging from the trees, replacing us in the awaiting chopper hovering in the clearing. In a rush of rotor-blown debris, the bird rose straight into the air, the sequence repeated by Huey after Huey until they had evacuated Bravo Company. Jungle silence quickly replaced their mechanized cacophony.

With daylight rapidly failing, we had no choice except to make camp for the night in a stand of bamboo and forget the bunker complex until the next morning. After humping a short distance into the triple canopy, Lennie Dotson dropped his pack beside mine, his steel pot bouncing when it hit the ground.

"Damn it! I'm sick to death of this crap," he said. "I haven't had a real shower in so long that red shit is oozing from my pores."

Though Dotson was twenty-three his Howdy Doody hair had already begun to thin. Red clay caked his growth of beard. I'd rarely heard him swear. Now his thin shoulders shook in a sudden angry quake. Along with red clay, orange freckles mottled the pasty skin on his thin arms. With a frown, he plopped against a bamboo shoot and closed his eyes. None of the other tired men seemed to notice.

"Get off your lazy ass, Dotson. You still got work to do."

Patterson our E-5, shake-and-bake squad leader, emerged from a tangle of vegetation, stumbling over to where we sat. Like Dotson's hair, his own was also curly but thick and orange instead of red. His eyes were also red, his blood-shot red.

"Get up," he said, kicking Dotson's boot. "String the claymores and trip flares before it gets too dark."

He swaggered away, not waiting for a reply.

"Little sawed-off dope head," Dotson said, pulling himself slowly to his feet.

"Small man complex," I said. "Don't sweat him."

"He'll find a grenade in his hooch some night if he doesn't lay off of me."

"Forget it, Lennie. You are a short-timer. You won't have to put up with him much longer."

"You'd think the little prick would be a little more civil on a person's birthday."

"It's your birthday?"

"Hell yes," he said. "Happy birthday to me."

"Happy birthday Lennie. Relax. I'll string the claymores for you."

"No way. I'm a big boy."

"Birthday present," I said, grabbing the bundle of claymores, flares, and tripwire, and then stepping out beyond our perimeter.

Monsoon season. Every night, just before dark, the temperature would drop a few degrees making it impossible for moisture-laden clouds to hold their burden any longer. Then it would rain, hard and heavy. I hurried out into twilight dimness beyond the perimeter, hoping to complete my task before the nightly deluge began.

First, I left the clackers in the shallow hole one of our men was digging in the loose earth. After walking three claymores to the ends of their wires, I faced them toward the jungle and secured the blasting caps into their respective sockets. There I left them, armed and deadly. Fifteen feet beyond the claymores I strung flares and tripwire in a semi-circle that joined with adjacent devices already set on either side. Finished, I started back to camp.

Light fails quickly in the tropics. It was almost dark when the unexpected happened. Someone tripped the wire behind me. There was a loud pop. Like a flaming torch, the detonated flare lighted the jungle. Thinking about the soldier sitting in the hole with his hands on the clacker I dived for the earth and yelled 'friendly' at the top of my lungs. Not before two bursts from an AK-47 sliced through my chest and shoulder.

All hell broke loose. As I waited, my face buried in the damp earth, for the claymore in front of me to detonate and blow me to pieces, the gunner in the hole opened up with a sustained burst from the M-60 machine gun. Zeroing in on the muzzle flash, our attackers cut loose into our position. Hot lead from two directions began whistling over my head, shredding jungle vegetation and filling the void around me with flying shards of sizzling shrapnel.

I tried crawling forward but found I couldn't move for the pain. My vision blurred and the explosions of light and sound around me began to dim. Weakened by rapid blood loss my mind slowed to a near halt, rapture replacing my fear-induced panic. Hot shrapnel whistling from every angle continued shredding my body. Even though I was keenly aware of its deadly effect, I felt no more pain than if I were high on Novocain in a dentist's chair. Though I sensed I was screaming for help, my impotent cries were only muddy gurgles in a raspy throat.

Two smoke bombs exploded nearby, one so close I felt the concussion. Dark streamers of smoke, pink and purple in normal light, wafted up through the vegetation. I knew that the Captain had summoned a Cobra gunship, hence the colored smoke to mark its attack pattern. When it arrived, it would come in hot opposite the streamers, mowing down plant and animal alike with twin mini-guns that would sound like revving chainsaws.

It didn't matter. My own reality was fading with the shank of the evening, and rising euphoria began replacing my fear. I found myself a casual observer to my own imminent demise. Then someone's hand touched my shoulder. I vaguely recognized the voice.

"Hang in there, Buddy. I won't let you die," he said.

Not waiting for my reply, Lennie Dotson wrapped his skinny arm around my shoulders, lifting me into a half crouch and began dragging me toward the perimeter. When he took a hit in the leg, he grunted with pain. His body flinching. Both our bodies vibrated from the impact when another bullet ripped through his shoulder.

Behind us, the Cobra had finally arrived and had begun flattening jungle vegetation with a buzz of bullets and hail of rockets. The attack lasted only a single pass. Mother Nature, as if pissed off by man and his puny attack, responded with a deluge of her own, quickly drowning out the noise of battle with the sudden eruptive dissonance of falling water.

When I opened my eyes engine drone, and tremulous motion told me I was in a Huey. We were already in the air, and an IV pierced my arm as I lay on my back in a litter. Blood soaked the hastily applied bandage around my upper body. When I tried to speak, I choked on my words, along with the gritty mud inside my mouth. The medic kneeling beside me put his hand on my chest.

"Hang on, sky trooper. You're going to make it."

When I cocked my head, I saw the green body bag beside me.

"Who. . . ?"

"Relax and just be glad it ain't you."

Struggling, I reached to grasp it.

"Show me," I said.

With an expression of resigned obligation, the medic unzipped the bag. Pulling back the flap, he let me see who it was.

Howdy Doody hair curled into green eyes staring lifelessly at the Huey's vibrating ceiling. It was Lennie. He was dead.

Chapter 24

When I awoke the next morning I found Amber, already dressed in her pink jogging outfit sitting at the concrete picnic table. From the damp vee-shape of her singlet, she'd already finished her morning run and was resting before taking a shower. She glanced suggestively at the sun, already high overhead, when she saw me drag out of the tent.

"Morning, Troop. Finally, decide to wake up?"

"Not quite the Hilton," I said, giving the canvas a backhanded slap. "At least the bumps are uniform."

"You'd whine about a sharp stick in the eye."

"Hey, an old sergeant of mine said when you quit whining, you're dead. What's on the agenda today?"

"Zekiel, but first a shower and some breakfast."

"Fresh out of the latter," I said. "Maybe I should run into town and pick up some groceries while you're cleaning up."

She grabbed the keys to the Jeep and tossed them to me. "Watch it. It's pulling to the right a little."

As I drove away down the dirt path to the highway, I watched her in the rearview mirror. She looked fit and tan as she disappeared into the tent to find a towel. Mary Ann and John Stewart had left their house, on their way down the hill. I didn't wait to see if they stopped to talk to Amber.

Foliage along the highway seemed different, almost as if it had changed overnight. Russet reds and golden browns dominated the evergreens, already locked in a wreath of basic colors. Overhead, the cloudless sky was as faded as an old pair of blue jeans. Further down the road, I found a produce seller propped against the front fender of his powder blue pickup. Bright green watermelons and yellow cantaloupes filled his truck. I bought one large melon and two cantaloupes.

When I returned to camp, I wheeled onto the dirt road leading to the tent and immediately noticed something wrong. Amber was still in her pink jogging outfit. Bending over her shoulders were Mary Ann and John Stewart. I held my breath when I recognized the object in Amber's hand. It was Bill's journal.

"What's up?"

"We found something," Amber said.

"Don't keep me in suspense," I said, depositing two bags of groceries and the watermelon on the tabletop.

"You weren't wrong about your brother. There was something else in his journal. It was hidden in the liner."

"How did you find it?"

"I didn't. Mary Ann did. She's the super sleuth."

Mary Ann beamed at Amber's compliment. "I knew Bill must have written something in there."

"A piece of black tape held the liner in place and kept these extra notes concealed," Amber said. "Mary Ann picked at it until it came loose."

"Read it to him," Mary Ann said.

John Stewart interrupted and said, "You don't have time to listen again. You're late for class. Your teacher will have your head."

"No sweat, Grandpa. Homeroom is the first period. It's just a study class."

"I don't care. You're supposed to be there. Run to the house and get the pickup. I'll take you to school."

John Stewart turned away from her frowning pout though not before tossing her keys to his pickup.

"What's it say?" I said.

Amber flipped through several loose pages and began to read. "The hidden trail is narrow and steep and leads into the Big Valley. I've checked my topo maps and the maps I got at BST. There are no other roads or trails, and the valley encompasses nearly a thousand square miles. It's totally isolated from the outside world."

Looking puzzled, Amber paused. "Maps from BST?"

"They own the land surrounding the National Forest," I said.

"Maybe that's why Bill broke into their office," Amber said.

"Of course. The company cuts their own logging roads on the mountain. They'd need maps for their loggers. Maps no one else would have."

Deep in thought, Amber continued reading. "The Big Valley is beyond the limits of my work. I need to check it out. Tomorrow I'll follow the trail and see where it leads."

Amber glanced up from the notes. "He used the notebook almost like a diary, recording what he saw. He dated the entries and even noted the time of day. This entry occurred the week before he disappeared."

"Before he sent me the diamond. Maybe he found it in the valley."

"Just a minute, Troop, there's another entry."

When I grabbed for the notebook, she yanked it away from me. Blowing me a kiss, she reopened the notebook and began again.

"The Big Valley is vast, much larger than I suspected. The trail begins near the top of the mountain just south of the BM triangle. Even though I knew exactly where to look, it took me two hours to find it. Trees are thick and huge and undergrowth all but nonexistent."

"Shit!" Amber said.

John Stewart was staring over my shoulder, and we didn't notice Mary Ann pulling up behind us in the truck. We all jumped when the brakes screeched, and she blew the horn. The truck's hinges needed grease. The door made a hollow thump when she slammed it behind her and hurried to join us at the picnic table.

"What?" I said.

"Missing pages. There are no directions to the trail anywhere in here."

"Keep reading," Mary Ann said.

"You can hear about it later," Stewart said. "You're late."

John Stewart hustled Mary Ann to the pickup, its springs protesting as the truck bumped along down the winding path to the highway. The engine backfired when Stewart shifted gears. Amber grabbed my arm when I flinched at the ensuing blast.

"I'm fine," I said.

Amber smoothed her short hair with her fingertips, adjusted her position on the hard concrete bench, and returned to Bill's notes.

"Once in the valley, I followed a south azimuth, traveling about five kilometers before finding a large clearing. Several crops, including maize and tobacco, are growing. Not wild but cultivated. I would like to know whose crop it is, considering my recent experience with the two moonshiners. I have moved along the periphery of the fields, traveling two more kilometers without seeing anyone.

"Plowed ground has a strange bluish hue, and I filled a vial with soil from the field located on the map at point 1-A. I am excited about my discovery. Bits of olivine, mica, and feldspar are everywhere. It's much larger than an isolated igneous extrusion and covers two hundred acres or more."

Amber paused, and I said, "Don't stop."

"That's all there is," she said.

"Sure?"

"See for yourself."

I took the loose notes and thumbed through them quickly. Finding nothing, I returned them to Amber.

Closing the notebook, she said, "Bill must have wanted the location to the trail into the valley badly enough to break into the BST office and go through their papers."

"They wouldn't have cooperated with him after he reported them to the sheriff. Not to mention his call to Washington."

"And we have about as much a chance as Bill had to get a look at those maps."

"So what do we do?"

Amber glanced at her watch and then at the sun. Without replying to my question, she went into the tent, returning shortly with a towel and bar of soap.

"First I shower, and then we eat breakfast. Afterward, we go see Zekiel."

I reread the loose-leaf notes three times while waiting for Amber to shower and dress. After a quick breakfast, we started up the mountain to Zekiel's shack, stopping at the roadside liquor store for another bottle of Jack Daniel's. This time I also bought a twenty-five-pound block of ice for the old man's icebox.

Zekiel's hound met us on the dirt road when we rounded the last bend to his shack. As before, Zekiel was sitting in his rocker on the front porch, smoking his corncob pipe. He blinked his big brown eyes and licked his lips when he saw the brown paper bag and a large chunk of ice.

"Zekiel," I said. "I'd like to introduce Amber."

"Your Pearl," he said, nodding his approval and smiling appreciatively at our gifts.

After petting the hound's big head, Amber stroked the black cat at Zekiel's feet. The cat arched its back and began a throaty purr. Zekiel led us inside, and I loaded the chunk of ice into the icebox for him. He grabbed two cold drinks, opened them, and placed them on his table for Amber and me. Straight up with no ice, he poured himself a healthy slug of Black Jack. Finally, looking smug and satisfied, he motioned us to sit before asking us a question in such a way I wasn't sure what he really meant.

"Found what you was looking for yet?"

"If you mean what happened to Bill, the answer is no. Not yet, at least."

Zekiel stroked the crystal ball on the table and a throaty chuckle emitted from deep in his sunken chest. "You want to know how to get down in the valley, don't you?"

Amber's skeptical expression suddenly changed. Leaning forward in her chair, she rested her elbows on the table.

"How did you know that?" she asked.

"Scryed it," he said, glancing at his crystal ball.

When Amber rolled her eyes, I ignored her disbelief and said, "Can you tell us?"

"There's a trail into the Big Valley. It's old and mostly grown over with creepers and brush. It's the only way in."

"Where is it?" I said.

Zekiel scratched his snow-white hair and said, "Though I'm old as these hills all I know about the trail into the valley is there is one. Some of the hill people know. They keep it secret. Don't never tell nobody. Not even me."

Amber continued to lean on the table. "Has anyone been in there that you know of?" she said.

Zekiel shook his head thoughtfully. "Too far to hike in. Can't carry enough supplies on your back. There are no roads, and the trees and brush are too thick and the valley walls too steep to ride in on a horse. The only way in is on the trail. Even then you'd need a couple of good pack mules."

"Zekiel," I said. "Bill made it down into the valley somehow. We think that's where we'll find him."

Zekiel's eyes, lips, and sunken mahogany cheeks drew together to paint a morose frown on the wrinkles of his wizened face. He shook his head again. Reaching across the table with both hands, he held them palms up until we clasped them. Closing his eyes, he began to tremble.

"Danger!" he said in a high-pitched unearthly whine. "Danger!"

Chapter 25

When Zekiel's convulsive fit finally subsided, he leaned back in his chair, shook his head, refusing to answer any more questions. Amber poured him another glass of whiskey and held it to his lips until he'd sipped a few drops. When his rapid heart rate abated, he put his hand over his eyes and moaned. Amber helped him to the old army cot in the rear of the shack. Minutes later, he was patting the head of his worried hound, preventing it from licking his hand draped lifelessly over the edge of the cot.

"I'm all right," he said.

"You sure?"

"After I drink some more whiskey."

Amber let him rest on her shoulder as he lapped Jack Daniel's with a thirsty tongue.

"Tell us what you saw," she said.

"My old eyes went dim on me," he said, grasping my wrist. "I know I can't stop you from going down in the valley."

Closing his eyes, he took another swig of whiskey.

"Please, Zekiel. Tell us what you saw before your eyes went dim," I said.

"The forest was burning, a wall of flames keeping me from seeing who was screaming."

He shook his head when I asked, "Was it me?"

"It was Mary Ann," he said. "She was dying."

Amber grabbed my arm, pulling me toward the door. We left Zekiel on the cot, his hound still licking his hand as he worked on the bottle of whiskey.

"Now what?" I said as Amber negotiated the steep incline back to the highway.

"Drive into Dill City and get the Jeep fixed."

"And then?"

"Talk to Sheriff Bonner again. Maybe he can get us a look at BST's map."

"I'm thinking we should call off the search," I said.

"Are you that frightened?" she asked.

"Not for myself. You heard what the old man said about Mary Ann."

"Surely you don't believe his malarkey."

"Do you?" I asked.

"Course not," she said. "He's been living alone too long. The moonshine has started affecting his judgment."

She smiled, reached across the seat and squeezed my hand when I asked, "You really think so?"

"If you feel Mary Ann is in danger, we'll leave her behind. Her grandpa probably won't let her go with us, anyway."

"Staying behind won't make her happy," I said.

"I'll tell her if you want me to," Amber said.

I shook my head. "I'll tell her."

Though the day was still bright and sunny, dark clouds had begun rimming the horizon. Distant thunder echoed against the valley walls as we headed toward Dill City. We easily found Jake's Body Shop. After a short conversation with tobacco-chewing Jake, we left the Jeep in his charge and hiked down Main Street to the Sheriff's office.

Bonner was leaning back in his chair, his big head resting in interlaced fingers and his feet sprawled across the top of his desk. One soiled white sock glinted through a gaping hole in the sole of his worn trooper boot. Unlike before, he smiled when we walked through the door. He even got up from his desk and poured us each a cup of coffee.

"Thought you might drop by," he said."Jake just called. Said he can fix the steering problem but can't get on the fender until next week."

"That's half our problem," I said. "Bill's journal mentioned a map of the mountain BST has."

"Think you can get us a look at it?" Amber asked.

"Why hell no," he said. "You two are about as popular over at BST as a lap dog with bad breath."

"Is there anything we can do short of breaking and entering like Bill did?" I said.

"Wouldn't advise you doing that," Bonner said. "I got an alternative for you."

We followed Sheriff Bonner down a hallway to a locked door. Humidity had begun flaking green paint off the wall. Stale air greeted us when he unlocked it with a jingle of many keys. A single bare bulb, too small to light the room, cast gloomy shadows on rows of steel-gray file cabinets. Amber glanced at me with bated anticipation as we watched him begin to open and shut various filing cabinets.

"Got my own map in here somewhere. Never know when you're going to have to apprehend a felon up in the hills."

He finally located a full-sized black and white copy of a topographic map and unrolled it in front of us. Hand-labeled marks overlaid the map with BST's logging roads. Somewhere on it was the location of the trail leading into the Big Valley. Sheriff Bonner rolled up the map, turned off the light and lumbered back down the hall to his office. He poured himself another cup of coffee and then rolled out the map on his desk.

"Could be anywhere on here," he finally said, scratching his chin. "You can borrow the map and look for yourself."

"We really appreciate it, Sheriff Bonner," Amber said.

"No problem. I got a copy back in the file cabinet." Bonner wheeled around and wagged his crooked index finger at Amber. "Don't you be telling anybody where you got this, you hear? Especially anyone from BST. I got enough trouble in this county without losing my number one campaign contributor."

"Your secret's safe with us Sheriff," I said.

"You folks get in trouble up there on the mountain you get me a message, though I'm telling you now there ain't no quick way I can bail you out. Thirty miles as the crow flies takes hours up those logging roads."

"What you need is a chopper," I said.

"We're civilized around here, son. Blake Tedford up the highway has a half dozen or so. Uses them to dust crops. But the trees are so thick up there they ain't no place to land."

"In Vietnam, they hovered over the trees and let the soldiers rappel down ropes."

Sheriff Bonner rubbed his big belly and said. "How'd they know where to go in?"

"Flares and smoke grenades."

Bonner snapped his fingers as if he had an idea and went to a large metal locker against the wall. It had three padlocks on it. When he finally got it open, I saw why. It contained an arsenal of shotguns, rifles, pistols, and automatic weapons. After fishing around in a box on the floor a minute, he found what he was looking for. He winked as he handed me two army-issue smoke grenades and a flare pistol.

"How about an Uzi or an automatic rifle?" he said, holding up a weapon for my inspection.

"Thanks, Sheriff. Not for me. Amber has her weapon. We hopefully won't need it."

"Don't say I didn't offer," he said. "You get in trouble then try getting a message to the hill folk. When you hear the helicopter, send up a flare, and set off one of these babies."

We thanked him again, left his office, and made our way back down Main Street. Jake had already replaced the Jeep's broken tie rod and apologized for his inability to repair the fender quite so fast. Amber assured him that he'd taken care of our most pressing problem.

Following a late lunch at Vera's, we started back to Turkey Gap. We met the yellow school bus at the entrance to the campgrounds and gave Mary Ann a ride from the road. On the way to the tent, we showed her the map.

"Let me hold it," she said.

She jumped from the back of the Jeep, not waiting for Amber to park. After spreading the map on the table, she waited for us to join her.

Because of the valley's immense size, the topo's scale was small and four-digit numbers, added with a black marker, labeled BST's logging roads. Something else was on the map: exact locations of Federal land marked for clear-cutting and each location bore the initials of G. Gray Townsend. I began to regret my promise to Sheriff Bonner.

Suppressing the notion of returning to Dill City, I continued instead to study the map. After ten futile minutes, I still had no inkling of how Bill had gained access to the valley.

Mary Ann said, "This is enough to get us started. We'll find the trail."

I drew a deep breath when Amber gave me a glance.

"You're not going with us," I said.

"You aren't serious," she said.

"As a heart attack. It'll be too dangerous. I can't let you go."

"You know I'm not afraid."

"You're not afraid of anything," I said. "Doesn't make any difference. You can't go."

"That's a bunch of bull," she said. "I've been on the mountain with you a half-dozen times already. Why is it any more dangerous now than it was then? Tell me," she said when I glanced away from her stare.

"Zekiel told us you would be in danger of being killed."

"You went to see Zekiel without me?"

"You were in school," I said.

"Don't matter none," she said. "I'm not scared and you're not going to stop me from going with you."

"Your grandfather won't let you when I tell him what Zekiel told us."

Mary Ann grimaced as she started up the hill to her house, stopping after ten feet.

"Grandpa wants you to eat supper with us tonight. Will you let me go with you If he says I can?"

"He won't?" I said.

"And if he does?" Amber folded her arms and rolled her eyes when I turned for her support. Mary Ann picked up on her reaction. "Amber, do you believe I'll get killed on the mountain?"

"I'm not superstitious. Like I told Tom, I think the old man's brain has been stewed by too much moonshine."

Mary Anne's smile disappeared when she returned her attention to me. "I'm going with you," she said. "And that's that. We're having beans and cornbread for dinner."

"Sounds wonderful," Amber said. "What time?"

"Grandpa likes to eat early. Soaked the beans last night and they've been cooking all day. Cornbread'll be ready in about an hour."

We watched her stroll away, up the hill. "That gives me time to jog a few miles before I shower," Amber said. "Want to come along?"

"So she's coming with us?" I said.

"She'll be fine," Amber said, squeezing my hand.

"You weren't much help," I said.

"You running or not?" she asked, ignoring my subtle accusation.

Deciding to worry about it later, I let the subject drop.

"If I ran a few miles before showering, we'd be late for dinner. Think I'll stay here and study the map some more."

"Suit yourself."

Amber disappeared into the tent, returning shortly in a fresh jogging outfit. With a backhanded wave, she streaked away through the trees. I watched her tanned legs until she was out of sight before turning my attention to the map. After twenty minutes, I knew no more than when I'd started looking. I'd focused my full attention on it when Amber returned and tapped my shoulder.

"Still sitting here?"

"My eyes are popping out of my head. For the life of me, I can't find the trail into the valley."

"We'll find it later. Now we better hurry or we'll miss the beans and cornbread."

When she tossed me a towel, I followed her to the washhouse, Zekiel's danger warning, and the elusive trail still very much on my mind.

Mary Ann had outdone herself and we feasted on stewed pinto beans, hot-buttered cornbread, fresh okra, and corn on the cob. Later we sat on the rickety front porch watching the stars as we listened to the musical creak of swinging chains and a night bird in a distant tree. John Stewart rocked intently as I told him about our meeting with Zekiel and his description of the trail into the Valley.

"Johnsons up on the mountain have some mules," he said.

"Would they rent them to us?" Amber asked.

"Nope. They'd lend them to you if I asked them to. They're cousins of mine."

Amber patted the top of my hand, and I realized how tightly I was gripping the arm of my rocking chair.

"Can you give them a call?"

"No phone up there. If you want, I'll run up with you tomorrow."

Mary Ann interrupted and said, "Grandpa, I'd like to go down in the valley with Tom and Amber."

"No way," Stewart said. "You can't miss school."

"You're being unfair, Grandpa," Mary Ann said, slapping the screen door with the back of her hand.

"Life isn't always fair, little girl. Now you go on in and do your homework."

Ignoring her grandfather, Mary Ann knelt in front of Amber's rocker and clutched her hand.

"Please convince Grandpa to let me go into the valley."

"Is it that important to you?"

"It's the most important thing I'll ever do my whole life," Mary Ann said.

Amber didn't bother asking for my opinion. Turning instead to the old man, she clutched his hand.

"Even if we knew how to find the trail, we wouldn't be ready before tomorrow. Can't you let Mary Ann miss two days of school, Mr. Stewart? We'll be back by Sunday night at the latest and you can see how much it means to her."

"Well. . ."

"Please, Grandpa," Mary Ann said, turning her attention to John Stewart.

"Your grandfather is right," I said. "The valley may be dangerous."

"All the more reason I should go along. The only person that knows more about the hills than Grandpa is me. Besides, I know where the trail is and I'm not telling unless I go with you."

Mary Ann's unexpected pronouncement caused us all to shut up and take notice.

"How do you know that?" I said.

"Take me with you, and I'll tell you."

"I can't do that without your grandfather's permission. Even then, I'm not sure it's a wise idea."

"We'll take good care of her, Mr. Stewart" Amber said, ignoring my concern. "I'm a law officer. If it weren't for Mary Ann, we wouldn't even know about the valley."

"You really know where the trail is or are you just kidding us?" John Stewart asked.

"Will you let me go?"

When Stewart drew a deep breath, his dark eyes twinkled in the moonlight.

"Okay," he said following a thoughtful pause. "When I go in, I'll write your teacher an excuse. I'll give it to him tomorrow for you. You might even learn something."

"Thank you, Grandpa," Mary Ann said, hugging his scrawny old neck.

"I'll get the map and Bill's notes," I said. "You can show us where the trail is."

"Not tonight," Mary Ann said.

"Why not?" I asked.

"I'll show you tomorrow, right before we're ready to leave and it's too late for you to change your mind about me going with you."

Chapter 26

That night before leaving Stewart's house, we decided to begin our trek first thing the next morning. Amber and I spent the remainder of the evening packing and preparing for the trip into the Big Valley. John Stewart would go with us to Johnson's house and arrange for us to borrow some mules. He would return Sunday afternoon and pick us up. Someone pounding on the side of the tent awakened us before dawn.

"I got things to do. You kids want me to take you up to see the Johnson's, you need to get up and get to moving."

The old man was sitting at the concrete picnic table when Amber and I crawled from the tent. Mary Ann was with him, though she didn't look quite so chipper. Mr. Johnson had brought along two cups of hot coffee that we gladly drank before hurrying off to the washhouse. Mary Ann, Bill's notes in her hand, had the map spread out on the picnic table when we returned.

"Well?" I said.

Mary Ann cleared her throat and began reading from the loose notes.

"The Big Valley is vast, much larger than I suspected. The trail begins near the top of the mountain, just south of the BM triangle. Even though I knew exactly where to look, it took me two hours to find it. Trees are thick and huge, and undergrowth all but gone."

Amber touched her forehead as she and I exchanged glances.

"What's a BM triangle?" she said.

Mary Ann pointed to a spot on the map. "Near the top of the mountain, south of the little triangle that pinpoints the government benchmark. Bill's BM triangle is a government benchmark."

"Of course," I said. "I should have known Bill would let us know where it was."

"I still don't know what you're talking about," Amber said.

"A permanent marker set in concrete by the government geological survey. Surveyors use them as reference points to measure elevations from."

Just below the triangle, a dashed line pointed into the Valley. Besides having faded with time, and along with the propensities of Sheriff Bonner's copier, it extended for no more than half an inch. Now a mile wide grin engulfed Mary Ann's face.

I told you that you'd never have found it without me."

Even after breaking camp, we were halfway up the mountain before the sun crested the treetops on the eastern horizon.

The morning was bright and crisp, the pale sky blue with no hint of impending rain. The house was a mile further down the highway, the road to it steep and narrow. The first sign of human habitation as we approached their house through the trees was the cackle of hens, gobble of turkeys and the corrosive stench of wallowing hogs.

House was a misnomer. Like the place Zekiel lived, Johnson's house was little more than a shack. My stereotypical vision of an Arkansas hill family paralleled something straight out of Lil' Abner. Reality didn't disappoint. If anything, the family of ten lived in squalor and poverty even more abject than I could have guessed.

Rafe Johnson and his wife, their moon faces all grins that instantly highlighted missing front teeth, watched from the ramshackle porch as we approached. Both had flame red hair with complexions to match and dime-sized freckles that looked almost like an affliction. Their resemblance was so remarkable they could easily have passed as brother and sister.

Rafe was shirtless beneath tattered overalls. A naked toddler lay in his wife's arms, its head buried beneath the loose fold of her flour sack blouse. It was suckling at her breast. John Stewart explained why we were there, not bothering to introduce us.

Rafe led us to a pasture behind the house, several of his children following us. All had freckles and red hair and looked just like their parents. A hand-split fence surrounded ten acres of hilly land all but devoid of trees. A makeshift stable, no less rickety than the house, provided shelter for six lop-eared mules corralled in the pen. We found Rafe's twang more pronounced than John Stewart's and I had to concentrate to make out what he was saying.

"These are my mules," he said. "Least the ones that ain't down in the low pasture."

"What do you do with so many mules?" I asked.

"Sell them. Best plow beasts in the world."

Looking at Rafe Johnson's house and the surroundings, I had a hard time believing the profession was very rewarding. With John Stewart's assistance, we picked out four animals. Rafe saddled three and threw a large leather pack for our supplies over the back of the fourth. We wasted no time unloading the Jeep and transferring our supplies to the bellowing beasts.

My mule had blinders attached to his harness, and I asked why.

"Ol' Flame's a pistol," Rafe said. "Don't like nobody on his back. Them blinders fool him into thinking there ain't nobody there."

"What if he finds out?"

"Why hell, he'll toss you right over his head and take a bite out of your butt," Rafe said, obviously amused by the possibility.

Mary Ann and Amber had already mounted their mules. Their mile-wide grins reflected their own amusement, enjoyed at my expense.

"Any advice?" I said as I put my foot in the stirrup.

"Ol' Flame's mean as a snake. Don't get in front of him and whatever you do don't get behind him. If he gets hard to handle, take a hickory stick to his head. And keep a tightrope 'round his neck, or he'll be back in the barn before you can say scat."

Armed with Rafe's comforting words and the braying of an angry beast, I situated myself on Ol' Flame's bony back. By now, the entire Johnson family had arrived to watch us depart up the hilly trail. Amber reined her mount and trotted over to where John Stewart stood with his elbow on a fence post.

"If we're not back by sundown Sunday, Mr. Stewart, get word to the sheriff. He'll know what to do."

The old man nodded and waved as we disappeared over the rise.

Mary Ann led the way, followed by Amber and the pack mule. Ol' Flame and I brought up the rear. Our slow going up the steep grade reminded me of many hot, single-file humps through Vietnamese triple canopy. What the belligerent beast beneath me might do if I fell off became more of a concern than encountering an NVA ambush.

Soon there was no discernible trail, only giant trees growing so close together that they left quite a squeeze for the mules and our packs. Mary Ann continued uphill at a steady pace.

"Mary Ann, you're not lost are you?" I said.

"I have Bill's compass," she answered over the braying of Ol' Flame. "I'm following an azimuth to the benchmark."

Of course. The forest was like Vietnam. Instead of jungle creepers and vines, so thick you had to whack your way through with a machete, the mountain environs were thick with tall trees. Compass navigation was the only way to stay on course in either place. Until that moment, it hadn't dawned on me how thick the forest would be. Having read Bill's notes more closely than I had, Mary Ann remembered to bring along the compass Bill had taught her how to use.

Trees became ever taller, their boughs blocking the rays of the sun. The mules, especially Ol' Flame, grew progressively apprehensive and their nervous brays began to sound like cries of frightened children. We soon had to dismount and lead the beasts the rest of the way. Ol' Flame refused to let me lead him, so we tied him to the mule in front to keep him going in the right direction.

Mary Ann pointed and said, "There it is."

"I don't see it," Amber said.

Neither did I. Mary Ann simply let go of her lead line and scampered up the slope. Blocking our view with her body, she knelt beside something in front of us. Amber tied the mules to a tree and joined her. Fallen leaves partially covered whatever Mary Ann had found. She crawled on her hands and knees, frantically digging with both hands to expose it.

There it was: a concrete post weathered by wind, rain, and time. Attached to the post was a brass marker bearing the name of the governmental agency that had placed it, along with the location's elevation at that spot in the forest. As quickly as Mary Ann had cleared away the leaves, she hurried down the slope toward the valley as she looked for the trail. It took us ten more minutes to find it.

"Let's go," Mary Ann said, bursting with a youthful exuberance that had deserted my own body ten years prior.

"Why don't we take a break and eat lunch," Amber said.

"Second the motion," I said. "I'm not tired, but Ol' Flame and the other mules need rest and a water break."

Amber rolled her pear-shaped indigo eyes in a way to which I had become accustomed. Mary Ann simply frowned, stopped in her tracks, and shook her head in disgust.

"See if you can find a pool of rainwater for the mules," Amber said. "We don't want to run short this early in the trip."

"No problem," Mary Ann said. "We've had so much rain lately there are clear puddles practically beneath every tree."

She tied the mules in a semi-circle around a large pool of water while Amber broke out baggies of leftover beans and cornbread. My butt had already suffered ill effects from Ol' Flame's bony back, and I collapsed into soft leaves, stomach first.

After lunch and a brief rest, Mary Ann said, "If we don't leave now it'll be dark before we make the base of the valley."

My arms and legs protested when I rose up from the soft pile of leaves. I began thinking about the tepid shower and already knew I'd miss it long before we made it back to the campsite. I had little time to fret as Mary Ann and Amber saddled up and started down into the valley.

Though the trail was old and barely visible, the mules seemed to know the route. They kicked loose rocks down the steep incline as they slowly picked their way like mountain goats down the narrow pathway. Thick gray cloud cover draping the valley became visible through the trees as we continued down the steep path winding along the side of the mountain.

Wildlife, scarce on the mountaintop, grew more plentiful the further we went. Chipmunks, squirrels, rabbits, and even foxes, seemingly unafraid of the mules or us crossed our path along the way. After another two hours, my butt was already so sore I thought it would fall off if we didn't stop soon. Finding no good place to do so on the steep and narrow trail, I simply endured.

Then it happened. The pack mule, walking behind the two lead mules though ahead of Ol' Flame, slipped in loose chert. Somewhere along the trail, his heavy pack had shifted. Now, the unevenly dispersed weight caused his left hind leg to buckle and then slip completely off the narrow ledge.

"Headache!" I yelled.

The line around Ol' Flame's neck, connecting it to the struggling mule in front of us, drew taut. I slid off Ol' Flame on the mountainside of the trail and grabbed the line in a desperate attempt to keep both animals from tumbling down the slope. Mary Ann was even faster. Reining her own beast to a halt, she thrust the bridle at Amber and dived for the stricken mule that was now on its side and struggling to regain its footing. At that point, only taut lines kept the mule from tumbling over the ledge.

The mule's heavy burden was pulling it toward the brink. From somewhere in Mary Ann's tight jeans she produced a knife and made two quick cuts with the sharp blade. Tearing loose from the animal the pack toppled over the ledge, relieving the beast of the offending weight, and allowing Ol' Flame to pull the frightened animal back up on the trail.

With some doing, we managed to calm the mule and redistribute the burden. Most of our food and supplies had taken the plunge into the Big Valley far below. When we started forward, I could only imagine what we would do without food for the next four days.

After three hours, we reached the thick layer of vapor. It felt like flying into a bank of clouds in a plane. It felt even more surreal from the backs of the mules. When the trail finally flattened and widened, I had no feeling in my rear. It, along with the loss of much of my sense of reality, had disappeared. Gray fog was eerily thick, the distinct odor of sulfur floating in the hollows. I had lost all sense of direction and was beginning to feel dizzy and claustrophobic.

"Hold up, Mary Ann," I said. "My legs are cramping."

"You wus," she said.

"Let's take pity on the old man," Amber said. "Besides, it's less than an hour before dark. We need to find a creek or pond and make camp."

"I'll make a quick circle," Mary Ann said.

Amber jumped off her mule and waited, holding the reins while I slid off Ol' Flame, desperately trying to remember how to walk. Mary Ann called to us through the fog. She was about fifty feet away though completely hidden in the misty veil surrounding us.

"Hey, I found a creek, and it runs into a pond."

"Eureka," Amber said. "I'm dying for a drink of cold water."

"Then you better hold on to your horses," Mary Ann said.

"Why is that?" I said.

"Cause it ain't cold; it's bubbling."

Amber and I picked our way through the fog toward Mary Ann's voice, realizing what she meant when we reached her. The creek bursting forth into the valley from somewhere high above us was cold. Not the pond. As Mary Ann had said, it was bubbling. I found out why when I tested it with my finger.

It was hot, very hot.

Chapter 27

Giant trees replete with remnant limestone ledges protruding like worn monoliths from damp earth gave way to a glade. Bathed in foggy humidity, ferns, lichens, and assorted bromeliads grew in profusion and gave the low-lying glade a look and feel of a lush botanical garden.

I knew that Arkansas had hot springs, though unaware of any located in this part of the Ouachita Mountains. Now, only a day's trek from civilization, we found ourselves cloaked in the wispy mist of a different geologic age and the giant head of a Tyrannosaur suddenly peaking through the fog would not have surprised me.

"It's like Yellowstone National Park," Amber said. "I think it's a geyser."

As she pointed toward the center of a pool, it began bubbling like a boiling pot, shooting a stream of hot water and steam thirty feet into the air. I couldn't stop staring.

"This must be the reason for the constant cloud cover over the valley. No wonder no one knows what's down here."

I could see Mary Ann was grinning when she said, "Hope there aren't any snakes around."

"You could have gone all day without mentioning snakes," I said.

"I don't know about snakes," Amber said. "I can tell you right now we're not alone."

Mary Ann drew closer to me as she gazed around trying to see what Amber saw.

"Up there," Amber said, pointing again.

On a ledge above us a yellow lizard, at least three feet in length lounged among brightly colored ferns. Purple and crimson moths, some with wings spanning a foot or more, flitted around above stunted shrubbery. Large frogs with translucent skin the color and texture of lime Jell-o floated on darker green lily pads that abounded in the bubbling pond water. And, there were flowers: water-blooming hyacinths whiter than polished ivory, and hothouse orchids, some as indigo as Amber's eyes.

I touched Mary Ann's shoulder and said, "It's getting late and I'm bushed. Let's find a place to make camp for the night. We can explore tomorrow."

We soon found a suitable spot near a cool pool of water on which to raise the tent. I helped Amber string a circular rope corral for the mules, and they seemed happy when we relieved them of their packs and saddles. Once Mary Ann had given them each a bag of oats, luckily saved from our near-disaster on the trail, they took to the rope corral with no fuss. With daylight rapidly waning, we relaxed and finished our beans and cornbread. Amber had put leftovers from lunch in her own pack and it was all we had left to eat.

"Too bad we didn't save the food," Mary Ann said. "Swamp grass and hot water won't be very filling by Sunday."

"I'd just like to get out of these dirty clothes," Amber said. "If anything, by Sunday night we're going to be awfully ripe."

"What did you say about a sharp stick in the eye?"

My muscles were sore from our extended mule ride, and I winced when Amber elbowed me in the ribs because of my remark.

"Personally, I could use a massage and soak in a Jacuzzi," I said.

Finishing her last spoonful of beans, Mary Ann said, "Not much we can do about the food. I spotted a pool of water over yonder and the temperature seemed just right. We can wash our clothes and soak our joints while they dry."

Amber and I required little convincing. We found Mary Ann's pool only a short hike from the tent. She led us to a shallow basin beveled by the relentless drip of slightly acidic water on solid limestone. Cold water from the creek and hot water from one of the thermal pools fed into the basin. What resulted was a near perfect temperature for soaking fatigued muscles.

Darkness had engulfed the glade, a chorus of frogs and crickets already holding sway. The perfume of night-blooming orchids filled the air as distant thunder sounded far up on the mountain. Neither Mary Ann nor Amber seemed the least modest about stripping and washing their clothes and I decided not to worry about it.

After washing away trail grime from our garments, we spread them to dry on the bank and eased up to our necks in hot water. When Amber switched off the lamp to save batteries, we got another surprise in a day already abundant with surprises. Lichen, growing everywhere on surrounding limestone, lighted the area around us with multi-colored phosphorescence.

"Magnificent," Amber said.

"It's like a fairyland," Mary Ann said.

Their words understated how I felt. Languishing in the luxury of the moment I reclined until only my eyes and tip of my nose protruded from hot water. My muscles relaxed as I breathed the lusty mixture of sulfur and orchids. Sometime later, Amber aroused me from the lethargy of my relaxation.

"I just had a bad thought. What if the whole valley is foggy like this? What happens if we can't find the trail or our way back up the mountain? It could happen, even if we go no further than we've gone right now."

Perspiration trickled down my forehead and I waited until it dropped off the tip of my nose before replying.

"We could circle the valley. Stay close to the mountains until we reach the trail again."

"Great idea, Magellan. And make it back here in about a month?"

"You're not suggesting we turn around and go back are you?"

"Of course not. We just need a plan."

"We still have the compass," Mary Ann said. "All we need to do is head straight south. When we reach the other side of the valley, we come back in the opposite direction."

"Genius," I said sarcastically. "What happens if we don't find what we're looking for? Forget the whole thing?"

Mary Ann's lower lip protruded into a full pout. Leaning against the limestone wall, she curled into a near fetal position with her arms clasped tightly around her knees.

"I know I'm dumb. It don't give you any right to be mean to me."

I had already noticed that Mary Ann's accent seemed to intensify when she was angry or upset. My not-well-thought-out remark had now made her almost incomprehensible.

"Hey," Amber said, sitting straight up in the pool. "Listen to us. We're starting to sound like cranky old men."

"More like cranky old women," I said, unable to help myself.

"Mary Ann, let's yank his hair out."

They both grabbed handfuls of my hair, their playful tugs igniting a wrestling match that ended with the three of us laughing so hard that I almost choked when Mary Ann pushed my head under water. Our antics relieved the tension. When we finally returned to camp in clean albeit damp clothes we all felt much better. My apology to Mary Ann and Amber also seemed to help matters.

Once in the tent, Mary Ann cuddled up in her blanket and Amber, and I crawled into the double sleeping bag.

After situating ourselves beneath the covers Mary Ann asked, "Are you two married?"

"No," Amber said.

"You sleep together. Do you love each other?"

Her question roused a nervous giggle from Amber. "We haven't exactly reached that stage yet. Right now, we're just lovers."

Amber's answer surprised me, and Mary Ann didn't immediately respond. As if needing further clarification she cleared her throat.

"Are you going to make love tonight?"

After the exhausting mule ride and our near disaster on the mountain, Mary Ann's questions were far too much for me. I reached over and switched off the lamp. My parting remark evoked giggles from both Mary Ann and Amber.

"Not to worry. I couldn't now even if I wanted to."

The trip into the Big Valley had left us out of sorts with each other and our first morning in the strange world found Mary Ann trying to satiate her hunger by nibbling on a flower petal. I was so sore I could hardly walk as Amber fidgeted like a nervous panther because she couldn't go for her morning jog. The mules had fared better overnight and seemed anesthetized by moist, sulfurous air. At least they'd had their breakfast.

Silver sheaves of slow rain draped our path and cleared away most of the fog as we saddled up and headed south. Thick clouds remained directly overhead, blocking sunlight except for isolated shafts that illuminated the valley like heavenly spotlights. The mules must have liked the rain because Ol' Flame brayed and kicked up his heels like a yearling.

We finally reached the edge of the glade and with it the end of the inherent fog. This portion of the Big Valley was as flat as the glade, the walking much easier and trees even larger. Because of the same thick cloud cover and extremely high branches, little sunlight filtered through to the ground. Here, unlike the thick forest around Turkey Gap, there was no undergrowth, vines or trailers to impede our progress and our mules ambled along on a thick mat of pine needles that cushioned their hooves like high-grade carpeting.

An armadillo startled the mules and seemed unafraid when it crossed our path. The valley, like the trail leading into it, was a haven for wildlife and abounded with diverse vegetation. Within a mile, we spotted a small herd of whitetail deer. They, along with rabbits, raccoons, and other assorted small animals regarded us as no apparent menace.

I had estimated the distance across the valley at fifty miles. Despite our attempts to speed them along, the mules lazily sampled tall grass and stubbornly refused to go much faster than we could have traveled on foot. By noon, after many rest and exploration breaks, we had yet to reach the center of the valley. We did find a grove of fruit trees, sagging from the weight of bushels of green pears.

"Lunch," Amber said.

"Don't let the mules loose beneath them. They'll bloat up like sheep in green clover," Mary Ann said, reining in her mount as it drew back its head and snorted.

"Let's tether them beyond the grove and walk back," I said. "Or else we'll have a stampede on our hands."

The mules, especially Ol' Flame, protested. After much urging, they finally continued past the pears. Just beyond the grove, we found a circular clearing, cloud-filtered light reflecting from spots in the dark blue soil. I seemed to remember something about blue soil. For the life of me, I couldn't remember what it was.

Though it was late September, the day was as warm as early summer when we emerged from the grove. Mary Ann tied her braids in a ball on her head and wiped perspiration from the back of her neck with her hand. Amber mopped the vee of her chest with a handkerchief. I was thinking how good a glass of iced tea would taste.

I noticed the clearing was furrowed and looked as if someone had just prepared it for seed. We tethered the mules and walked into the open field to investigate. Forgetting heat and fatigue, Mary Ann sprinted ahead, suddenly emitting an eardrum-shattering squeal. It halted Amber in her tracks and caused me to wrench a muscle in my neck when I jerked around. Amber backed against me and grabbed my hand.

"What the hell!" I said.

Mary Ann didn't answer. Instead, she crouched on her knees, digging with both hands in the plowed earth. She glanced up from the field, grinning like a deranged person, and held up a shiny stone.

"Look what I found?"

"What?" Amber asked.

Mary Ann came running and handed Amber a pomegranate red crystal.

"Don't know. It's sure pretty."

Amber turned the crystal in her palm with an index finger and handed the crimson stone to me. I held it to the light, rotating it slowly. All fire and sharp edges, it seemed to have a life all its own.

"If Dr. Quinn was here," Amber said. "He'd know what it is."

"Or Zekiel."

Mary Ann squealed again. She had returned to the furrowed field and was crawling on her hands and knees. She'd found a second crystal, this one vivid green. Amber rushed to the clearing, knelt beside her and began sifting through the earth. Struck by the fever, I joined them. In minutes, digging in a frenzy of discovery, we each had handfuls of crystals and had totally lost track of time. With our thoughts riveted on the search for gems, we failed to hear someone approaching from behind.

Had we glanced up we would have seen the circle of strangely dressed men watching us from the edge of the clearing. They went unnoticed as our fervor continued, unabated. When one of the men cleared his throat, our minds quickly returned to the present. Jumping like frightened rabbits, we turned to see who it was.

Chapter 28

We remained on our knees in the dirt, staring into the eyes of a huge, strangely dressed man. Buckskin lacing intertwined the holes in his garment, replacing buttons in his brown wool tunic. Pants of the same material extended to his ankles and bright feather anklets highlighted his dirty feet. The big fellow's straight black hair extended to his shoulders, framing his hooked nose and olive complexion. His eyes were anomalously blue. He spoke to us in a hard to understand dialect.

"What are you doing in our field?"

Despite the strangeness of his dialect, I managed to comprehend his question. The big fellow wasn't alone. Ten similarly dressed though smaller men encircled us. It revived recent memories of our confrontation with the loggers. At least they weren't armed.

"I asked you a question. What are you doing in our field?"

Mary Ann jumped to her feet, attempting to sprint past the men surrounding us. Grabbing her elbows, they pushed her back into the circle. The big fellow pointed to Mary Ann.

"It's forbidden to dig here," he said. "You'll destroy our crops."

Amber had the same look in her eyes as when she'd kicked ass at the biker bar. The men had no weapons. I put a hand on Amber's shoulder.

"They aren't armed," I said. "Let's ride this out and see where it takes us."

Amber nodded. "They had just better keep their hands to their selves."

"You?" I said, glancing at Mary Ann.

"I'm all in," she said. "Maybe they can tell us what happened to Bill."

"Okay, then. Let me handle this. Who are you?" I asked the big man.

"Bring them," he said, not answering my question.

The men closed around us, one of them prodding me with a thump between the shoulder blades.

"I'm Tho-mas," I said.

Ignoring me, one of our captors gave me another push to keep me moving in the right direction.

"What now?" Amber asked.

I could only shake my head and follow the big man who was already moving away through the forest at a rapid clip.

"Go with them."

The mules had heard the commotion and were braying nervously. Seeing the beasts for the first time, two of our captors dropped behind to fetch them. We continued along a trail, the trees larger than any I had ever seen, their lowest branches fifty feet from the ground.

"Where are you taking us?" I said.

The men continued to ignore us, except for gentle prodding to keep us moving in the right direction. Hazy fog cloaked the space between the ground and tree limbs. For the first time since earlier that morning, I smelled the prevalent odor of rotten eggs.

Rough-hewn ledges of rock between the trees and bubbling artesian water formed crystal pools along the path. Unlike pools in the glade, no wisps of steamy vapor marked these as hydrothermal.

For nearly an hour, we continued through the forest before reaching a small clearing. There the large man stopped, allowing us a moment of rest. Mary Ann and Amber scooted closer to me. Amber's face was red, probably from anger, while Mary Ann's olive complexion was white with concern. Our captors circled around us with frowns and folded arms. When our eyes adjusted to the brightness, I noticed a village in the distance. The village consisted of many houses, some large and some smaller, but all constructed of cut stone laid with mortar.

After a brief rest, the big fellow motioned toward the village. A bevy of children tagged along with our procession. Unlike the stoic band of men, they laughed and pulled at our clothes, acting as if we were part of a parade contrived for their entertainment. Some of the children wore pants and tunics, while others only breechcloths.

Truck gardens and abundant greenery surrounded the houses and multi-colored flowers hung from baskets in trees. The village could have passed for an early-American town. We soon reached a single large building, facing the clearing from where we had come, and separated from the others by an unpainted fence.

Through the distant haze, I could see the mountain front. The big fellow opened the front door and led us down a dark hallway to a windowless room in the back. Our captors herded us into a room, the door slamming behind us as they departed. Trying the door, I found it locked.

"What now, Troop?" Amber asked.

The room sounded hollow, her voice echoing off bare walls.

"See if there's another way out of here," I said, fumbling in the darkness.

Mary Ann said, "Who are these people?"

"Throwbacks from another century if you ask me," Amber said.

"Some of them look like Indians," I said. "Is there a tribe around here?"

"Grandpa's part Indian. Don't know what tribe, though."

"Hope they don't have tomahawks."

Amber's off-handed quip failed to diffuse our concern. When the door opened, Mary Ann grabbed my arm. It was the big fellow, stooping through the door. The oil-burning lantern he carried cast shadows on the wall and revealed the three of us huddled together. The big man wasn't alone.

The older of the two men was much smaller than the big fellow, the younger man probably about the same age as Mary Ann. Both had black hats in their hands, and each had shoes that looked like a cross between boots and moccasins. They both had pale blue eyes.

The older man had Eurasian facial features and a dark beard with a hint of gray covering much of his face. The younger man's hair was auburn, his complexion fair. When he spotted Mary Ann, he smiled warmly. When he did her neck flushed, her bright red blush visible even in the dim lantern light.

"Who are you and what are you doing here?" the older man asked in the same guttural language as the big fellow.

I responded with slow words and expressive gestures. "I'm Tom. My friends are Amber and Mary Ann."

The little man nodded, apparently having no trouble understanding. He didn't bother introducing himself. Instead, he grabbed the big fellow's elbow and hustled him back into a corner where they launched into a spirited, although whispered, conversation. His younger companion, still smiling, stepped forward and shook my hand.

"I am Wat," he said. "Where did you come from?"

"The mountains," I said.

"How did you find your way here?"

"We followed a trail on the north end of the valley," I said.

"Ah yes," he said. "Then you came through the Land of Steam."

"I'll say we did," Mary Ann said, stepping closer to the young man.

From the looks in both their eyes, I could see they were instantly smitten with each other.

"Why are you holding us here?" I asked. "I assure you, our intentions are peaceable."

"You were digging in the fields. Leon thinks you were raiding our crops."

"We lost our food on the mountain. Though I may be half-starved to death, I wasn't stealing your crops. We were digging there cause we found these."

She opened her palm, revealing a handful of shiny gems. They locked eyes again, and both smiled.

"I believe you," Wat said. "Father, these people weren't raiding our crops. I'm sure of it."

"That is not your conclusion to make. We caught them in the act."

"They were gathering these," Wat said, grabbing Mary Ann's wrist and holding it out for his father to see.

"There were no crops in the field for us to steal," I said.

Wat's father glanced at Leon and his tone was stern when he replied.

"You are not from the valley. We worry that strangers will come to do us harm, perhaps set a destructive fire."

"We aren't here to set fires or harm your crops," Amber said. "We're looking for Tom's brother, Bill. He disappeared, and we think he may be here, in the valley."

Amber's statement instantly got the men's attention. The smaller man grabbed the arms of Wat and Leon and hustled them back into the corner for another whispered debate.

When they returned, the older man asked, "Do you have proof of this?"

I reached for my wallet and showed them an old but recognizable snapshot of Bill.

"Bill is my brother. We came from far away to find him. This is our first time into your valley."

With grave expressions, the three men studied the picture of Bill.

"What is this?" he asked.

Amber glanced at me and then back to the older man.

"It's called a photo, taken with a device called a camera. Do you know what a camera is?" she asked.

Wat's father didn't answer. "May I borrow this?" he asked.

I removed it from my wallet and handed it to him. To the vocal protest of Wat, they ordered us to remain in the room. Shutting the door behind them, they left us in darkness. They returned within the hour.

"My name is Caleb," Wat's father said. "Leon and I are village elders. We have discussed the situation with Pastor Gray. Tonight you can prove your innocence before the people of the village."

"And how will we do that?" Amber said.

Caleb shifted his weight from one foot to the other and stared at the floor. "By submitting your story to the serpent. He and the Lord will decide if you are telling the truth."

We had no time to discuss or worry about Caleb's cryptic message. Shaking his head when I asked him to explain, he led us instead to another house. After Leon had left us, we went inside with Wat and Caleb, to a dining room.

"Wat says you are hungry," Caleb said. "Please seat yourselves. We will feed you as a gesture of trust."

Caleb motioned to the large wooden table, pushed Wat out the door, and left us alone. Amber and Mary Ann looked at each other, barely able to suppress nervous laughter.

Mary Ann said, "I can hardly understand a word he's saying."

"It's English," Amber confirmed."Just different from the way we usually hear it spoken. Without outside influences, there would be nothing to cause it to evolve."

"What do you mean?" Mary Ann asked.

"Imagine how it would be if you hadn't seen another group of people for many years," Amber said.

Mary Ann's eyes widened, and so did mine. "You think these people have never had contact with the outside world?" I said.

"They have no regional accent that I can identify," Amber said.

"What do you make of the talk of snakes? Do these people have something to do with Bill's disappearance?"

Amber drummed the table with her knuckle. "Though something bothers me about this whole thing, Wat seems friendly enough."

"What bothers you?" Mary Ann said.

"Snakes imply devil worship. We've seen it for years around Brannerville; secret ceremonies, sacrifices, and midnight cattle mutilations. Maybe these people are part of some blood-crazed satanic cult. If so, it's also very possible we may have found Bill's murderers."

Chapter 29

Although there was only one small window in the room, abundant light filtered through a skylight in the vaulted ceiling. Prisms of quartz, drawing radiant energy from outside the house, surrounded the strange skylight. A woven rug covered the rough-hewn wooden floor. The chairs and table looked hand-carved.

Before we could discuss Amber's assessment of our situation, a girl peeked through the door and interrupted our conversation. She stared at us a moment before stifling a giggle and slamming the door behind her. We listened to her footsteps as she ran away down the hall.

Caleb soon returned with a woman and the giggling girl. Both females shielded themselves behind the little man. At least until he'd introduced them as his wife, Elizabeth, and daughter, Virginia. Virginia came forward and curtsied. Elizabeth hurried away, quickly returning with bread and a large pot from which she served us each a bowl of very tasty soup.

After encouraging us to help ourselves, Caleb told us they'd already eaten. The homemade bread and vegetable soup were delicious. Caleb watched from the doorway, nodding and urging us to enjoy the meal. Having already missed breakfast, we needed little motivation to devour the soup, bread, and cool water from pottery mugs.

Elizabeth and Virginia also watched us eat. Their long dresses consisted of the same woven fabric as Caleb's clothes. Lacy caps as I imagined our English ancestors might have worn, crowned their heads. Like Leon, feather bands decorated their wrists and ankles. Before we had finished eating, Wat joined his family at the door.

Caleb, Virginia and her mother were short, though Wat was at least six feet tall. Elizabeth had olive skin, characteristic of many of the others. Virginia and Wat's were milky white. Instead of Virginia's auburn hair, Wat's was scarlet red. Freckles complemented Virginia's hair, her Irish complexion, and her pale blue eyes. There was no communication problem between Wat and Mary Ann. They chattered like magpies, ignoring everyone else. When we finished the last of the soup, Elizabeth and Virginia cleared the table.

"Now we must prepare for tonight's meeting. Wat will take you upstairs," Caleb said. "The two misses will accompany Virginia."

Caleb reacted to my hesitation with a broad grin. "They will be safe. Virginia will take good care of them. After resting, we will attend the meeting together."

Along with the warm food in my belly and the friendly way Caleb and his family had treated us, I largely discounted Amber's cult theory. Neither she nor Mary Ann seemed particularly worried, laughing like old friends as they followed Virginia out the door.

Wat and I climbed a narrow stairway near the back of the large house to a bathroom on the third floor. Virginia's big yellow cat followed us up the stairs, chasing after a make-believe mouse when we reached the hall.

A quick glance around the bathroom revealed Caleb's people were not as primitive as I'd thought. A marble tub and basin occupied part of a wall, along with a toilet. Metal pipes connected the fixtures and supplied running water to the room. One of the pipes was hot to the touch. After our visit to Johnson's farm, finding a large house in the valley with indoor plumbing truly amazed me. While I waited on the edge of the tub, Wat opened a cabinet that had beautifully wrought metal hinges. From it, he handed me a stack of fresh towels.

"You have hot water?" Wat nodded, and I said, "Where does it come from?"

"I will show you tomorrow. When you finish bathing, you may go to the room down the hall. The meeting does not begin for several hours, and you can rest until time to dress for supper. I will place some clothes on the chair for you to wear."

Wat backed out of the bathroom and shut the door behind him. I listened to the creak of wooden stairs as he descended. Just what the doctor ordered, I decided. A hot bath appealed to my aching muscles. Water entered the large tub through ornate metal valves. A cork-like fitting stopped the bottom drain. I turned on both taps and waited for the tub to fill. When it did, I stripped and pivoted into steaming water.

I didn't expect the heat affronting my bare rear-end. Shrieking like a scalded dog, I yanked myself out of the tub. Then I stood there, staring at the water as if it had suddenly become a fiery demon. Laughter at the door interrupted my shock. It was Wat, his hand on his mouth, trying to contain his mirth. Feeling suddenly foolish, I also grinned.

"That water's hot enough to scald the hide off an elephant," I said, rubbing my blistered rump.

Wat measured a small distance between his thumb and forefinger and said, "A little is all you need." After removing the stopper with a wire hanging on the wall, he said, "Now you must start over."

"How?"

Wat only shook his head, handing me a bar of soap before exiting the room and leaving me alone again. Once half the water had drained, I replaced the stopper and turned the tap. This time I was careful to obtain the desired temperature and was able to complete a delightful soak without further incident.

Wat had also provided a straight razor, mirror, and comb. After shaving and combing my hair, I wrapped a towel around my waist and sauntered down the hall to the only other room on the floor. A metal bed, polished wood dresser, and a single chair occupied most of the room. A pleasant breeze blew through the only window. It was open and covered with transparent cloth that apparently kept out flying insects.

I gazed out the window and took a deep breath of mineral-laden air. Late afternoon light reflected off distant mountains, and I marveled at the diverse combination of colors it created. Billowy clouds covering the valley weren't dark and ominous but more like a hazy mist rising lazily from the surface of an overheated hot tub.

Filtered sunlight imbued the mist with a distinct mixture of purple and pink, and I realized that reflections through the clouds were causing the interesting variations in lighting and coloration so prevalent in the valley. The panorama it created resembled a Kodachrome print a color-mad developer had processed.

I stood looking, awed by the beauty of this primitive place that seemed as if it were almost on another planet and unrestricted by Earth's physical laws. Again, I breathed deeply, savoring mineral-laden air, before examining the room. A pottery vase filled with red flowers occupied one end table. I dipped a finger into the water, tasting it. Like the air, it had a pleasant, decidedly mineral flavor. My warm bath and the pungent breeze through the open window relaxed me, and I reclined on the bed. Soon I fell into a sound sleep on the soft feather mattress, not stirring until the ringing of a bell aroused me from my stupor. When I opened my eyes, I found the room dark and the mountain front no longer visible through the window. Silky curtains flapped in a cool evening breeze when Wat appeared at the door.

"It's time for supper. Then we will attend the meeting," he said.

"How many people live in your village?"

"Not many," he said.

"Wat, you don't believe we were vandalizing the crops, do you?"

"No, but it's not for me to decide."

"Tell me about this meeting we are to attend. What will happen to prove or disprove we are telling the truth?"

Wat glanced away from my thoughtful stare and said, "I cannot tell you. If you are truthful, then everyone will know."

"Did you ever meet my brother Bill?"

"You will learn everything in due time. For now, that is all I can tell you."

Wat lighted a lamp on the dresser and left me alone in the room. I dressed in the strange garments draped over the chair and instantly felt like a guest at a masquerade ball. The clean buckskin garb fitted well though I refrained from wearing the feathered anklets. Despite thoughts to the contrary, I began to worry about the impending meeting and Caleb's veiled reference to the serpent. Trying to suppress my nagging doubts, I hurried downstairs.

When I reached the meandering hallway, I became disoriented. After unsuccessfully trying two doors, I finally reached the dining room. There I found everyone, including Amber and Mary Ann, waiting for me at the table. Plates of food were already in place, and their savory aroma whetted my appetite.

"Sorry I'm late," I said, grabbing the chair I'd occupied at lunch.

Like Virginia and her mother, Amber and Mary Ann also wore dresses. Like my own Natty Bumpo costume, they resembled clothes from a different century. It was the first time I'd seen either of them in a dress. When I winked at Amber, she made a face, refraining from shooting me the bird.

After Caleb's prayer, Elizabeth began passing food to the right. It became quickly apparent from the varied and succulent dishes on the table that Caleb's village had never wanted for sustenance.

Satisfied with the fresh vegetables straight from Elizabeth's garden, Amber bypassed the carved turkey. Mary Ann dawdled with her spinach, making mooneyes at Wat throughout the meal.

"Caleb," I said. "What's the name of your village?"

"Carbonica," he said.

"Have you lived here long?"

Instead of answering my questions, he held up his hand and shook his head.

"Please. I can tell you no more. You must first pass the test at the meeting. Then we will answer your questions."

Virginia fidgeted in her chair and picked at the carrots on her plate as if dying to ask us a thousand questions. Her father's stern demeanor and Elizabeth's determined silence discouraged her from doing so. Like everyone else, she remained silent during the remainder of the meal.

After clearing the dinner dishes, we gathered in the front parlor. Caleb bowed his head and led us in another prayer before exchanging a silent signal with Elizabeth and starting for the front door. I followed him after a quizzical glance at Amber and Mary Ann. When we reached the porch, Wat replaced his father in the lead. Mary Ann dropped back and edged closer to me. Without stopping, she cupped her hand and motioned me to tilt my head toward her so she could whisper something in my ear.

"I talked with Wat," she said. "Whatever happens in the meeting, try not to panic."

Chapter 30

People from the village began joining us as we followed the path to the meeting hall. No one seemed to pay us the slightest attention. From the numbers joining our procession, I realized I'd vastly underestimated the valley's human population.

Based on the beds of brightly colored flowers surrounding the path, the valley seemed inhabited by a group of professional gardeners.

Pink and purple light filtering through the clouds painted the horizon and capped the village like the vivid background of an O'Keefe painting. The spectacle of color mesmerized me, and I could tell Amber and Mary Ann were also impressed. Dazzled by the light show, we continued along the brick path until we reached the front of a large building that looked like an antique church. Caleb left us, strolling away to the rear of the building.

Fully two stories tall, with a large limestone porch jutting from the massive wooden doors, this building was easily the largest building in Carbonica. Four fluted columns, devoid of ornamentation, supported a simple molded cornice. Like the porch, gray limestone comprised the building's primary construction material.

We followed Wat, Elizabeth, and Virginia through the large doors into the interior of the church. Stairs on either side of the room led to a second level. Another stairway snaked into a dark basement. Finely polished wood railed the stairways and paneled the walls.

Some of the crowd went directly upstairs. Wat led us down the long aisle to the front of the church. We followed Virginia and Elizabeth as they filed into a front-row pew. A small metal plaque on the pew bore a single engraved word: Dare.

Having removed my hat upon entering the church, I glanced around hat in lap. The large room was now nearly full, and I estimated the main floor and balcony capable of seating five hundred people. A wooden gate separated us from the front of the church. Behind the gate, the floor elevated into several sub-levels raised ten feet or more above the pews. On the highest level, a massive wooden pulpit dominated the otherwise spartan setting.

Two large chairs flanked the pulpit on a sub-level of the stage. A larger, more ornate chair, sat beside it. The low hum of persistent conversation ceased when four men dressed in dark robes filed in from behind the stage and took seats in the chairs. A theatrical pause transpired before a fifth person entered and occupied the pulpit chair. That person was Caleb, dressed like the others in a flowing black robe.

The room remained silent as we waited for someone apparently aware of how to elicit a dramatic effect on an audience. The sudden and unexpected sound of someone bursting through the curtains startled me, along with the rest of the congregation. A tall man swept into the room, his shoulder-length white hair flowing over his shoulders as if it had a life of its own.

The congregation remained silent. I stared at the man's pale skin and striking blue eyes that seemed to burn with an inner fire. The wooden platform creaked beneath his weight, and I thought it might collapse when he crossed it. Once behind the pulpit, he stood in silence for more than a minute, his gaze touching everyone in the room.

The pastor singled me from the crowd with his sullen stare. His spreading robe accentuating his great stature, the man played with the congregation like an actor acutely aware of the subtlety of high drama. With arms fully outstretched above his head, he locked his gaze on the people in the balcony to his right.

Seconds passed before he turned away, arms still fully outstretched, and stared at those in the balcony to his left. The mesmerized congregation sat like mice in a viper's gaze. Like everyone else, the white-haired man dressed in black had riveted my attention. Soon his eyes lost focus, and he gazed at the rafters. His booming voice filled the hall with the rumble of a single word.

"Peace."

"Peace," the congregation chanted.

Seconds later the echoes of the man's deep voice had barely ceased reverberating from antique walls. Though he lowered his arms, everyone's eyes remained transfixed on him, their attention concentrated on his every movement. With his dramatic entrance complete, he launched into a rousing hell-fire and brimstone sermon. No sound disturbed his words as he danced about the stage using his entire being to communicate with the congregation. His booming voice vibrated from the walls and ceiling like a pure note from a jazz man's horn. My eyes followed him as he darted across the stage, admonishing the congregation with a frenzy of motion and paroxysm of religious fervor.

As the mesmerizing performance continued, a large rectangular box in front of the pulpit began to draw my attention. It sat alone on a small table, cloaked in a mysterious swath of black cloth. The preacher continued to work the audience, repeatedly returning to a spot behind the box, touching it, stealing an occasional glance at it as he planted a subliminal message in everyone's mind. Finally, he stopped behind the box and spread his hands directly over it.

I was ten feet from the preacher with flowing white hair and clearly saw him raise the box's hinged lid. With more than a touch of drama, he inserted his right hand into it.

"Someone amongst ye has sinned," he closed his eyes, raising his clenched hand high above his head. "The stench of sin is strong. Come forward and handle the serpent."

I suddenly sat bolt upright in the pew, the hairs on my neck straightening as a cold chill swept down my spine. A huge rattlesnake, fully seven feet in length, draped from his outstretched hand. A mournful sob came from the back of the church. I hoped he hadn't heard it.

The sorrowful cries became persistently louder until everyone turned to see the face of the person causing the disturbance. It was a girl, not much older than Virginia and certainly not Mary Ann. Her mother didn't attempt to console her, and the thundering voice of the preacher interrupted my thoughts.

"Come here, daughter."

I stole a glance at the girl. She sobbed even louder as her mother pushed her gently away from her, then crossed her arms and looked away. The girl moaned, her eyes begging someone to intercede. No one did and the girl's sobs dissolved into a woeful wail.

"It's time to confess your sin to the congregation and ask for divine forgiveness."

Tears had swollen the girl's face puffy and red. Instead of pity, her mother appeared embarrassed and stared at the floor. She pushed her into the aisle.

"No!" wailed the girl, struggling to retain her seat.

An older man beside her grabbed her shoulders and whispered something in her ear. Her bottom lip quivered as she stared through teary eyes one last time at her mother. The older woman shook her head, riveted her gaze on the floor, and pushed the girl's hand away when she reached it out to her.

"It's time," said the preacher. "Come forward now."

The girl shook as she made her way to the aisle. She covered her face with her hands and approached the altar. After opening the gate separating the stage from the rest of the church, she ascended the stairs, still sobbing uncontrollably.

"Stand before me," commanded the preacher. She did, looking up tearfully into his angry eyes. "Turn and face the congregation."

The girl turned her back to the preacher who looked even taller when back-dropped against her. She cringed, as did half the congregation when he draped the writhing reptile across her shoulders. For a moment, I thought she would faint.

"Now, you must confess your sin before the congregation, God and the Serpent of Justice," he said.

I felt paralyzed and apparently so did the girl. The rattlesnake slowly coiled the back portion of its body around her right arm. Its head darted over her left shoulder to her chest. Its lidless eyes were six inches from her face, and her sobbing ceased, replaced by cold sweat dripping down her forehead.

"Confess now, and I will take away the serpent." When she tried to speak, her voice cracked with fear. "Talk to us. It is all right," the preacher said.

"I let James touch me. Please forgive me, Father," she said in a near stuttering whine.

"From whom are you asking forgiveness?" asked the preacher.

"The good Lord, my family, and the people of the colony," she said in a stammer.

"And will you engage in this sin again?"

"No, I promise it will never again happen."

"Quiet," he said. "Now we shall see if the serpent believes you."

The girl stood frozen as the reptile stared directly into her eyes. Its tongue darted as if tasting the odor of fear in droplets of sweat dripping down her cheek. The snake's head brushed the girl's face before loosening its grip on her arm and slowly encircled itself around her neck. It remained there for only a moment before uncoiling and dropping with a dull thud to the floor.

"Go my child and sin no more."

The girl slumped forward as if a supporting rod had dropped from her back. Tears gushed from her eyes. Clasping her hand over her mouth, she ran down the aisle and out the door of the church.

The preacher picked up the snake and raised it above his head. Total silence engulfed the congregation. This time he stared directly at me.

"Strangers have come to our colony from outside. As the Lord teaches, we have broken bread and offered them shelter. Now we must know if their hearts are pure and free of sin and treachery. Who amongst you will bare his soul to the Serpent of Justice?"

My own mouth dropped open. Sweat trickled off the tip of my nose. I was powerless to move. I stare straight ahead, sensing every eye in the church suddenly focused on me. Wat grabbed my arm and whispered into my ear.

"One of you must take the test of the Serpent," he shook me gently as he spoke. "Pastor Gray expects it to be you since you're the man and the elder."

I couldn't stop my hands from shaking. My thoughts returned abruptly to the dark hole in Vietnam with Honeyboy's dead eyes and broken body engulfed in a writhing pile of poisonous snakes. I locked my hands on the front of the pew and swallowed hard to keep from vomiting. Thousands of imaginary needles prickled my skin. I felt like a person about to have all his teeth extracted without the benefit of Novocain.

Amber seemed even more frightened. I took another deep breath and tried to stand. My legs responded like warm rubber beneath my weight. I fought to keep from fainting and started for the aisle like a doomed murderer preparing to walk the last steps to the gallows.

My heart raced at the thought of touching the slithering reptile. Maggots of anxiety crawled beneath my skin. Blood rushing from my face left my lips cold, my hands clammy. I was already dead and felt like a silent corpse, blasted in its grave by an ice-cold winter chill. Before I could take a step, someone put a hand on my shoulder. It was Mary Ann.

She pressed past me to the aisle, proceeding straight to the altar where the preacher waited with the reptile undulating in his grasp. She threw open the gate and strolled up the steps toward the man in the robe. I could only stand there like an idiot, incapable of any action except to watch. Wat grabbed my arm and eased me back into the pew.

I could neither move nor scream. As in my nightmares, only a feeble gurgle emerged from deep in my throat. Mary Ann stopped in front of the blue-eyed man whose features seemed sharp as the reptile's fangs. Without hesitation, she took the rattlesnake from his hands and faced the congregation. With the reptile held high above her head, she moved it in a slow arc.

In a strong, unwavering voice she said, "The Lord protects his flock, and the Serpent guards us against lies and deceit."

"Amen," chanted the congregation in unison.

Mary Ann handed the snake to the preacher and returned to her seat.

The service lasted another hour. The time didn't matter because I remained in a frightened haze until the preacher returned the snake to the box. Finally, it was over. When we filed from the church, Mary Ann grabbed my elbow. I could only respond with a thin smile.

"Thanks," I said. "That's two I owe you."

Mary Ann only grinned and said, "I'm not afraid of snakes. Wasn't nothing to it."

She put her shoulder under my arm and supported me as we returned to Caleb's house. Caleb met us at the front door with a big smile and outstretched arms.

"You have passed the test of the Serpent," he said. "You will stay with us for as long as you wish and tomorrow we will show you the valley."

Amber blew me a kiss as Virginia led her and Mary Ann to their rooms. Wat helped me up the stairs where I sprawled on the bed feeling humiliated, worthless and stripped of every ounce of honor and dignity. For one brief moment, I seriously considered throwing myself out the window.

Chapter 31

Somewhere between self-loathing and mental flagellation, I fell asleep on the bed still dressed in the period costume. Depending on one's conception, it was either early morning or late night when a noise outside the room revived me to semi-consciousness. I stared out the window at the dim figure of someone tearing at the cheesecloth, trying to get in. It took me a moment to realize I wasn't dreaming and that someone really was outside on the sill.

"Tom, are you awake? I'm stuck in this damn cloth."

It was Amber. Jumping out of bed, I yanked the bottom of the cloth and pulled her into the room. When she was safely on the floor, I released my hold around her waist then stuck my head out the window to see where she had come from.

"How in the world did you manage that?"

Amber grinned impishly and said, "There's a small ledge outside the window. My room's on the other side of the house. I followed it around."

"The ledge can't be more than a foot wide," I said.

"I wanted to see you."

"You're nuts," I said, leading her by the hand to the edge of the bed.

I pulled Amber into my lap, and she wrapped her arms around my neck and squeezed.

"I was lonely sleeping by myself."

"I missed you, too. After what happened, I decided to find a rock to crawl under," I said.

"I talked with Mary Ann. She's not afraid of snakes. Wat told her what to say to the congregation."

"I wondered about that. Still, it was my job to face the music. I feel terrible about having put Mary Ann through it."

"You were on your way. She just pushed ahead of you and took your place."

"I'm not sure I'd have made it if she hadn't."

"You did better than me. I couldn't move."

With Amber still in my arms, I reclined until the soft pillow cradled my head. She pressed against my chest as I stared at the ceiling.

"Sorry I'm such a coward," I said.

"You're no coward. You wouldn't be here if you were."

"I don't feel like much of a man right now."

"Everyone has something they fear above all else. You'd have never let us down in a bind."

"We were in a bind."

"If you'd had to handle the snake, I'm sure you would have done it."

"I'm not so sure about that," I said. "Maybe, just maybe, I could have. Anyway, thanks for believing in me."

"You think these people killed Bill?" Amber asked, changing the subject.

Her body was soft and warm against my chest. I could feel her heart beating to the slow cadence of a trained runner.

"I doubt that Wat and Caleb are capable of murdering anyone. I don't know about the preacher. That was a pretty wild ceremony."

"You bet it was. I've still got the creeps," Amber said. "He's the strangest man I've ever seen."

"Same here."

"His name is Pastor Gray. Wat told Mary Ann when he was showing her around."

I drew Amber even closer, kissed her and stroked the back of her neck with my fingers.

"Wat is showing us more of the valley tomorrow. We'll possibly scratch up some answers such as where these people came from?"

"Maybe we'll even find out what happened to Bill," I said.

"And why no one in Brannerville or anywhere else seems to know about this village," Amber said.

She closed her eyes. Soon her muscles relaxed, and her breathing became a gentle timpani. Fatigued by worry, she fell asleep against my chest without saying a word. Rain began falling outside the window, the wind whipping the cheesecloth covering. It didn't matter. Amber was out for the count. I rolled her off my chest and covered her with a quilt.

As I stared at the ceiling, listening to the quiet sound of Amber's breathing and the pounding of rain against the roof, I wondered how I would return her to her room before the others awoke. I needn't have worried. Like a strong sedative, the rain and day's events lulled Amber and me into a deep sleep. When I awoke the next morning, the sun was out. Amber was gone. I was alone.

Once out of bed I gazed out the window at the bright reflections rising in the eastern sky. When I wiped my hand across the sill, I found it damp with morning dew. My shirt was also damp. For the first time since arriving in the valley, I realized how excessive the humidity really was. As I gazed across the clearing, I marveled again at the strange lighting produced by morning sun piercing dense cloud cover. This was surely the primary reason why the valley and the people occupying it had remained hidden from the outside world. Discovery would be difficult, even by satellite, and that is assuming someone was looking for it in the first place.

Contemplating the valley's isolation, I went down the hall to the bathroom. There I found my own clothes, clean and hanging on a peg. This time when I filled the tub, I took extra precautions with the temperature before soaking. When I finished, I felt better than I had since before the snake ceremony. I even caught myself whistling as I strolled downstairs to the kitchen. As before, everyone was at the table and awaiting me.

Elizabeth's thick porridge covered with milk was simple and delicious. After breakfast, Caleb brushed his hands together and got up from the table. Stopping at the door, he scratched the side of his nose and winked at me.

"I am glad you passed the test last night," he said.

"Thanks to Mary Ann."

He gave my shoulder a fatherly pat and said, "She is a brave girl, though I think you would have done as well."

"Thanks. I'm glad we didn't have to find out." Caleb chuckled and leaned against the wall. "Can you tell me now about my brother Bill?"

"You look very much like him," he said. "He stayed with us a week and listened to our conversations with a strange device. He returned to the mountains, and we never saw him again. I am very sorry that he is missing. That is all we know."

Amber asked, "Will you show us the valley?"

"Wat will guide you and answer your questions. I have business elsewhere or I would go with you."

Within the hour Amber, Mary Ann and I tagged along behind Wat as he led us on an exploratory trip through the valley. I lagged behind Wat and Amber to have a word with Mary Ann.

"You're the bravest person I know," I said.

Mary Ann blushed and entwined my arm as we continued through the forest. The morning was a hive of activity. Carbonicans were everywhere, tending their gardens, walking along manicured pathways, and generally portraying a semblance of activity. We went the opposite direction from where we had entered the valley and soon arrived at a large building that blended with the rocks and trees surrounding it. We found twenty people busily at work inside.

On the far side of the building, a forge blasted as workers removed a cauldron of molten metal. Others worked at benches creating objects from the foundry's product. A smiling little man with a baldhead soon joined us. He looked enough like Caleb to have passed as his brother.

This is John," Wat said. "He is our head smithy."

John pumped our hands and led us on a tour of the foundry, answering all our questions in a clipped version of the valley dialect.

"We convert ore from the mines into metal. Our artisans craft metal into objects for use in the colony."

I stood beside a table where a man formed what looked like a door hinge. The artisan acknowledged our curious stares and handed the hinge to me. I hefted it, feeling its weight. Like steel, the metal was smooth though dark black in color. Amber, unaware of the many abandoned mines in the hills, appeared puzzled.

"Where do you find ore to smelt the metal?"

John shook his head and rubbed his carbon-coated hands on his leather apron.

"The Lord has provided everything we need right here in the valley, including many different types of ore and abundant coal for stoking the furnaces."

"Fascinating," Amber said.

We exited through a door in the back and immediately entered the front of another large building. This building housed a different communal project: a pottery plant. The chief potter escorted us on another quick and interesting tour. The pottery factory employed many people, some working at a large kiln while others created objects for everyday use or works of art.

After leaving the second building, we continued along the path until we reached a mill by the bank of a roaring river. The operation of the mill was similar to the other two plants we'd seen. Twenty or so workers labored to turn out various milled grains. The wonderful aroma from the nearby bakery returned my thoughts to the loaves of Elizabeth's delicious bread.

We visited many similar mini-factories, all manufacturing items of need for the people of the valley. All were located along the mountain front and hidden among the trees and rocks. We continued on the path until we reached a bridge across the river. I stopped for a moment, puzzled by everything. Here within a giant valley far from civilization, camouflaged by giant trees and shrouded by thick cloud cover, we'd found a colony of self-sufficient people apparently lost from mainstream society for decades, maybe centuries. Scratching my head in disbelief, I hurried to catch the others.

After a brisk fifteen-minute stroll, we rounded a bend in the trail and approached yet another large building, this one also partially hidden by trees. The giant room was the valley's version of a modern greenhouse where a veritable jungle of plants grew in profusion. Wat led us down rows of plants, both fruit, and vegetable, pointing with pride to a tomato vine with a ripe tomato the size of a grapefruit. Cantilevered partitions encompassed portions of the roof and upper walls. Despite the greenhouse's extreme humidity, a gentle draft of air made the room infinitely bearable. Wat explained.

"The partitions open and close allowing optimum lighting and air flow. Because of this design, we are able to grow fruits and vegetables year-round."

It was then that I realized we hadn't seen a single fireplace or even a chimney since arriving in the valley. We'd yet to feel even the slightest of chill, despite the advancing season.

Chapter 32

Many things about the valley I found hard to believe. One was the moderate temperature this late in the fall. The other was the anomaly presented by the lack of radiators or heating vents in the greenhouse.

"How do you keep the plants from freezing? Doesn't it ever get cold here in the winter?" I finally asked.

"The valley is protected by the mountains, and there are ways to prevent damage from the cold."

"Such as?"

"You will soon see for yourself, I promise."

Purple morning glories, pink hydrangeas, and yellow roses covered the tabletops like a flowering carpet. Carbonican horticulturists were everywhere, working with grasses, vines, grains, and even weeds.

"Our scientists have developed many ways to increase the yields of our crops," Wat said. "We are able to produce just the right amount of many varied vegetable products. There is little or no waste."

After exiting the building, high on oxygen and flowery perfume, we rejoined the winding path paralleling the river. Wat, Mary Ann, and Amber raced forward, hurrying toward some unknown destination. I hobbled after them, the memory of Ol' Flame's bony spine still firmly impressed in my sore butt.

"Wat," I said. "How much does a bushel of grain cost in the valley?"

Wat and Mary Ann were walking with their arms linked, enjoying the stroll through the hazy valley. My question seemed to perplex the young man. He waited for me to catch up.

"I do not know what you mean," he said.

"What do you use for money?"

My question seemed to perplex him.

"We work for the common good of the colony. No one goes without. The elders see to that."

Amber was climbing on a nearby boulder. Becoming interested after she'd caught a snippet of our conversation, she slid down the gentle rock face on her fanny and joined us.

"You mean the valley is governed like one of those social communes in the Great Depression."

When Wat raised a palm, Mary Ann giggled and punched him with her elbow.

"I have never heard of the Great Depression," he said. "Everyone works at what they are best suited. The joint effort of all provides for our needs."

"Is your father the headman?"

"Father is the governor of our colony. He and the Board of Elders guide us."

"And what happens when somebody breaks the law?" Amber asked.

"Do you mean sinning?"

"Not exactly. Like when two people fight or someone steals something from another person."

"There is no need to steal. Everyone has whatever they need for the asking."

He walked ahead, pulling Mary Ann along by the hand.

"Wait, Wat," Amber said, sprinting to catch them. "Is Pastor Gray part of the governing body? He seems very powerful."

"He guides our spiritual needs and directs us when we sin."

Wat seemed to attribute no particular prominence to Pastor Gray, though the man with flowing white hair seemed so much more to me and I couldn't get him out of my mind.

We crossed the river, leaving the persistent forest and entering an area characterized by sporadic clearings interspersed between the rocky terrain and sprawling tree line. Thick clouds seemed even closer to earth, and flocks of sheep and goats grazed in the clearings. Shepherds with crooked staffs looked after the herds and seemed to recognize Wat when we passed.

Wat was quick with a quip and a smile and could have been a presidential contender or perhaps a future governor of the colony. Evidence of the colonists' handiwork appeared everywhere. Fruit trees, arbors of grapes and beehives abounded. Thick clouds shrouded the valley, though everything beneath them shouted the presence of skilled, civilized people.

The river originated in the mountains. When we reached the first low-lying foothills, an ethereal mist wafted overhead, quickly engulfing us. The mist finally thickened to the consistency of hazy soup, reducing visibility to only a few feet.

With fog dimming our vision, we drew closer together. Amber grabbed my shirt and held on. Gone was the thick carpet of pine needles and the terrain became ever steeper as we approached the mountains. We soon found ourselves in the midst of many circular pools of steaming water. One of the pools spewed steam and water high into the air. We stopped along the path to watch it erupt.

"It's beautiful," Amber said.

Shrubs and stunted trees comprised what little flora remained. Moss and lichens coexisted on weathered boulders and multi-colored orchids dangled from vines. Mineral-rich water, unusual vegetation, and twisting violet-colored mists created the distinct image in my mind that we had suddenly entered Alice's Never-Never Land. Several large metallic pipes emerged from the pools and trailed away into the distance, back toward the village. I rubbed my rear end, remembering the hot bath water.

"I should have realized," I said. "You heat your houses with steam generated from hot water."

"And our factories and greenhouses," Wat said.

"That explains why there are no chimneys on the houses," Amber said.

Amber's simple observation had escaped me completely until I saw the greenhouse. It was so obvious that I felt like a dummy. Wat knew a shortcut through the Land of Steam, and we soon left the mist, finding ourselves in the rolling foothills south of the mountain front.

Down the hill were several houses similar to those in the main village. Just as I brushed away the last swirl of mist, a slender boy with red hair and freckled face spotted us. Before we knew it, many children were running to greet us, calling Wat by name. Wat affectionately rubbed his hand through the boy's red hair. The procession led us to a large stone house, and we entered without knocking.

We were tired and hungry after hiking all morning. Wat's uncle and aunt owned the house, and they had anticipated our arrival. Wat's Aunt Sara, waiting for us in the parlor, hugged him before leading us to the kitchen. She had prepared a hearty lunch of bread and goat's cheese.

After lunch, we rested on the front porch, drinking icy water from an artesian spring that gushed from a hole in a nearby wall of solid rock. I couldn't recall another glass of water that had ever tasted better.

"How long have your people been in this valley?"

"Forever," Wat said simply.

"I understand why," Mary Ann said. "It just has to be the most beautiful place on earth."

Mary Ann and Wat exchanged a warm, undisguised glance.

"Where are we now?" Amber asked.

"There are several mines near here. My Uncle Jeb directs ore extraction."

Wat had to wrestle his hand from Mary Ann's grasp to point up the slope in the direction of the mine. My next question was as blunt as a club. Amber must have thought my inquiry too abrupt because she turned away so she wouldn't have to make eye contact with Wat when he answered.

"Wat, do you know what a gun is?"

My question puzzled the lad, so I held up my arms to mimic a hunter aiming a rifle.

"Though game is abundant in the valley, we mostly eat vegetables. Our hunters are skilled with bow and arrow, and that is what they use."

As the reason for my question struck home, Mary Ann frowned at me and folded her arms.

"You'd never kill anyone, would you Wat?" she said.

"That is one of the Ten Commandments. There has never been a murder in the valley."

It seemed obvious to me and certainly to Amber and Mary Ann that the act of murder was almost inconceivable to Wat. I was sorry I'd broached the subject and sure that no one we'd met, with the possible exception of Pastor Gray, could kill anyone.

Wat was soon ready to go. After shouting farewells to his aunt and waving to the multitude of children that followed us all the way back to the path in the foothills, he began a brutal pace that only Mary Ann's youth and Amber's conditioning could match. I labored a hundred yards behind, my calves and thighs already sore from the hike. From the hillside village, he led us to the mountains to examine one of the mines his uncle operated. It hummed with activity from a dozen workers extracting unbelievable quantities of ore.

Valley miners had accomplished what modern miners had failed to do: develop a successful method of following sinuous veins that laced through the mountain. The visit to the mine provided a brief respite to my sore muscles.

"It is late," Wat said. "We must hurry."

"Hey, I thought that's what we were doing," I called after them as they started up the hill.

Wat followed the steep wall and soon began climbing a narrow path carved in solid rock. Our ascent took us a hundred feet above the valley floor. As we continued along the hazy trail, we soon encountered the first low-lying clouds. With our vision dimmed by the fog, we reached an abrupt bend in the mountain-front.

Around the bend, an unexpected sight confronted us: a spectacular waterfall plummeting five hundred feet down the side of a vertical rock wall. At the base of the trail, tons of falling water crashed into a clear pool. A rainbow bracketed both sides of the fall.

A circuitous river, the same one we'd crossed earlier Wat informed us, snaked away from the pool. I guessed it was part of the same system forming the grotto where Mary Ann and I had found Bill's journal. This waterfall was much larger, its crashing water exploding into a fine mist that dampened our clothes, even as high as our lofty vantage.

"This is truly spectacular," Amber said.

"Beautiful," I said. "How are you going to top this?"

Wat and Mary Ann were still holding hands. "Follow me, and I will show you," he said.

The trail led under the waterfall and communication ceased when we ventured beneath the thundering turbulence. Wat and Mary Ann disappeared in a misty shroud. Amber, trying to avoid getting drenched, sprinted along the path behind the crashing water. I bumped into her when I exited the opposite side.

As I recovered my balance, I realized she was gawking at something in front of us: the gaping mouth of a huge cavern that an eon of slow erosion had incised deeply into the very face of the mountain.

Chapter 33

Falling water and hands of time had sculpted a gigantic opening into the mountain, a cavern that incised a gap in the cliff the size of a football field. Mary Ann and Amber stared at the giant chasm. I just stood there with my mouth open while Wat grinned and kept walking into the black corridor. Behind a boulder near the entrance, he produced several awaiting torches.

Wat led us beyond the mouth of the cave. For the next hour, we traced a path through a maze of delicately shaped stalactites and stalagmites hanging from the roof and protruding from the floor. Frozen torrents of pink alabaster walled the giant cave's visually spectacular rooms and antechambers. Everything we saw appeared totally devoid of human debasement that I'd seen in the few caverns I'd visited.

Although totally lost in reflected darkness, I had the distinct impression we were descending rather than climbing. I found I was correct in this assumption and had to shade my eyes when we exited into the sunlight at the base of the waterfall.

When Wat kept going, I sat on a rock and yelled, "Uncle."

I apparently wasn't the only tired soul in the group.

"Water sure looks good," Mary Ann said, looking over the ledge at the pool below. "Got time for a swim?"

"We have time," Wat said.

Amber and I were not surprised when Mary Ann stripped and dove into the water from the ten-foot ledge. Her action almost sent Wat into terminal shock. His pale skin went suddenly whiter than the alabaster on the cavern walls. His neck and face flushed bright crimson.

I grabbed his arm, shook him, and said, "You okay?"

By now, Amber was barely able to restrain herself from bursting into laughter.

"I'm tired," she said. "Let's join Mary Ann."

Amber leaned against a boulder and began removing her boots. Wat gave us each a momentary nervous glance, and then hurriedly stripped off his own clothes. Without waiting to see if we were watching, he performed a perfect swan dive into the pool.

"You think we're doing the right thing?" I said. "I don't remember having much control when I was eighteen."

"You still have no control," she said, slipping off her blouse and tossing it into my face. "Anyway, who's going to chaperon us?"

Before I could answer her question, she followed Wat off the ledge, barely raising a ripple when she entered the water. I joined them, wondering what had happened in my life that I had gone skinny dipping more times in the last two weeks than I had all the rest of my years combined.

We found the water wonderfully clear, its temperature crisp. Fully twenty feet deep, the rock-bottomed pool encapsulated water the hue of burnished turquoise. After swimming ten quick laps to impress Mary Ann, Wat climbed a nearly invisible trail along the ledge's rocky face. When he disappeared, Mary Ann climbed the ledge and hurried after him. In a moment, she was also out of sight.

"Know what I think?"

"Tell me, Troop," Amber said, her wet body sending tactile messages to my brain when she pressed against me.

"Unless we want to answer to the good Pastor Gray and his scaly friend, I think we better go see what they're doing."

"How old do you think Wat is?" she said.

"Old enough."

"Maybe you're right," she said.

Amber vaulted out of the water, onto the ledge. I made my own exit much more slowly and then hurried after her up the narrow trail. Around a turn in the path, we found the two youngsters in a deep circular pool, the water so blue it almost looked unreal. It was a natural hot tub, with wispy fingers of steam wafting from its surface.

Amber slipped into the pool with barely an upward glance from Wat and Mary Ann and reclined slowly until the hot water reached her neck. Remembering my episode in the bathtub, I probed the surface cautiously with my toe before committing myself. Then I sank to my neck and issued a satisfied sigh.

On the ledge above us, two snowy egrets perched on the stunted limb of an elm, loosely rooted in rocky soil. The birds seemed like a watercolor mural painted on the pale blue sky. High above the egrets, swallows chased a swarm of insects raised from their hiding place by a sudden gust of wind. When distant thunder echoed against rock walls, we ignored the light mist of rain that dimpled the water and sent radiating circles across the surface of the pool.

When I finally climbed out of the hot water and followed Amber up the path to retrieve my clothes,

I found the steamy mineral water had worked wonders on my sore muscles. For the first time in a week I felt revived, and twenty years younger. As we trekked back to the village, it seemed as if I had somehow left all my problems behind in the hot mineral water. Maybe they had dissolved away. High above us, the egrets floated in the breeze amid pink and purple clouds.

When we finally reached the first stone house of Carbonica, it was late. Although physically tired, the soreness in my legs was gone. We found Caleb and Elizabeth sitting in rockers on their front porch. Sensing our fatigue, Elizabeth went immediately into the house and returned with a pitcher of cold water. Still shy Virginia hid behind her skirt.

"What do you think of our valley?" Caleb asked.

"It's much larger than I imagined," Amber said. "I feel as if we only saw a small part of it."

"It takes several days to circle the valley," Caleb said. "You'll have to stay longer to see the rest."

"We have to start back tomorrow," I said. "If we can impose on you for one more night, that is."

"Stay for eternity if you wish," Caleb said.

From the sincerity in his voice, he meant it. After a long drink of ice-cold mineral water, we retired to our rooms for a rest before dinner. Exhausted from the long hike, I barely responded when the bell on the wall began to ring. I went to the bathroom and splashed water on my face, trying to shake the cobwebs loose in my brain.

After dinner, we returned to the porch and watched a wonderful light show created by brilliant sunlight through translucent, chalcedony clouds. We continued to watch until darkness completely covered the valley. Nightbirds warbled in the distance, and a fruit bat chased insects in the dim lantern light. A misty breeze cooled the evening air.

"What do your people do when they get sick?" I asked.

Caleb puffed on his long-stemmed pipe, extending his short legs over the edge of the porch.

"There is rarely sickness here. The valley is a healthy place. We have little need for anything other than poultices and unguents we produce from roots and herbs."

"We didn't see the school," Amber said. "Where do you teach the children?"

Caleb cocked his head slightly and puffed on the pipe until a circle of smoke billowed from the bowl.

"Children learn everything they need to know from the elders, Pastor Gray and whomever they apprentice themselves to when they get older."

Amber had another question, and I wondered why I hadn't already thought of it myself.

"Caleb, you detained us when we first arrived because you thought we might have destroyed some of your crops. Wat told us today you have little or no crime here."

"An act of vandalism occurred in one of our fields high on the mountainside, not here in the valley. We thought the mountain people were responsible. When we found you digging in the field, we naturally suspected you."

"What did they do to the crops?" I asked.

"They tore down a field of corn and destroyed what was there. We were afraid they might start a fire out of maliciousness in the valley."

"Does that frighten you?"

Caleb puffed introspectively on the pipe. "It is the one thing in the world we fear the most."

"You know about the outside world," I said. "Does anyone ever leave the valley?"

"No reason to leave. We have everything we need right here."

Virginia sat cross-legged on the porch beside me. The solitary game she played looked similar to ball and jacks, except that brightly colored stones replaced the usual metal jacks. I did a mental double take when I realized one of the stones looked very familiar.

"Can I see?" I said, pointing to the stone.

She handed it to me, and I rolled it against my palm. Its sticky translucence left no doubt in my mind. It was a rough diamond similar to the one Bill had sent me.

"Do you know what this is?" I said, showing the stone to Caleb.

"Crystal," Caleb said.

I returned it to Virginia, and she said, "We find them in the clearing."

Amber listened to our conversation and grinned dumbly at the little girl's statement. Then I remembered Dr. Quinn's words.

"You'll find diamonds where you find the blue earth."

The plowed field with the strange blue hue was an extinct, volcanic plug. Hundreds, maybe thousands, of perfect ice-blue diamonds remained for the taking within ten feet of the surface of the ground. These people were sitting on a fortune in diamonds, greater perhaps than the vast deposits of South Africa. The irony was that they didn't care.

That night I sat, wide awake, on the edge of my bed. Moonlight reflecting through clouds produced an eerie glow that penetrated my gauze-covered window like dancing wraiths. When Amber appeared on the ledge, I shook myself awake and grabbed her hand to help her into the room.

"You're going to break your pretty neck one of these nights."

"But you're glad I'm here, aren't you?"

"I was just thinking about closing my eyes and stepping out the window myself."

"Thought so," she said, sitting in my lap on the edge of the bed. "I've been considering these people. I've reached a conclusion."

"Don't keep me in suspense. My mind's beginning to wander," I said, stroking Amber's cheek.

"I've decided I'm totally and completely confused."

"We're no closer than we were a week ago to finding out what happened to Bill," I said.

"Unless one of Pastor Gray's snakes got him," Amber said.

"These people aren't capable of murder," I said, ignoring her levity. "I'm sure of it. It's like we've found Shangri-La, right here in Arkansas."

"They have a near-perfect communal society and don't even know what money is," Amber said.

"And almost no illness nor crime. Where do these people come from?"

"Don't know. It's not hard to see why they've gone undetected. This place is so remote it could just as well be in the heart of Africa. What trees don't cover, clouds do."

"And all the houses, buildings and even the people's clothing seem to blend with the surroundings," I said. "I don't know if it was their intent to do so. The result is near perfect camouflage. It's like they're part of the forest itself."

"You're right," she said."

"One more thing I noticed."

"What?"

"It puzzled Caleb when you asked about their schools. He didn't know what you meant. I imagine it's because they simply rely on elders providing knowledge on a need-to-know basis."

Amber considered my observation. "Now that you mention it I haven't seen a single book since we've been here."

"Except. . ."

"Of course, the Bible in the church. I should have thought of that," Amber said.

Sliding abruptly off my lap, she strolled to the window, gazing into darkness, trying to decide what to do. Finally, she removed the candle from the nightstand and started for the door.

"Where are you going?" I asked.

"To take a look at the Bible."

"Now?"

"Right now," she said, exiting into the dark hallway without waiting for me to follow her.

Chapter 34

Amber glared at me when the door slammed shut behind us with a bang.

"Hold it down, Troop or you'll wake everyone in the house."

"Hey, you too."

My retort prompted her to punch me in the arm causing us both to have to muffle our laughter. We somehow managed to creep down the creaky staircase without waking anyone. When we reached the front door, I groped in the dark for the handle. As we headed down the deserted lane toward the church, full moonlight lighted the opalescent sky much like Zekiel's smoky crystal ball. There were no lights in any of the houses.

"No wonder everyone in the colony has so many kids," Amber said. "They all hit the sack when the sun goes down."

"That's a fact," I said as we reached the church. "Good thing for us."

The stone structure seemed more indigenous to a New England hamlet then the eerily lit tranquility of a remote Arkansas forest. I turned the latch on one of the heavy front doors and found it unlocked. As we eased into the darkness of the church's interior, a rush of cold air swept over us.

Fishing a candle out in my pocket, I lit it, my thoughts returning to the reptile box. I hoped the good Pastor Gray hadn't let the big rattlesnake loose on the floor to guard the church against intruders. I forgot about the snake when we reached the massive old Bible nestled on the lectern. As Amber carefully opened the book, I held the candle for her.

The book was more than old, it was ancient, its type and paper snatched from a different era. Amber thumbed to the front plate of the book. Elaborately printed it bore the inscription: Imprinted in London for the Queen Mother— Elizabeth I, 1587. There was a faded note at the bottom of the page written in what must have been Old English.

"Lucke, Deare Raleigh, to seak worldes of golde, for praise, for glory."

The inscription was signed Virginia and even the dim candlelight reflected disbelief in Amber's indigo eyes.

"Tom, could this possibly be the original handwriting of Elizabeth I?" She answered her own question. "I believe it's a note to her lover, Sir Walter Raleigh."

Almost immediately, I had a second shock. A giant hand grasped my shoulder. When I jerked around, I found myself staring into the big face of Pastor Gray. His glare, like a blue-eyed, avenging angel, heated the back of my neck.

"What is it you seek, my children?"

"A look at the Bible," I said, stammering the obvious.

Pastor Gray's long white hair, lighted by candle reflections in a stained glass window, bounced with a strobe-like effect.

"In the midst of darkness?" he asked. "Why not wait until morning?"

I had no answer and didn't want to explain that it was because we were afraid of him. Amber managed to give him a feeble, although apparently acceptable answer.

"We were discussing the Bible and couldn't contain our curiosity until morning. We meant no harm."

Gray released his grip. "Did you discover what you sought?"

"Partially," I said, finding my voice. "Maybe you can answer some questions for us?"

"Perhaps," Gray said, turning toward the door at the back of the stage. "Come with me."

Amber gave me an uneasy glance and shook her head ever so slightly. Pastor Gray didn't wait for an answer and was already ducking through the door. Amber nudged me toward his office where he motioned us to sit and then slumped into the chair behind the small desk facing us.

"What questions can I answer for you?"

"Tell us about your colony. Where your people came from."

Gray's expression grew solemn. Folding his hands in his lap, he stared hesitantly at Amber and me. Apprehension glazed his voice and darkened his face.

"Why do you wish to know?"

"Curiosity," I said. "We would never do anything to harm your people."

Gray's demeanor gradually changed to passive acceptance. The weight of a secret kept for centuries appeared to lift from his shoulders. Leaning back in his chair, he gazed at Amber and me.

"What I'm about to tell you is unknown to the others of the colony. We are descendants of another colony that failed long ago. Roanoke."

I leaned forward with my elbows on the desk and so did Amber, her mouth open as we listened to Pastor Gray verbalize what we both already suspected.

"That was more than four hundred years ago," Amber said.

"Yes," Gray said. "We are descendants of Raleigh's second colony on Roanoke Island."

"How is that possible?" I asked.

"The year was 1587, although it doesn't really matter. A group went to re-colonize Roanoke that the original colonists had abandoned the prior year. The scheduled supply ship never came.

"Our ancestors were resourceful and thrived in their new surroundings. They had little worry of survival until supplies arrived. At least until the second year when sickness struck the colony. Many died, their bodies thrown into the sea to prevent the spread of the infection. Indians, known as the Croatans assisted the colonists. The disease also struck them, killing many and the colony's survival seemed bleak.

"The Governor, not knowing what else to do, sent two exploratory groups along the coast to seek respite from the disease. One man returned from each group. Both told stories of fierce Indians that had captured most of their parties, killing them slowly with horrible techniques of torture. The colonists were gentle people, mostly farmers. The tales of the wild men terrified them. The Croatans, a tribe of fishers and hunters, were also terrified.

"Events worsened. A marauding band of savages had followed the returning survivor of one of the exploratory patrols. The colonists fought off the small group though not without casualties on both sides. Fearing the return of a larger raiding party, the governor ordered the migration to an island off the coast.

"When wild Indians crossed to the island and slaughtered many of the colonists, the governor abandoned hope of rescue from Mother England.

"Those escaping the massacre fled west, the only safe direction from the island. The remaining Croatans joined them. The course they followed was long and arduous. Many died on the trek. After wandering for two years, the survivors reached this valley. It was a haven then as it is now.

"Food was abundant. There was metal for crafting and hot water pools that became the life's blood of the colony. The rest you know or can decipher. Our ancestors stayed and prospered though always with a fear of what lay beyond the valley."

Gray paused, exhausted from his discourse. Sinking back into his chair, he again grew silent.

"There are no wild Indians beyond the valley, Pastor Gray. Has no one left the colony in all these years?" I asked.

"Many of the mountain people are descendent of families from this valley. Our crops grow at all levels of the mountain. Some even grow on the mountains surrounding the valley."

"Yet no one has betrayed the secret," Amber said.

Gray sat up straight in his chair and leaned forward, placing his hands on the desk.

"And neither will you. You must seal your promise with an oath of blood."

Pastor Gray straightened to his full intimidating height and glared at us, a sudden look of wildness in his eyes. It was the same cold chill I felt when the rattlesnake wrapped itself around the girl's neck. Gray retrieved something from beneath his desk. By candlelight, we gazed at the bleached skull of a giant viper staring at us through eyeless sockets. Its gaping mouth revealed two dagger-like fangs.

"Place your arms on the desk," Gray ordered.

Amber cleared her throat and laid her left arm on the desktop. I stretched my right arm beside hers. The Pastor grasped them in his enormous left hand and drew them together. Brushing back our sleeves, he flipped our palms face up and grabbed the grotesque skull from the desk.

Pastor Gray bowed his head. "By my own blood taken by the serpent, I swear silence forever. Say it," he said.

"By my own blood taken by the serpent, I swear silence forever," we said.

"Again," Gray implored.

"By my own blood taken by the serpent, I swear silence forever."

After repeating the oath, Gray used the serpent's fangs to trace four connecting cuts on the fleshy side of our forearms. Dagger-like teeth incised the skin until bloody diamonds appeared simultaneously on each of our arms.

"In the presence of the Serpent of the Lord these sinners have sworn a mortal oath of silence. Let your mark always remind them and make strong their oath."

He released our arms and slumped back into his chair. I had one more question for him.

"We came to the valley looking for my brother. Is there anything you can tell us about where he might be?"

Gray's answer was little more than a whispered response. "Your brother stayed for only a short while. We have not seen him since he departed."

We had solved one puzzle while yet another remained unanswered. Thanking Pastor Gray, we returned along the pathway to Caleb's house.

"This blows me away," Amber said, glancing at the bloody diamond etched in her forearm. "Oath or no oath, no one would ever believe us anyway."

"These people aren't responsible for Bill's disappearance," I said. "Not even Pastor Gray or his snake."

Chapter 35

Despite having had only three hours of sleep, I felt rested when I awoke the next morning. I found my clothes in the bathroom, washed and pressed. Steam rising from the sink evoked memories of geysers and hot springs as I daubed hot mineral water on my face. Like Caleb's offer for us to remain in the valley forever, I hoped the memories would remain as long. I looked out the window, one last time. Our days in the valley had not dulled my awe inspired by the beautiful surroundings.

I was the last to arrive for breakfast, and everyone exchanged knowing smiles when I took my place at the table. After breakfast, we thanked the Dares for their hospitality and prepared to hike out of the valley. To prevent us from losing our way Wat had volunteered to go with us to the mountain front. Amber and I knew the real reason, and so did Mary Ann.

Rafe Johnson's pig and mule farm lay forty miles in the distance. My sore muscles ached every time I thought about the trip. A crowd of curious villagers waited in front of Caleb's porch, wanting one last look at us before we departed. Pastor Gray was there with a rare smile on his usually stoic face. Wat appeared from around the garden pathway on one of our mules, leading the others behind him.

"Never thought I'd be so happy to see that bandit," I said when Wat handed me the reins to Ol' Flame.

I shook Caleb's hand. "Though we've only known you a short while, we'll miss the valley."

"It would please us if you would visit us again someday."

"I'll be back," Amber said.

"Go with God," Pastor Gray said.

The villagers waved, and children chased after us until we were well away, into the trees. Wat took the lead, urging his mount in the direction of the mountains. Behind us, the laughter of children died away as we plunged into the thick growth of trees between Carbonica and the mountain front. Light mist soon became gentle rain that barely wet our shirts and did nothing to dampen our spirits. Two turkey buzzards circled high above us, disappearing completely when their flight paths took them into the clouds.

The rain soon ceased, and a lark warbled in a tree as we passed beneath. When Wat and Mary Ann slowed and dropped back behind me, I took the opportunity to talk with Amber. Feeling suddenly rambunctious, I whacked Ol' Flame on the rear and raced ahead to catch her.

"Seems doubtful we'll ever learn what happened to Bill," I said, slowing to a trot beside her mule. "Maybe he really did have an accident like Sheriff Bonner said. He could have fallen off a cliff or into a mine pit."

"Mary Ann doesn't think so. She says he knew the hills too well for that to have happened."

"She could be wrong."

"That doesn't make it any less frustrating."

Amber raced ahead for a moment and then reined in her mule so that I could catch up to her.

"If you feel there's something to gain by staying longer, I'll take a few more days of vacation."

"We've done all we can. Someday I'll sort things out."

"You will," she said.

"At least I think I've finally shed my phobia of dark holes in the ground. The trip through the cave yesterday had no adverse effect on me."

"Then you're almost home free," she said, trotting away.

Shortly before noon, we reached the Land of Steam and the foothills surrounding the valley. Ol' Flame balked when he entered the fog bank, and I had to yank the reins to keep him from wheeling around and trying to take a chunk out of my leg. We stopped beside a clear pool for a rest before starting our ascent of the mountain trail.

Wat and Mary Ann barely touched the food Elizabeth had packed for us. Instead, they sat on a rock above the pool, holding hands. We were close to the waterfall we'd visited the previous day, and the sound of falling water through the fog sounded like distant thunder. I called Wat and Mary Ann and told them we needed to go.

"You do not have to return the way you came," he said. "There is a short route to the top of the mountain."

"How short?"

"Much less than an hour," he said. "You won't be able to find your way alone so I will go with you."

After three days in the valley, we began a winding ascent up a narrow trail replete with switchbacks and hairpin turns to the top of the mountain. Wat reluctantly left Mary Ann's side and joined Amber and me in the lead. Shortly, we reached the waterfall and the end of the narrow trail.

"What now? The trail to your Uncle's village is too narrow for the mules. They'll never make it."

"Yesterday I did not show you the entire cavern," he said. "It honeycombs the mountain. Some of the corridors lead out of the valley."

Wat hopped off his mule and led him into the dark lower entrance of the cavern. Ol' Flame didn't like following me and yanked a mouthful of hair from the back of my head. When I pulled him into the cave, he rose up on his hind legs, not calming until Wat had lighted a torch.

The cavern's acoustics magnified every drip of limy water, and every step the mule's hooves made. About fifty feet into the cave the tiny hairs on my neck stood on end and the perspiration dripping down my forehead turned icy cold. Despite earlier prognostications, my dark companion had returned. Again, fear gripped my neck with icy fingers and squeezed.

"How much farther," I called out.

When the echoes died away in the hollows of the empty corridor, Wat said, "Not far."

Amber must have noticed the urgency in my voice because she handed the reins of her mule to Mary Ann and joined me.

"Take my hand and close your eyes," she said. "I'll guide you the rest of the way."

The gentle pressure she exerted on my hand calmed me as much as the torch had calmed Ol' Flame. I opened my eyes to a flash of blinding sunlight. We had finally exited the corridor on a plain overlooking the valley. When my dilated eyes adjusted to the light, I stared down into it. For the first time, I realized its true nature. It was a preserved caldera capped by a thick nimbus issuing from its still hot bowels. I realized I was holding Amber's hand in a tight grip.

Wat mounted his mule and slapped its rear, directing him into thick shrubbery surrounding the valley overlook. We plunged after him, bushes brushing against us and threatening to make the obscure trail too narrow to pass. The distance was short, and we quickly exited near the top of the mountain at the intersection of two narrow logging roads. Thick shrubbery camouflaging the trail to the cavern opening popped back into place, cloaking the entrance to the valley.

"Do you know where you are now?" Wat asked.

"Not far from the trail leading down to the mines," Mary Ann said. "It's where we went the first day on the mountain."

"Then we're not far from Johnson's farm."

Mary Ann glanced at the sun and said, "Grandpa will be waiting for us."

"I will ride with you as far as the farm," Wat said, reluctant to leave us.

As we started down the dirt-paved logging road toward Rafe Johnson's farm, Wat and Mary Ann dropped behind Amber and me. Shielded from radical weather changes by mountains and thick clouds, the valley's controlled environment was rarely too hot or too cold. Now, we'd returned to reality in the outside world. I realized as much when a cold wind whistled down the back of my neck.

The blast of refrigerated air also affected Ol' Flame. Like a skittish colt, he suddenly reared back on his hind legs and began to buck and spin. I clenched my knees against his ribs and clutched the reins with both hands, yelping in terror as the ornery mule arched his back, cleared the earth with all four hooves, and sent me tumbling over his head. Every bone in my body popped, and the fillings in my teeth rattled when I landed on my back. Amber and Mary Ann rushed to assist me while Wat grabbed Ol' Flame's halter and somehow managed to subdue him.

Amber knelt beside me, cradled my head in her lap.

"Tom, are you all right?"

I wriggled my fingers, arms, and shoulders. "Nothing broken except my confidence," I said, sitting up slowly. "Think I'll walk the rest of the way."

Before the words died on my lips, we heard the rumbling engine of a vehicle coming up the road. Shortly, an old pickup truck rounded the bend, and I remembered the encounter with the strange hermits my first day on the mountain. The truck appeared from around the trees and screeched to a halt in front of us. Seeing me sitting on the ground, the lone man in the truck got out and came over.

He had the same strange grin on his face as before as he bent forward at the waist like a person with a bad back. Despite the chill in the air, he wore no shirt beneath his torn overalls. Motley gray-streaked his dirty brown hair. Chewing tobacco trickled down his chin, staining his lips and facial stubble. As he limped toward us, grinning like an idiot, I noticed his prominent facial tic. It imparted a grotesque expression to his otherwise twisted face.

I glanced at Mary Ann and then at Wat. Amber's expression was apprehensive. The closer the man approached the more overpowering grew his body odor. He knelt beside Amber and leaned forward, invading my space. When he spoke, his foul breath made me wince.

"Folks need some help?"

"We have things under control," I said.

"Got something in the back of my pickup I'd like to show you."

"Though we don't mean to be rude, were in a hurry," I said.

"Only take a minute," he said, motioning us to follow as he limped away toward the truck. "Come see. You ain't going to believe this."

Wat helped me to my feet, and we followed the man to the truck. Still grinning like a moron, he waited for us. Something flopped around on the truck bed, and curiosity overcame my suspicion. It was a giant fish and obviously very much alive.

"A big 'ol catfish," said the hermit. "Caught it on a trotline. Weighs forty-six pounds."

We edged around the bed of the truck for a better look, trying to ignore the man's offensive odor. The fish was four feet long with two whisker-like appendages near its mouth. I empathized with the creature, forgetting its imminent peril when something hard and metallic pressed against the small of my back.

I turned around slowly and found myself staring into the one eye of the hermit's friend. He had a shotgun pointed directly at me. Like his partner, he was grinning like a lunatic.

Chapter 36

It took another moment before Amber, Wat and Mary Ann realized we weren't alone. When they did, the man fanned the barrel of the gun and grinned. A quarter-inch gap separated his two front teeth.

"Looks like we caught ourselves a mess of fish today."

I raised my hands and pressed back against the truck. The man with the shotgun was tall and dressed exactly like his partner.

"What the hell do you think you're doing?" I asked.

Their laughter sounded maniacal, and the big man said, "Taking whatever you might have, that's what. He fanned the barrel of the shotgun. "Strip."

Amber gripped my hand, sensing dire trouble. She still had her pistol in the pocket of her jacket, and she reached for it. A painful mistake. One Eye slammed the barrel against the side of her head. I grabbed her as she sank to her knees in the dirt.

"Let her go," One Eye said.

When I failed to react to his command quickly enough, he nailed me with the butt of the shotgun. My ears rang, though I somehow remained conscious. I could hear Mary Ann's loud stream of invectives and was subliminally aware that Wat had bolted toward the mules.

Despite his size, One Eye had the reflexes of a cat. Tossing his partner the shotgun, he sprinted after Wat, made a flying leap, and tackled him from behind. Not before Wat had untied Ol' Flame and slapped him across the rump.

Ol' Flame rose up on his hind legs to show his disgust. Before One Eye could subdue him, the mule knocked him off his feet with a well-placed kick. I watched the beast disappear down the forest trail.

With Amber out cold and me in a stupor, our assailants didn't bother requiring us to strip. They quickly went through our pockets, retrieving Bill's diamond and Amber's pistol.

"This one's from the valley," One Eye said, looking at Wat. He'll tell us how to get down there if we have to skin him alive to do it."

I regained consciousness on the floor of a musty cabin with my hands tied behind my back. Bailing twine secured my ankles, my right shoulder red with blood dripping from the side of my head. For a moment, I almost faded back into unconsciousness.

Like Zekiel's shack, cardboard and yellowing newspaper covered the flimsy walls. Amber and Mary Ann were beside me on the floor, Amber managing a weak smile when she saw me open my eyes.

"We're in trouble, Troop."

"You okay?" I asked, unable to rub the egg-sized knot on the side of my head.

"Just a glancing blow. They got my pistol. Mary Ann's fine. They have Wat outside."

Bailing twine also bound Amber and Mary Ann. Mary Ann remained silent when I shifted my weight to get a look in her eyes. She was lost in thought, a desperate expression painted on her face.

"You okay, kid?"

Mary Ann nodded, her cheeks wet with tears. "They're killing Wat," she said.

"No, they're not," I said, edging closer. "Just think positive."

"We've got to do something," Amber said.

I stopped struggling and looked around the disheveled room, hoping for inspiration. When it wasn't forthcoming, I sank back against the wall. Mary Ann stopped crying and stared at me with accusing eyes.

"Those are the men that killed Bill. The rest of his journal is over on the floor. Now they're killing Wat."

A dozen loose-leaf sheets lay crumpled in a corner and vibrated in the draft wafting through the blazing fireplace.

"No one is going to hurt us," I said a bit too loudly to inspire much confidence.

"Yes they will, and there's nothing we can do about it," she said.

"I'll think of something."

"What can you do?" she said between sobs. "You're as passive as a moonbeam."

Her words stung me to the marrow of my soul although I could do nothing to stem her sobs of anguish or convince her otherwise.

"They probably found Bill's journal on the trail. It doesn't mean anything."

Mary Ann took a deep breath. In a minute, her sobbing ceased.

"One of them is wearing his boots."

"Listen," Amber said. Unmistakable sounds of someone taking a vicious beating came from just outside the open window. "We have to do something, or they'll kill him. And then us."

It was then that I saw the means of our escape in the flames of the fire. Without explaining, I inched across the dirty floor and thrust my wrists into the fireplace, hoping the rope would catch fire and pull apart before my skin did.

Amber and Mary Ann watched as I bit my lip to keep from crying out in pain. My temples and the veins in my forehead throbbed. Slowly, the fire ignited the twine and burned through it. With wrists free, I dived forward and rolled through the dirt on the floor to extinguish the fire.

Sounds of violence outside the shack had ceased. I quickly untied my ankles and rushed to Amber's side, fumbling with her bindings. As her wrists pulled free, the door creaked open, One Eye entering. When he saw my hands were loose, he pointed his shotgun. I didn't wait for the resultant blast.

Many years had passed since I'd broken a leg playing high school football. There are some things you don't forget. Blocking a tackler was one of them. I slammed into the giant's knees with the full weight of my rolling body. When he bounced against the wall and fell on top of me, I realized I had caused him no serious damage. He hoisted me up and then slammed me to the floor.

Amber was fumbling with Mary Ann's bindings though I knew she had no time to complete the task.

"Get the hell out of here! Get help." She seemed frozen in place. I drew myself up and screamed at her. "Run, damn it! Do it now!"

Mary Ann began screaming and kicking the wall with her feet. The smaller man heard the commotion and came limping in from outside the cabin. The diversion was all Amber needed. Diving through the opening between us, she managed to make it out the door, though not before cat-quick

One Eye grabbed the collar of her blouse. She didn't stop as he ripped it off her back.

The moon was full and yellow and cast a golden glow on the clearing outside the shack. Amber stopped and looked back at the struggle still going on inside before sprinting away into the forest's darkness. I could only hope she was running the race of her life, though I had little time to think about it.

Pain ripped through my shoulder like a red-hot shell fragment. One Eye had clamped his teeth on my shoulder and was attempting to bite through my arm. When his partner tried to grab my flailing feet, I kicked him in the face. Losing his footing in the dirt, One Eye rolled us both across the floor.

I managed somehow to scramble to my hands and knees and crawl toward the blazing fireplace. One Eye had my ankle, trying to pull me into his grasp. Kicking free, I grabbed the remains of Bill's journal, shoving my hand into the fire until flame engulfed dry paper. When I thrust the burning ball beneath the ragged curtain on the shack's lone window, the tattered cloth burst into flame.

"That's for what you did to my brother, you dirty bastards!"

One Eye kicked me in the head and then quickly extinguished the fire with a bucket of sand he retrieved from behind a door.

"Nice try," he said.

As I crawled toward Mary Ann, One Eye bounced my face off the floor. Grabbing a handful of Mary Ann's hair, he dragged her out of the cabin. Little Man kicked me in the ribs and followed him.

One Eye tossed Mary Ann into Little Man's grasp and then hurried to the dog pen where the coonhounds were raising holy hell. Grabbing a frightened hound, he dragged her out of the pen by the collar and held Amber's blouse to her nose. When the animal had Amber's scent, One Eye pointed her toward the dirt road leading to the shack.

After one long mournful bay at the moon, the hound raced away down the hill. One Eye opened the pen and held the door as the remaining hounds hurried after her. I could hear their howls long after they'd disappeared into the night.

"She won't get far," One Eye said. "Let's take care of these three and then we'll go get her."

Wat was unconscious against a tree and Little Man tossed Mary Ann on top of him. One Eye's hands seemed larger than the base of a skillet and about as rough. I was almost out for the count, as the giant man dragged me to the tree beside the two youngsters.

From a well, he hoisted a wooden bucket of water with one effortless yank on the rope. He tossed half the bucket over Wat's head and the rest over mine. Wat regained consciousness. Beaten nearly senseless, he groaned and clutched his ribs. Mary Ann could do little except draw close to him and continue to sob.

Though Wat's face looked like raw hamburger, I could do no more than stare up into the face of the massive, pig-eyed man. For my troubles, he delivered a vicious boot to my kidney. My body ached, raw blisters popping up on my hands and arms, as my mind kept repeating one set of repetitious childhood sentences: Run Spot run. See Spot run. Run Amber. . .

"Get some rope and then herd them down to the mineshaft," One Eye said as he dragged me off the ground.

Little Man cut the rope binding Mary Ann's ankles and wrists then nudged her with the barrel of the shotgun until she moved. Yanking Wat off the ground, he shoved him forward. After jamming the gun barrel into Mary Ann's ribs, he directed the youngsters toward a vertical mineshaft behind the house. As I faded in and out of consciousness, something deep within the marrow of my being urged me not to give up.

Chapter 37

Prodded by the shotgun, Wat and Mary Ann trod a narrow path to a large hole in the ground. I was still dazed, so One Eye dragged me up the sharp cherty path as tortured thoughts seeped from my brain. It didn't take someone fully cognizant to understand what was about to happen.

The hole was a funnel-shaped pit that looked like a gravel-strewn anthill. I struggled to stand, and my effort earned a vicious whack across the back of my head with an ax handle. The impact sent yet another electric jolt through the throbbing nerve-endings of my beleaguered brain.

"Stop it," I said.

One Eye's fitful laughter sounded even more harrowing as it resonated from his phlegm-filled lungs.

"You're a real smart ass. Let's see just how smart you are." Knotting one end of a rope around my waist, he tied the other end around the trunk of a tree on the edge of the pit. He tossed another rope to his squatty partner.

"Tie them up, face to face. Make it tight then give me the other end."

Little Man did as told. One Eye tied the other end of the twenty-foot rope around my waist. Soon,

I was tied to the tree and Wat and Mary Ann were tied to me.

The old shaft formed a circular hole in the ground fully fifty feet across. Shaped like a funnel, it sloped ever steeper until it reached the dark, vertical pit, fifty or sixty feet below the rim. Decades, maybe centuries had passed since miners had worked the mine. All that remained were loose rocks and stunted bushes growing on the ever-steepening slope culminating in the dark hole that could easily lead straight to hell.

Wat and Mary Ann waited, five feet from the mouth of the dank pit. When I called out to Mary Ann, One Eye slapped me across the bridge of the nose to shut me up.

Steel, reflecting in the moonlight, glinted in my half-closed eyes. It was a large knife with a blade at least eighteen inches long. One Eye held it to my neck, and I waited for him to cut my throat. Instead, he sliced a crescent swath across my chest. With mind and body already numb, I barely felt the sharp blade's bloody bite.

"Bring the gun," One Eye said. "He makes a move, blow his head off."

To my surprise, One Eye slipped the knife into my belt then grabbed Wat and Mary Ann, tossing them down the incline toward the vertical shaft. Mary Ann screamed. As the echo died in the hollow of the pit, the weight of two bodies on the other end of the rope snatched my legs out from under me. The rope around my waist kept me from following Wat and Mary Ann down the flint-covered slope. One Eye smiled as he cut the rope halfway through.

"Now, you got yourself a real problem. You can use the knife I give you to cut yourself loose, or you can wait till your lifeline breaks and those two suck you into the mineshaft with them. Whatever your choice, those two will be dead by the time we get back with your woman."

Amber understood she was now our only hope. One Eye had ripped the blouse off her back. He hadn't managed to stop her as she sprinted down the narrow dirt road leading away from the shabby cabin. They could only watch a glimmer of light reflecting from her churning legs as she hurtled a pile of brush and disappeared into the forest.

The distance down the hill to Rafe Johnson's farm was less than six miles. Many times Amber had run six miles. On a track, she could have spanned the interval in less than forty minutes. She'd never run the distance downhill through a forest at night pursued by two psychopaths and a pack of baying hounds. As she floated through the trees, no one had to tell her whom the hounds were following.

Realizing that her only chance was flat-out speed, she deserted the forest for the open center of the rocky logging trail. Her body responded, and she moved like an apparition awash in silvery luminescence.

One Eye's hoarse laughter mingled with Mary Ann's moaning pleas as loose gravel tumbled in a mini-landslide over my head. As I sprawled against the sharp rocks, the full implication of our deadly dilemma filtered into my swollen brain.

For the moment, the partially severed rope supported our weight though I knew it wouldn't last for long. There I hung, my arms aching as gravity pulled us toward certain death in the dark abyss. My body strained from burns, beatings and the combined weight of Wat and Mary Ann pulling on the rope. Mary Ann's weak voice made my misery even more intense.

"Help us, please help us," she called.

"Hang in there, Buddy. I won't let you die," a voice above me said.

As if someone had suddenly snatched his soul from the netherworld to inspire me Lenny Dotson's tremulous body floating above the chasm's rocky slope appeared.

"Lenny," I said. "Is that you?"

"Hang in there, Buddy. I won't let you die."

"I can't Lenny. I'm hurt and this rope's about to break."

"Hang in there Buddy," his voice said, trailing away into darkness. "I won't let you die."

Honeyboy's lifeless body, dangling from the end of a rope, joined Lenny. Maggots crawled from his mouth as darkness reflected from his lifeless eyes. Around his neck, a viper coiled.

"Please help us," Mary Ann called from deep in the pit.

On the brink of unconsciousness, I wrestled with the Devil, dragging myself back to reality. Far down the mountain, I imagined Amber running for her life. The moans of two youngsters suspended from the rope around my waist echoed from the pit behind me. I suddenly found myself shouting, and my trembling voice erupted in a strangely guttural cry.

"Hang on Mary Ann. I won't let you die."

When I glanced up the slope, I saw Lennie again. He had a can of gasoline and he was dousing the cabin with it.

Amber, her legs powered by large doses of both fear and adrenaline, was running the race of her life. She had covered a distance of nearly three miles in fifteen minutes, twice the time it took Little Man and One Eye to set the hounds loose and throw Wat and Mary Ann into the pit. Now they were after her in the pickup.

Amber had fallen twice, tripping once on a root and diving into the soft undergrowth. The second time she wasn't so lucky. Slipping in loose gravel, she'd skinned her knees, elbows, and bare chest.

A broken leg or even a sprained ankle would have resulted in her demise and her concentration focused single-mindedly on the trail. Baying hounds registered only subliminally as she plunged down the moonlit path, though her subconscious kept reminding her that the two killers were rapidly closing the gap.

Amber's training told her she was halfway to Johnson's house. It kept her going, even faster than an excellent distance runner could have run. When she reached the mountain's edge, the winding road grew narrower as it plunged steeply into the valley below. The rattle of pickup and bay of hounds closed behind her and the steep road forced her to slow her descent.

The logging trail took a hairpin loop. Realizing the killers would catch her unless she did something drastic she exited the road in a near-plummet down the rocky slope. Oblivious to danger and desperate to reach the farm before the killers caught her, she hurdled boulders and fallen branches in a limb-risking gallop.

The shortcut worked. When Amber reached the logging road, she knew from the bay of hounds that she had put extra distance between herself and her pursuers. Now the road was flat, and Amber pushed forward in a sprint. Johnson's farm lay just ahead. John Stewart would be there. They would have their own shotguns. With dogs and truck close behind, she pushed even harder.

Rounding the last corner, Amber expected to see Johnson's house with their animals grazing beneath the bright light of the full moon. Seeing nothing but trees, her heart almost stopped. With lungs bursting, she dropped to her knees, looking desperately for salvation. Behind her, lights of the pickup cast their deadly pall on her as One Eye wheeled around the corner. Ahead of the truck raced the pack of hounds.

Amber's strong heart quelled a brief impulse to give up. Springing to her feet, she tried a desperate tactic usually reserved for cornered animals. Running straight at the pack of hounds, past the approaching truck, she hurdled the beasts, then sprinted up the road to the only place that might still provide haven: the cavern entrance to the valley.

One Eye spun the pickup around, barely avoiding the pack of confused hounds, as Little Man got off a single shotgun blast at Amber's fading figure. Buckshot flew harmlessly over her shoulder as she rounded a turn in the steeply winding road, releasing in her a much-needed burst of adrenaline. Spurring her forward, it allowed her to cover the uphill mile to the turn-off in less than six minutes.

Reaching the trail to the cavern she plunged into the forest, hoping darkness would cloak her path. Subliminally, she wondered if Tom, Wat, and Mary Ann would survive, even if she managed to reach Wat's uncle before collapsing from exhaustion. She had little time to ponder the thought as she plowed headlong into a tree.

Chapter 38

The half-severed rope had somehow managed to continue holding the combined weight of Wat, Mary Ann and me. Knotted muscles cried out as I used the rope to try to pull our combined weight to the tree. Loose gravel had shredded my hands and they were sticky with blood. Every time I considered giving up, Mary Ann's desperate cries made me renew my efforts.

Multiple cuts stung my body. Flies, attracted by sweat and body heat, swarmed around my head. As I locked out the near impossibility of Amber returning with help, the rope supporting us finally separated and we began a slow-motion slide toward the precipice. My feet dangled helplessly over the ledge as I reached for my belt. Before we plunged into dark oblivion, I grabbed the knife and exercised my last chance for survival.

When Amber had sprinted past her pursuers, One Eye slammed on the truck's brakes and skidded sideways in loose gravel. After turning the confused hounds, they followed Amber back up the logging road. They'd almost caught her when she plunged off the trail.

"Get the hell out there and go after her," One

Eye said. Seeing his little partner limp slowly toward the trees, he followed him out of the truck. When he reached him, he was gazing at something on the ground.

"Look here what's waiting for us," he said.

One Eye bulled his way through the undergrowth and joined him. Amber was lying in a pile of pine straw, bare-chested and unconscious. Nearby lay the cavern's mouth.

"Well kiss my ass if she didn't just lead us to the valley door," One Eye said.

Something behind them averted his attention. The killers' shack was on fire, billowing smoke and intense flames turning the darkened sky as bright as day. As they used their hands to block the glare, an ear-splitting explosion shook the trees.

"Damn his sorry hide," One Eye said.

"Least we got the girl," Little Man said.

"We got shafted is what we got," One Eye said, glancing back at the fire on the mountain.

"What'll we do?"

"I'll get the girl. You get your ass down in the valley and set it on fire."

"Why?"

Little Man's head snapped when One Eye backhanded him.

"Cause we need a distraction, that's why. Something to give us a chance to get the hell out of here before firefighters and police start swarming the mountain."

Something soft and wet was licking Amber's face as she began regaining consciousness. She blinked and stared into the brown eyes of a hound. She froze when she realized someone was standing over her. Not ready to quit and admit failure she struck out with both feet in a violent frenzy. She managed to connect with someone's shin before a familiar voice caused her to cease her struggles. The discernible accent of familiar voices pacified her. It was Caleb and Pastor Gray, and they weren't alone.

Leon and his men gathered in a circle around her. Gray's jacket draped her bare breasts. When Amber's blurry vision focused, she recognized the two killers. Leon had personally dispatched the large killer, lifting him bodily off the ground and knocking him unconscious with a single vicious head-butt. Up the mountain, the flame still licked the horizon.

"Caleb!" Amber cried. "Up the hill! Tom, Wat, and Mary Ann! Please hurry."

Caleb and his men had horses. Without further question, they saddled and raced up the logging road to the destroyed shack. When they reached the smoldering fire, they spread out to cover the surrounding area.

When Caleb's men arrived, they found me suspended half-in and half-out of the chasm's dark mouth. With strength derived from two long-dead souls, I had ripped the knife from my belt and driven its long blade deep into the hard earth. They found me in a trance-induced stupor, holding on to the knife. After pulling Wat and Mary Ann from the precipice, they had to pry my frozen fingers from the knife's stag horn handle.

* * *

Later that night Amber and I huddled beneath a blanket. The villagers had taken Wat and disappeared into the valley. Police took Mary Ann by helicopter to a hospital in Little Rock where John Stewart waited. The once isolated mountaintop hummed with activity. A dozen or more people had come in logging trucks. They were busy searching the premises with high-powered lights.

When Sheriff Bonner and his men arrived by helicopter they found the three of us waiting for them, Little Man and One Eye hog-tied on the ground. As Amber and I watched, a police officer pulled himself from the pit that had nearly become my grave. He had rappelled into the hole, searching for evidence. With a flurry of waving arms, he explained to the others what he had seen. Minutes later Sheriff Bonner joined us.

Though I had barely spoken since our rescue, Amber had recounted the story of the killer's capture, carefully omitting details of the people from the valley. After having witnessed her performance with Bear Townsend, Bonner had little trouble believing Amber was quite capable of capturing the two men. He removed his hat and grinned.

"We were in the air ten minutes after John Stewart notified me that dang mule had come home without you. We were looking for a flare. The burning shack served the purpose. We found enough bones in that pit to put those two away for good. Looks like they've been at the same game a long time."

"Your Valley Monster?" Amber said.

"Sure seems like it," Bonner said, pumping Amber's hand. "I just want to say for myself and everyone that we think that you two are mighty brave people. I'm going to personally see your boss in Brannerville gives you a commendation."

"Thanks, Sheriff," she said.

"How the hell did you manage to light that shack on fire? The loggers said there was gasoline all over the place."

"Divine intervention is all I can tell you," I said.

Sheriff Bonner didn't comment. Instead, he rocked back on his boot heels, his hands stuffed in his pant pockets, his coal-gray stare unnerving.

"I guess you saw G. Gray's initials all over the logging map? The day after I give it to you, I had a warrant filed for his arrest. Cuffed him myself and put him in jail."

Amber and I exchanged glances. "You didn't have to do that for us," Amber said.

Bonner chuckled. "Hell, girl, he was out in an hour and mad as a wet hen. But he's in trouble now, and he knows it. I got thirty years of dirt on that man."

"What about your career?" I asked.

"Hell, you two got me to thinking about all the kids around here that cough like twenty-year smokers, and about my mama and brother that died of cancer before they were sixty-five. Somebody had to do something, and I didn't trust those crooked Washington senators to do it."

"Will Townsend go to prison?" I asked.

"Why hell no!" Bonner said. "But he's got his ass in a real crack, and I spread the manure thick enough so that even he'll have a hard time covering up its smell. I suspect we're going to see some real changes around this county before long. Townsend's a sick man. When he dies, he'll likely spend eternity hung upside down in the smokestack of one of his own factories."

With that, he tipped his hat and walked away. I was still very much in a state of shock. Amber and I remained huddled together until another helicopter arrived and transported us to Little Rock. Shaken but safe, our ordeal had ended, and I finally knew what had happened to Bill.

Chapter 39

Scant hours later, we were safe at a hospital in Little Rock. When I awoke the next morning, the first thing I saw was Amber's smiling face.

"You okay, Troop?" she said.

"Don't know," I said. "I haven't tried to move yet."

"Your doctor says other than a few thousand bruises, contusions, cuts, and lacerations, you'll be fine."

"What about my head?" I said, wincing as I rubbed the bump on my forehead with my free hand.

"He said of all the patients he has examined you absolutely have the hardest head he's ever seen," Amber deadpanned.

With some difficulty, I sat up in bed. "How are you doing?"

"My muscles are so sore that I have to walk backward when I climb the stairs. Otherwise, I feel great."

"And Wat and Mary Ann?"

"You saved their lives."

"You saved all our lives," I said.

Amber's expression changed to a look of concern. "Caleb and the others took Wat before Sheriff Bonner, and the police arrived. Mary Ann is physically fine."

"Physically?"

"She's in a state of shock and hasn't spoken since the rescue. She just lies in bed staring at the ceiling."

"Help me out of bed," I said.

"Tom, no. The doctor says you should stay flat on your back for at least forty-eight hours."

I pulled back the covers and pivoted my legs off the bed and onto the floor. My face must have looked like the aftermath of a nuclear attack, and even Amber winced at the deep cuts on my legs.

Seeing her face, I said, "I look worse than I feel."

"Please get back in bed, Tom."

"I'm going to see Mary Ann. Will you help me?"

"You're incorrigible."

Amber put her shoulder under my arm and helped me out the door. A nurse offered her assistance. I waved her away. Halfway to Mary Ann's room, we passed an open door. I stopped and glanced inside.

"What are you doing?" Amber asked.

"I see something I need."

Amber held on as I entered without knocking and approached the surprised patient's bed.

"Hi, I'm Tom. This is Amber Armstrong."

The man in bed smiled weakly, nodding as I shook his hand. The flowers in the room indicated a man with many friends. The bouquet nearest his bed contained a dozen yellow roses.

"I have a friend that loves flowers. It is a little late to visit the florist. Can I borrow one from you?"

"Sure," he said. "I have a room full."

"I just need one," I said, taking a single yellow rose from the vase beside the bed.

Mary Ann's door was half-open. We found her lying in bed, staring at the ceiling, her face white and pasty. John Stewart nodded as we entered.

Pulling away from Amber's grasp, I shuffled to the bed's edge and kissed Mary Ann's forehead. Her face revealed no sign of recognition as I closed her fingers around the yellow rose.

"It's all right, Mary Ann. Those two monsters are behind bars and never coming out again. Amber, Wat and I are okay. Your daddy sent you a yellow rose so you would know it's so."

It took a moment for Mary Ann to react. She finally did. Amber and I watched tears appear in her blinking eyes. My own eyes clouded when she grabbed me in a tearful embrace.

Mary Ann's smile relieved my worries as the night nurse shooed us out the door. Amber let me lean on her shoulder as she helped me down the hall. When we reached the lobby, she braced me against the wall and backed away. Her half-averted eyes told me she had something on her mind that she needed to tell me.

"Tom, can you make it on your own?" Amber's body language had prepared me for a shock, though her question took me by complete surprise.

"I'm not going to like this, am I?" I said.

"The University has offered me a teaching position starting next semester. I'm going to take it."

"I'm thrilled for you." Seeing her glum expression, I said, "Now tell me what's wrong."

"You'd make a great detective," she said. "I've never been much for commitments. Two in one year is more than I can handle. It's either you or my poetry. You finished a close second. I'm sorry, Tom."

Amber's muscles stiffened as she let me brace my palms on her shoulders though resisted my embrace. Her sudden detachment caught me like a direct gut shot.

"I never asked for a commitment," I said, loosening my grip.

Amber Armstrong, neo-pop poet/police officer, gently freed herself from my grasp and backed away a step. After glancing at the floor behind her for a moment, she faced me again and smiled. Before walking out of my life, she gave my butt a suggestive pat.

"Troop," she said. "You gave us all one hell of a ride."

Chapter 40

Late August heat held New Orleans in its grip, the temperature wavering somewhere between hot and explosive. Too early for an afternoon shower, I found a tall stool at Gil LaPierre's bar in the French Quarter.

Even at this early hour, the drunk on the stool beside me was already railing about politics and I tried to ignore him. Hippolyte Culotta, the French Quarter mailman, pushed through the door from the street, grinning when he saw me. Giving me thumbs up, he handed me two envelopes, one regular and one thick manila.

"Thought I might find you here. Got yourself two letters from Arkansas."

He pronounced Arkansas, Au-koon-saw. Sweat dribbled down his baldpate as he propped his foot on my stool and waited for me to open the letters.

"Slow day, Hippolyte?" I said.

"Just curious," he said. "Didn't know you had people in Au-koon-saw."

Seeing he was not going to leave until I opened the two envelopes, I tore away one end from the manila envelope and yanked out the contents to find it contained only a picture. Hippolyte and Gil drew closer to get a look. It was an oversized glossy of Mary Ann's grandfather sitting in a rocking chair. He was holding a baby. Behind John Stewart, Wat and Mary Ann stood. The mountainous background seemed very familiar.

Though there was no letter, the inscription on the back of the picture told the story.

~Thomas Logan Dare, newly born~

Hippolyte and Gil elbowed my ribs and gave each other high fives, congratulating me as if I were the proud father. I hardly noticed, desperate to tear open the letter with the Brannerville postmark. Denying their very vocal protests and my own very urgent need for a double shot of straight Black Jack I backed away from the bar, the letter still unopened.

"Thanks, Hippolyte," I said, waving as I hurried out the door, not stopping until I had reached a nearby alleyway.

Though the letter was long, one paragraph caught my eye. It was all I needed to see.

"Guess I miss you more than I thought I would, Troop. I have a few open weeks between semesters. Spend them with me? Love, Amber."

Leaning back against old stone masonry I took a deep breath and closed my eyes. When I opened them again, heat lightning was flashing in the distance.

It hadn't rained for a month in the Big Easy and puddles of water from a gardener's hose steamed off of Bourbon Street like a breath from a dragon's mouth. The Quarter lay deserted except for a black shoeshine boy chasing a single tourist up the street. When I reached Esplanade, the bang of a snare drum sounded from around the corner. I peeked to see the commotion.

Ten old black men, each with a brass or woodwind instrument, had gathered. The very picture of withered age, they all had snowy white hair. At first, I thought they were lining up for a jazz funeral. Instead, they were preparing to march up Bourbon Street.

They stood in formation in the center of the cobbled thoroughfare, stopping traffic, both auto and pedestrian. The old man with the drum had arms as spindly as the drumsticks he held in his hands. Didn't matter because he nailed into the instrument with a strong beat. A reluctant chorus of trumpet, trombone, and clarinet joined in, producing for a moment an undisciplined drone that sounded like a cross between foghorn and cry of the wild loon.

Then a lone cornet, accompanied by a strong blast from the trombone, began weaving a steady strain through the fracas. Strengthened by the cumulative effort, the old snowy-haired trumpet player began the recognizable strains of "Over in Glory Land," and the spindly old men marched around the corner, music from their instruments welling forth from their horns as true as ever produced by any sullen youth.

With tapping feet, I swayed to the hypnotic beat of a century past. Then, clutching Amber's letter and the picture of Wat and Mary Ann to my heart, I danced up Bourbon Street along with the old men.

End

About the Author

Born on a sleepy bayou, Louisiana Mystery Writer Eric Wilder grew up listening to tales of ghosts, magic, and voodoo. He's the author of eleven novels, four cookbooks, many short stories, and Murder Etouffee, a book that defies classification. His two series feature P.I.s adept in the investigation of the paranormal. He lives in Oklahoma near historic Route 66 with wife Marilyn, three wonderful dogs, and two great cats.

If you enjoyed reading A Gathering of Diamonds, please check out the French Quarter Mystery Series, Paranormal Cowboy Series, and all of Eric's books.